P9-DCN-750

PIECES *of the* HEART

PIECES
of the
HEART

New Chicano Fiction

Edited by Gary Soto

CHRONICLE BOOKS

SAN FRANCISCO

Introduction copyright © 1993 Gary Soto. Stories copyright © by individual authors.
Compilation copyright © 1993 by Chronicle Books. All rights reserved.
No part of this book may be reproduced in any form without
written permission from the publisher.
Glossary prepared by Michael Bradburn-Ruster and Myrna R. Villa.
Page 179 constitutes a continuation of the copyright page.

Printed in the United States of America.

Library of Congress Cataloging-in-Publication Data

Pieces of the heart: new Chicano fiction/edited by Gary Soto.
p.   cm.
ISBN 0-8118-0068-7
1. American literature—Mexican American authors.   2. Mexican Americans—
Literary collections.   I. Soto, Gary.
PS508.M4C524   1993   810.8'086072—dc20   92-19164
                                                           CIP

Book and cover design: Kathleen Burch
Composition: Burch Typografica
Cover image: Carmen Lomas Garza: "A Medio Dia/Pedacito de mi Corazón"
("At High Noon/A Little Piece of My Heart") © 1986 by Carmen Lomas Garza

Distributed in Canada by
Raincoast Books
112 East Third Ave.
Vancouver, B.C. V5T 1C8

10 9 8 7 6 5 4 3 2 1
Chronicle Books
275 Fifth Street
San Francisco, CA 94103

Table of Contents

Introduction

Gary Soto

When I think of the stories that make up this collection, I think of young and beautifully single-minded writers sitting at a Formica-top table pressed to a kitchen wall. On this table lie a loaf of bread wrapped in orange-colored plastic, a single banana sugar-flecked and soft, a pair of oily pliers, some bills, some coupons clipped from newspapers—the daily paraphernalia that piles up on a kitchen table for no apparent reason except that the writer walks past that table a dozen or so times each day. As I see it, it's the late 1970s when much of the *movimiento*, the Chicano movement, had lost ground, both in the community and in the university. There was a sense of stasis and the repetition of slogans that were tired and out of breath. People pulled back and were less committed, politically and otherwise; the older generation of activists having grown weary.

These writers, all in their mid or late twenties at the time, pulled back as well. Or, perhaps, they never put forward an obvious political commitment because the writing life of the 1970s was not a public life. It was, and is, utter loneliness and uncertainty. These writers were getting by on their wits, poor-paying jobs, and the free fruits of the world. Their lives were not a smear of brie on a stone-ground cracker. They were in for the long haul—the 300-page novel and the short story collection with a bloody heart. They were not kidding themselves. This was nerve-wracking work, even competitive work, for the Chicano writer in California was looking to see what the writer in Texas was putting to the page. On some days, there's not enough White-out to shake and correct a story.

It was a writer's life, a meager beginning that worked from a rich memory but an irregular present. Perhaps the writer didn't sit down at a kitchen table but a space in the oily garage-turned-studio, the living room, a shed in the backyard wired with electricity, a cubbyhole near the back door where a squat washing machine stood. And the city was Los Angeles or El Paso, Chicago or San Francisco, or a mining town that clung economically, as strong as gravity, to a mountainside in New Mexico. Invariably, the writers were creating from the passion of memory and imagination stories whose subjects live first on a piece of typing paper, later to spring on the imaginations of readers.

The writers in this anthology have created stories that are important first to themselves as works of art and, second, as possible extensions to the reader's own story. They are carefully written. They are fresh and open to new experience. They are more ambitious in exploring the mysteries that make up the personalities of people than the Chicano short fiction of the late 1960s and early 1970s, which, as we look back, was obsessed with the question of political identity. This obsession, however real and passionate, was short-lived because such questions don't go far in short stories.

In a short story, a writer must remember to tell a good story. The characters must be recognizably human, and, therefore, complex in their weaknesses and occasional strengths. Moreover, a dramatic and purposeful action, however minimal on the surface, must occur. Short stories are not about issues; they are about people in the flush of active living. The hope of every writer is that the details compound to accumulate symbolic weight. In the end, what a writer hopes to create is a dramatic moment that will be difficult to condense into an easy summary. Not every moment is grasped. Not every character accounted for. In the hands of a talented writer, the reader may feel that something remarkable has happened to the sense of being.

Curiously, while I was compiling these stories, I noted that almost all of them concerned family and are, I suspect in a few instances, autobiographical. A door is thrown open and slammed shut. A husband is at the wife's throat, and the wife is making a fist of bitter words. Memory won't let the poor writer be. Family is forever in the backdrop, hurting or being hurt, taunting or being taunted, accusing and being accused, disappointing or being disappointed. Often family life is not happy, and stories are better for it. As another writer remarked, "Happy literature has no history," a point of truth with these stories because each has a dark kernel at its center. This is true of Ana Castillo's long and richly magical "La Loca Santa," the story of a mother and her child who, although dead, magically decides to remain in the family; Víctor Martínez's "The Baseball Glove," the story of two brothers, one ambitious and the other not, who end up picking chiles; Rosalie Otero's "The Closet," the story of a girl forced to give up a bedroom to her visiting aunt; Sandra Cisneros's "One Holy Night," the satirical story of a pregnant girl exiled in a small town; Helena María Viramontes's "The Jumping Bean," the story of a tireless father and his lazy children; Dagoberto Gilb's "Hollywood!" the story of a father trying his best to entertain his family cheaply at a winter beach.

The other stories are by Alberto Alvaro Ríos, Daniel Cano, Diana García, Jack López, Edna Escamill, Mary Helen Ponce, Carlos Flores, Guy Garcia, and Danny Romero—writers with richly varied stories that throw off the worn image of the Chicano solely as the *vato loco*, lowrider, *campesino*, or selfless mother.

Readers will be surprised. The worlds of these stories are not the expected. An example is Daniel Cano's "Somewhere Outside Duc Pho," a Vietnam story with a narrator from East L.A. He wakes from surgery to mumbling gossip that Jesse Peña, a Chicano from Texas, has left his platoon to run with the Vietcong. The buzz of gossip spreads, the sightings become frequent, and the myth of Jesse Peña grows with the metaphor of soldiers shooting at themselves—the enemy.

José Antonio Villareal's *Pocho*, a coming-of-age novel published in 1959, is arguably the start of modern Chicano writing. This novel appeared and then disappeared and resurfaced with the *movimiento* of the late 1960s, when it was required reading in classrooms. This book was followed by other prose collections, including the now-recognized classics *No Se Lo Tragó la Tierra* by Tomás Rivera, *Bless Me, Ultima* by Rudolfo A. Anaya, and *The Road to Tamazunchale* by Ron Arias, novels that were published in the early 1970s and that enjoyed a large and eager audience. A number of other prose collections were published that decade by small presses in editions of two or three thousand copies, but it was not until the 1980s that we saw a surge of major prose collections. One such work was *The House on Mango Street*, a collection of vignettes that brought Sandra Cisneros, a native of Chicago, to the forefront of critical and popular acclaim. Her stories were deftly told, cleverly constructed, and enjoyable and their characters somehow familiar to the reader. It awakened a major renaissance in Chicano literature.

The books by Chicano writers have been nudging over waves like ships—a book here and a book there. Now it's the 1990s and we have strong evidence of work that has paid off. The writers have remained committed and have done their best over the years to produce stories that reflect a life they know and have felt. This collection, then, introduces fifteen short stories by Chicano writers, some of whom are only now being recognized. These are not "Hispanic" writers, the buzzword of government officials and media, but Chicanos, or Mexican Americans, who have the courage to assert: "Sí se puede."

For me, and perhaps these writers, it is always the beginning, always the start of something in which there is no arrival. It's a brave act to keep the rush of words going. I keep thinking of the late 1970s, when these writers began. This was before the computer and the throw of amber light, and before Fed-Ex, fax, e-mail, or copy machines in the home. They were sitting by the typewriter and the evidence of work was a fleck of White-out on a knuckle. On a hard day, the typewriter keys would bunch up, standing in salute. There was so much to say that in eagerness the writer was pressing down all the keys at once.

PIECES *of the* HEART

The Waltz of the Fat Man

Alberto Alvaro Ríos

Noé's house trim was painted blue, good blue, deep and neat, with particular attention to the front door, that it should stand against spirits. He kept the house in repair and hired a gardener in the three seasons, spring and summer, a little in autumn. In this place it was a gray wind after that, a time for planting things in the ground to save them, or to hide them.

His personal appearance suffered nothing from the attentions to his house, as Noé kept on himself a trim mustache and a clean face, and neat clothes for which he thanked Mrs. Martínez, patronizing her for a quarter of a century. From ironing his clothing, she knew the shape of his body more than he did, and for her consequent attention to detail in that regard he was appreciative—just the right fold in the collars, a crease moving a little to the left along his right leg, the minor irregularities and embarrassments. And he was doubly thankful as she never said a word to him about it.

His was a body full of slow bones, after all, and Noé moved as if long fish swam in a small place.

He did not think himself fat, but he felt himself heavy, in a manner he could not explain to anyone. His body, to be sure, was overweight, but he did not feel it to be something of the stomach or thighs; rather, it was a heaviness that came from the inside out, manifesting itself to the world as the body of a fat man.

On his best days, Noé could make that weight look like muscles. On those days he could make his stomach go into his chest and his shoulders, and people would believe anything he had to say.

Noé had a business as a butcher, but it was too much for him, a sadness cutting the meats. He had become a butcher, after all, purely for social reasons. It was a civic service, and he wanted to do good things. But it was not a good choice, given what he desired, which was simply to be part of the town.

To be sure, people patronized his shop and took him up on his offer of extra services and niceties, but they did not finally stay very long to talk, not in the way they stayed for coffee and to warm themselves at the baker's. Noé could see them in there, with their mouths open and their eyes rolling along a line of laughter.

He could not say why the townspeople were like this, exactly. Perhaps it was his full size, or something about his looks, or about being the butcher in a town and being too good at his trade. But the whole of his life was that no one cared much for him, or even spoke to him very much, and when he attended wakes, which he did because he was a courteous man, he left indentations in the kitchen linoleum, which would not go away.

Noé knew that in the people's minds he was simply an irritation though he tried not to be.

In whatever part of the town he walked, people spoke behind their hands and pointed when they thought Noé couldn't see them. But his eyes were fat as well, and because of that, he could see more.

~~~~~~

When Noé danced he wore a blue suit and was always alone, always at the same place outside of town, by the river reeds.

He danced with the wind, which was also cruel, like the women of the town, but the wind, at least, did not have a face. He locked the trunks of his arms with the branch arms of the black walnut trees, which, also like the women of the town, did not bend around to hold him, did not invite him to another, softer room.

But neither could these arms of a tree leave Noé so easily. Nor could they so quickly give him over cruelly to the half-hot tongues of the weeds so that they might talk about him and make their disapproving sounds.

When he danced this dance he let out, with a small noise, his thin girl, which he kept inside himself. This is what had made him look fat, the holding in, the keeping in of the noise inside himself, his desire to speak freely of his needs as a human being in the company of other human beings. This was his thin girl.

And Noé would let her out and they would dance the dance of weddings into the night.

~~~~~

Noé took to wearing his blue suit to the shop because he thought he looked better. He did this in case someone would look at him and think the better of him, think him something of a fine man after all.

Then his plan for the blue suit grew into a great deal more, taking the wearing of the suit as some small license. It was the license, he thought, of a regular man. And he tried what he imagined to be the secret work of a regular man in the company of a regular woman.

When he shook the hands of women he did so vigorously, hoping to see movement on their bodies, some small adventure to take his breath, some nodding yes, some quiet dance of the upper body. This first adventure of a man.

His was a modest plan and worked a little. The shaking of the hands was, however, the most Noé did. It gave him so much, and he thought the intimate movements of a woman to be so loud, there in front of everybody, that he could go no further.

But it is also why Noé attended wakes so faithfully, sometimes as if they were the whole of his social life: in comforting a bereaved wife he could—properly and in front of everyone so that there was no question of propriety—kiss her on the cheek.

Even then, after the hour of praying for the deceased and thinking about what he would do, by the time his moment was at hand, his attempt at kissing was a dizzied missing of the mark. His lips to the cheek were so clumsy and so fast that the kiss was more of something else, something not quite anything, something in keeping with his life after all.

~~~~~~

The butcher shop through the slow years began to change, as did Noé himself. He had taken up in his house the collecting and caring for clocks, because, he said to himself, they had hands, and in so many clocks was a kind of heaven, a dream of sounds to make the hours pass in a manner that would allow him to open up shop again the next day.

His nighttime dream became a daytime dream as well. He did not keep the clocks, could not keep them, finally, only at home. As with Noé in his blue suit, the shop also began to find itself dressed differently, hung with clocks, first one, of a plain dark wood, and then two, and then a hundred. Each of them with two hands for him.

There was a blue clock, cuckoos, and to the side of the scale, 28-day anniversary clocks, large-faced numbers where once there had been letters in the sections of an illustrated cow.

What Noé knew and did not say was that here was the anniversary Mariquita, the schoolhouse Mariette, Marina the singular blue, Caras with her bird tongue. Armida had hands that sometimes rose outstretched to the two and ten like the blessing arms of Christ, sometimes lowered to the five and seven of desire, one hand shorter, in the act of beckoning him, a *come here, Noé. A come here, I've got something to tell you, Noé, come on, don't be afraid.*

This was no butcher shop, the townspeople would say to themselves, not with clocks. One or two clocks maybe, but not so many as this. It would not have been so bad except that he was the only butcher in town, and people had to make use of his services. An unofficial inquiry was opened as to whether or not there was perhaps a law, some ordinance, prohibiting such abuses of the known world, but no one could find any reference that applied to the walls of a butcher shop, other than cleanliness. And of that, there could be no discussion: Noé did not neglect the clocks and therefore did not neglect the white-sheeted bed of his walls.

~~~~~~

One evening in winter as Noé was closing up his shop, having wound the clocks for the night and having left just enough heat in the stove that they would not suffer, he heard the blue clock falter. So much like a heartbeat had the sounds of the clocks come to be for him that he was alarmed and stumbled in his quickness to reach the clock, though it could not move and was not falling. It called to him nonetheless as a wife in pain might call to her husband: honey, it said, please.

He reached it too late, he thought, though it was simply a clock, and he laughed at himself.

Noé tried winding the clock again, thinking the unthinkable, that perhaps he had missed its turn in his haste to leave. But that was not it: the spring was taut, and there was no play.

He took it down from its nail and looked at it from different angles in his hands but he could see nothing extraordinary. There was no obvious damage, no one had dropped it without telling him and rehung it, no insect had been boring into its side. Its blue was still blue, without blemish.

He took it to the counter and measured out some butcher's paper in which to wrap it, deciding that he would take it home to see to its difficulty. He put string around it and made a good blanket of the paper, which, he always said, should comfort what was inside. As he picked it up he could hear the workings move and he resolved to be wary of its delicacy.

He need not have done it, but he warned himself, as if he were his own mother. He put the clock in the crook of his arm, closed and locked his door, took a deep breath in the cold air, hunched his shoulders, and began his walk toward home.

He had errands, but they could wait. He was, in any event, the last of the merchants to close for the evening, so he would have been out of luck anyway. Save for the clock, this was how his evenings most often came to an end, the closing of the door and the walk toward home.

An occasional voice greeted him, and he returned the hello, but it was the conversation of single words, friendly enough, and that was all.

⌇⌇⌇

Some theorized later it was the soldiers, who were common in those days and who hung around with nothing better to do, that it was they who had been paid, because they never did anything for nothing but would do anything for something, those soldiers from that kind of army.

There was nothing tragic, of course, nothing for which any charges could be drawn, in much the same manner that nothing could be legally said about what Noé had done to his butcher's shop. You get back what you give, someone was later reported as having said. Someone, but not anyone in particular. That's how it was told to the captain of the police.

Noé was walking home with his package, which no one could have known was the blue clock. No one but perhaps the soldiers, and only then if they had been nosy enough to have been watching through his window, which had been recently broken and was full of cardboard patches, easy enough to hide behind.

The package's aspect was of a ham or a roast of some sort, a good rabbit, something simple and natural in the arm of a big man walking home to dinner.

Darkness had set and the moon was new. He cast no shadow and made his way quickly as he left the last of the downtown buildings. The ground was neither muddy nor dry, resembling something closer to a woody mulch, and through him passed a moment of gardens from some time in his life, gardens he had passed through or that his mother had kept. It was a simple feeling and brought a prickling to his skin.

He next passed by the stand of walnut trees and wild oleander, which was white-flowered in the summer.

The oleander called to him, *Noé.*

At first it was so quiet he said to himself he did not hear it, *Noé.*

Noé, the oleanders said, louder this time, and he stopped to look. Though it was dark and the moon was hidden, he was not afraid.

His size was such that he had never been made to be afraid, not at a moment like this. It was, if one could read his face, a curiosity, this sound that was reminiscent of his name.

Noé. He heard it again and stopped and turned to it, saying who was there, what did they want, that perhaps he could be of some service.

No one answered, so he reached his free hand into the leaves and moved them around. He heard the sound and saw what in the dimness seemed like a rabbit running into the underbrush.

Ha, he said, and let it go. He turned again to walk, pulling his coat back up onto his neck.

Noé. It was a whisper, this time he was sure. Not a voice, but more of a breath. A half-breath, but unmistakable in its enunciation.

As a child, Noé might have crossed himself, and as he was sometimes his own mother, he had the impulse, but he just stood there, once more.

He put down the clock in order to enter the oleander more fully and see what was what, but he found nothing, only branches and the small noises of startled birds and lizards.

When he came out he could not find his package, though he concentrated with his eyes and with his hands. It was not there.

A voice whispered once more, *Noé. You know me,* it said, *you know who I am.*

Noé no longer moved around. He listened and he waited.

Noé. He did know the whisper. He had in fact heard it many times. He knew the whisper better than the voice of his neighbor, whom he had seen a thousand times.

He would not have believed any of it had this not been the blue clock. Marina, his blue, who had made so many places for herself in his life. Not big places, but so many, her hair color on the trim of his house, the color of her eyes in his suit, and so on. She was the blueness inside him, the color of his appetite, the color both of what filled him and what he needed more of.

Marina, he said.

Noé.

He stood there and waited.

Do you love me?

Noé did not answer.

You can love me if you love me like a horse, said the whisper. *Can you be a horse, Noé? Can you show me how you are a horse?*

Noé stood there, quietly. Then he stamped his foot, gingerly at first, unsure and sure at the same time.

Is that it, Noé, is that all the horse you are?

Noé stamped his foot harder and made a noise with his nose and partway through his mouth.

Yes, Noé. And are you more of a horse still?

If this were anything but his blue clock, Marina, he would have gone and given the moment up as the ghosts of this place. Or children, or who knew what. But he could not.

And then he heard the laughter of the soldiers as they could no longer contain themselves, camouflaged so well in the oleanders. He heard the laughter, but did not bother with it. He turned and went home without the clock.

~~~~~

He had gone away from home once before, from his family. He had to. One thing and another, right or wrong, these things hadn't mattered. It was simply too much to stay.

He had, in some manner, become an exponent to a regular number. He was ordinary, times ten or times twenty, always too much. And his desire carried an exponent as well. He wanted everything to be nice, to be only the Golden Rule, but times ten, and that was too much. He had no sense of himself, and yet he was everything. In that sea of mathematics he had drowned a sailor's death.

And now he had to go away again. The tide had come up and caught him once more. He sold what was left of his business at a loss, finally, to Mr. Molina, who had a scarred face and who wanted to do the work. There was an art in the cutting, and it took Noé, because he was a courteous man, the afternoon to teach the profession's immediate intricacies to Mr. Molina, who had had no idea there was so much to learn.

That same night Noé bought a brown horse and rode it as far into the following days and weeks, as far into the future as he could, because he could not wait to see what was there. He arrived at the circus, and in it he made his life again.

But he almost did not make it. A man and a sparrow, each puts a shoulder to the wind, each to his own intention—a sparrow to fly, a man to run. Noé on this night was inbetween. Even with his weight he felt himself lifted, as if he were in league with angels at the edge of heaven, not quite deserving but sneaking in with some help through a back door, hoping to go unnoticed again, as he had felt when he had come to the town. But it was not heaven, these places.

He stopped because the circus people were the first to wave him down, all of them standing near the road, as if this were the place and they knew him and they had been waiting, and what took him so long and had he not heard them calling into the night for him.

They had called him without telegraph or telephone. Something stronger.

His mustache curled up from the wind and his body, which had sometimes seemed fat, was hardened, tense in that moment from the cold that had made him hold his breath and flex his muscles for the whole distance of the ride.

He arrived as a beast, almost, something crazed and unshaven, out of breath.

Or as a beast on top of a man, as if the horse itself were more human and asking for help.

His was a body full of slow bones still, but if it had taken his lifetime up to now to be slow, now the other foot was coming down, and it was fast. It was the other half of himself now, for the rest of his years.

This was, after all, the place. And in that moment of kicked-up dust and of noise, he began his real career, this life with a whole company of half-size men, two-bodied women, and all the rest of the animals who danced.

One Holy Night

Sandra Cisneros

About the truth, if you give it to a person, then he has power over you.
And if someone gives it to you, then they have made themselves your slave.
It is a strong magic. You can never take it back.

—Chaq Uxmal Paloquín

He said his name was Chaq. Chaq Uxmal Paloquín. That's what he told me. He was of an ancient line of Mayan kings. Here, he said, making a map with the heel of his boot, this is where I come from, the Yucatán, the ancient cities. This is what Boy Baby said.

It's been eighteen weeks since Abuelita chased him away with the broom, and what I'm telling you I never told nobody, except Rachel and Lourdes, who know everything. He said he would love me like a revolution, like a religion. Abuelita burned the pushcart and sent me here, miles from home, in this town of dust, with one wrinkled witch woman who rubs my belly with jade, and sixteen nosy cousins.

I don't know how many girls have gone bad from selling cucumbers. I know I'm not the first. My mother took the crooked walk too, I'm told, and I'm sure my Abuelita has her own story, but it's not my place to ask.

Abuelita says it's Uncle Lalo's fault because he's the man of the family and if he had come home on time like he was supposed to and worked the pushcart on the days he was told to and watched over his goddaughter, who is too foolish to look after herself, nothing would've happened, and I wouldn't have to be sent to Mexico. But Uncle Lalo says if they had never left Mexico in the first place, shame enough would have kept a girl from doing devil things.

I'm not saying I'm not bad. I'm not saying I'm special. But I'm not like the Allport Street girls, who stand in doorways and go with men into alleys.

All I know is I didn't want it like that. Not against the bricks or hunkering in somebody's car. I wanted it come undone like gold thread, like a tent full of birds. The way it's supposed to be, the way I knew it would be when I met Boy Baby.

But you must know, I was no girl back then. And Boy Baby was no boy. Chaq Uxmal Paloquín. Boy Baby was a man. When I asked him how old he was he said he didn't know. The past and the future are the same thing. So he seemed boy and baby and man all at once, and the way he looked at me, how do I explain?

I'd park the pushcart in front of the Jewel food store Saturdays. He bought a mango on a stick the first time. Paid for it with a new twenty. Next Saturday he was back. Two mangoes, lime juice, and chili powder, keep the change. The third Saturday he asked for a cucumber spear and ate it slow. I didn't see him after that till the day he brought me Kool-Aid in a plastic cup. Then I knew what I felt for him.

Maybe you wouldn't like him. To you he might be a bum. Maybe he looked it. Maybe. He had broken thumbs and burnt fingers. He had thick greasy fingernails he never cut and dusty hair. And all his bones were strong ones like a man's. I waited every Saturday in my same blue dress. I sold all the mango and cucumber, and then Boy Baby would come finally.

What I knew of Chaq was only what he told me, because nobody seemed to know where he came from. Only that he could speak a strange language that no one could understand, said his name translated into boy, or boy-child, and so it was the street people nicknamed him Boy Baby.

I never asked about his past. He said it was all the same and didn't matter, past and the future all the same to his people. But the truth has a strange way of following you, of coming up to you and making you listen to what it has to say.

Nighttime. Boy Baby brushes my hair and talks to me in his strange language because I like to hear it. What I like to hear him tell is how he is Chaq, Chaq of the people of the sun, Chaq of the temples, and what he says sounds sometimes like broken clay, and at other times like hollow sticks, or like the swish of old feathers crumbling into dust.

He lived behind Esparza & Sons Auto Repair in a little room that used to be a closet—pink plastic curtains on a narrow window, a dirty cot covered with newspapers, and a cardboard box filled with socks and rusty tools. It was there, under one bald bulb, in the back room of the Esparza garage, in the single room with pink curtains, that he showed me the guns—twenty-four in all. Rifles and pistols, one rusty musket, a machine gun, and several tiny weapons with mother-of-pearl handles that looked like toys. So you'll see who I am, he said, laying them all out on the bed of newspapers. So you'll understand. But I didn't want to know.

The stars foretell everything, he said. My birth. My son's. The boy-child who will bring back the grandeur of my people from those who have broken the arrows, from those who have pushed the ancient stones off their pedestals.

Then he told how he had prayed in the Temple of the Magician years ago as a child when his father had made him promise to bring back the ancient ways. Boy Baby had cried in the temple dark that only the bats made holy. Boy Baby who was man and child among the great and dusty guns lay down on the newspaper bed and wept for a thousand years. When I touched him, he looked at me with the sadness of stone.

You must not tell anyone what I am going to do, he said. And what I remember next is how the moon, the pale moon with its one yellow eye, the moon of Tikal, and Tulum, and Chichén, stared through the pink plastic curtains. Then something inside bit me, and I gave out a cry as if the other, the one I wouldn't be anymore, leapt out.

So I was initiated beneath an ancient sky by a great and mighty heir—Chaq Uxmal Paloquín. I, Ixchel, his queen.

~~~~~~~

The truth is, it wasn't a big deal. It wasn't any deal at all. I put my bloody panties inside my T-shirt and ran home hugging myself. I thought about a lot of things on the way home. I thought about all the world and how suddenly I became a part of history and wondered if everyone on the street, the sewing machine lady and the *panadería* saleswomen and the woman with two kids sitting on the bus bench didn't all know. *Did I look any different? Could they tell?* We were all the same somehow, laughing behind our hands, waiting the way all women wait, and when we find out, we wonder why the world and a million years made such a big deal over nothing.

I know I was supposed to feel ashamed, but I wasn't ashamed. I wanted to stand on top of the highest building, the top-top floor, and yell, *I know.*

Then I understood why Abuelita didn't let me sleep over at Lourdes's house full of too many brothers, and why the Roman girl in the movies always runs away from the soldier, and what happens when the scenes in love stories begin to fade, and why brides blush, and how it is that sex isn't simply a box you check M or F on in the test we get at school.

I was wise. The corner girls were still jumping into their stupid little hopscotch squares. I laughed inside and climbed the wooden stairs two by two to the second floor rear where me and Abuelita and Uncle Lalo live. I was still laughing when I opened the door and Abuelita asked, Where's the pushcart?

And then I didn't know what to do.

~~~~~

It's a good thing we live in a bad neighborhood. There are always plenty of bums to blame for your sins. If it didn't happen the way I told it, it really could've. We looked and looked all over for the kids who stole my pushcart. The story wasn't the best, but since I had to make it up right then and there with Abuelita staring a hole through my heart, it wasn't too bad.

For two weeks I had to stay home. Abuelita was afraid the street kids who had stolen the cart would be after me again. Then I thought I might go over to the Esparza garage and take the pushcart out and leave it in some alley for the police to find, but I was never allowed to leave the house alone. Bit by bit the truth started to seep out like a dangerous gasoline.

First the nosy woman who lives upstairs from the laundromat told my Abuelita she thought something was fishy, the pushcart wheeled into Esparza & Sons every Saturday after dark, how a man, the same dark Indian one, the one who never talks to anybody, walked with me when the sun went down and pushed the cart into the garage, that one there, and yes we went inside, there where the fat lady named Concha, whose hair is dyed a hard black, pointed a fat finger.

I prayed that we would not meet Boy Baby, and since the gods listen and are mostly good, Esparza said yes, a man like that had lived there but was gone, had packed a few things and left the pushcart in a corner to pay for his last week's rent.

We had to pay $20 before he would give us our pushcart back. Then Abuelita made me tell the real story of how the cart had disappeared, all of which I told this time, except for that one night, which I would have to tell anyway, weeks later, when I prayed for the moon of my cycle to come back, but it would not.

~~~~~~

When Abuelita found out I was going to *dar a luz*, she cried until her eyes were little, and blamed Uncle Lalo, and Uncle Lalo blamed this country, and Abuelita blamed the infamy of men. That is when she burned the cucumber pushcart and called me a *sinvergüenza* because I am without shame.

Then I cried too—Boy Baby was lost from me—until my head was hot with headaches and I fell asleep. When I woke up, the cucumber pushcart was dust and Abuelita was sprinkling holy water on my head.

Abuelita woke up early every day and went to the Esparza garage to see if news about that *demonio* had been found, had Chaq Uxmal Paloquín sent any letters, any, and when the other mechanics heard that name they laughed, and asked if we had made it up, that we could have some letters that had come for Boy Baby, no forwarding address, since he had gone in such a hurry.

There were three. The first, addressed "Occupant," demanded immediate payment for a four-month-old electric bill. The second was one

I recognized right away—a brown envelope fat with cake-mix coupons and fabric-softener samples—because we'd gotten one just like it. The third was addressed in a spidery Spanish to a Señor C. Cruz, on paper so thin you could read it unopened by the light of the sky. The return address a convent in Tampico.

This was to whom my Abuelita wrote in hopes of finding the man who could correct my ruined life, to ask if the good nuns might know the whereabouts of a certain Boy Baby—and if they were hiding him it would be of no use because God's eyes see through all souls.

We heard nothing for a long time. Abuelita took me out of school when my uniform got tight around the belly and said it was a shame I wouldn't be able to graduate with the other eighth graders.

Except for Lourdes and Rachel, my grandma and Uncle Lalo, nobody knew about my past. I would sleep in the big bed I share with Abuelita same as always. I could hear Abuelita and Uncle Lalo talking in low voices in the kitchen as if they were praying the rosary, how they were going to send me to Mexico, to San Dionisio de Tlaltepango, where I have cousins and where I was conceived and would've been born had my grandma not thought it wise to send my mother here to the United States so that neighbors in San Dionisio de Tlaltepango wouldn't ask why her belly was suddenly big.

I was happy. I liked staying home. Abuelita was teaching me to crochet the way she had learned in Mexico. And just when I had mastered the tricky rosette stitch, the letter came from the convent which gave the truth about Boy Baby—however much we didn't want to hear.

~~~~~

He was born on a street with no name in a town called Miseria. His father, Eusebio, is a knife sharpener. His mother, Refugia, stacks apricots into pyramids and sells them on a cloth in the market. There are brothers. Sisters too of which I know little. The youngest, a Carmelite, writes me all this and prays for my soul, which is why I know it's all true.

Boy Baby is thirty-seven years old. His name is Chato which means fat-face. There is no Mayan blood.

I don't think they understand how it is to be a girl. I don't think they know how it is to have to wait your whole life. I count the months for the baby to be born, and it's like a ring of water inside me reaching out and out until one day it will tear from me with its own teeth.

Already I can feel the animal inside me stirring in his own uneven sleep. The witch woman says it's the dreams of weasels that make my child sleep the way he sleeps. She makes me eat white bread blessed by the priest, but I know it's the ghost of him inside me that circles and circles, and will not let me rest.

〰〰〰

Abuelita said they sent me here just in time, because a little later Boy Baby came back to our house looking for me, and she had to chase him away with the broom. The next thing we hear, he's in the newspaper clippings his sister sends. A picture of him looking very much like stone, police hooked on either arm . . . *on the road to* La Grutas de Xtacum-bilxuna, *the Caves of the Hidden Girl . . . eleven female bodies . . . the last seven years . . .*

Then I couldn't read but only stare at the little black-and-white dots that make up the face I am in love with.

〰〰〰

All my girl cousins here either don't talk to me, or those who do, ask questions they're too young to know *not* to ask. What they want to know really is how it is to have a man, because they're too ashamed to ask their married sisters.

They don't know what it is to lay so still until his sleep breathing is heavy, for the eyes in the dim dark to look and look without worry at the man-bones and the neck, the man-wrist and man-jaw thick and strong, all the salty dips and hollows, the stiff hair of the brow and sour swirl of sideburns, to lick the fat earlobes that taste of smoke, and stare at how perfect is a man.

I tell them, "It's a bad joke. When you find out you'll be sorry."

〰〰〰

I'm going to have five children. Five. Two girls. Two boys. And one baby.

The girls will be called Lisette and Maritza. The boys I'll name Pablo and Sandro.

And my baby. My baby will be named Alegre, because life will always be hard.

~~~~~

Rachel says love is like a big black piano being pushed off the top of a three-story building and you're waiting on the bottom to catch it. But Lourdes says it's not that way at all. It's like a top, like all the colors in the world are spinning so fast they're not colors anymore and all that's left is a white hum.

There was a man, a crazy who lived upstairs from us when we lived on South Loomis. He couldn't talk, just walked around all day with this harmonica in his mouth. Didn't play it. Just sort of breathed through it, all day long, wheezing, in and out, in and out.

This is how it is with me. Love I mean.

The Pan Birote

Edna Escamill

Nobody wanted to get up early and wash with cold water just because it was Sunday and they had to go to church. All over the barrio, kids were trying to get away from equally determined *mamás*, who were torturing them with wet, smelly cloths and big-toothed combs that tore out their hair along with the knots.

El Güero y El Prieto were already cranky because the afternoon before they had gotten the mean Father for confession and had to tell him all their bad words, bad thoughts, and bad actions. Who knew if a bad word was said fifty-eight times or one hundred since last week? And was it their fault if the other boys wanted to run *en bola* past the girls on the way home from school and grab their *nalgas*? And how couldn't they have wanted the same thing even if they hadn't actually done it? The Father punished them as though they had done the bad stuff too; the darn mean priest made them say so many Our Fathers and Hail Marys that they were still in the church after all their friends had left, smirking at them, and it was dark when they came out. They had to run all the way home chased by *espantos*!

As soon as they got free of Abuelita's hands, the boys were outside fighting and throwing dirt at each other. Abuelita yelled at them, *"No dejan ni alistarse! En lugar de dar gracias a Diós están peleando en día de misa? Ya verán!"* I can't even get ready in peace! Just wait till I get you! she threatened.

At last, the old lady was ready along with that brat, Chiltepín, who had to have her braids done every morning. Abuelita corralled them all into the kitchen for inspection and they set out, Abuelita dragging Chiltepín by the hand and the boys following behind, shoving and hitting each other every chance they got. They had just invented a game out of kicking rocks when Abuelita yelled at them to stop wearing out their shoes. They ran around, itchy and hot in their wool suits, tagging each other just to get away from her eyes for even a second. Abuelita made one more appeal to God to give her *paciencia* and walked faster.

It was difficult to feed and care for three children who acted *como el demonio*, like the devil, and assaulted life without thinking of the consequences. And this Sunday the whole world would be there to get the *pan para los pobres*, the bread for the poor. This was why she was going to this church so far away—watching for *alacranes* and *víboras* at every step. *Los niños* acted *como si no tuvieran ojos*, as if they were blind!

Abuelita looked forward to those moments in God's presence when she could rest and believe in His ultimate plan for her. The children didn't have these expectations. They lived the cruel reality of the moment, but with the grace of the child who looked with bright new eyes at each day. So they did not yet suffer as she did, watching the years go by without being able to make things better and feeling guilty for everything that went wrong.

"*Ay, Diós mío, ayúdame!*" God help me! She tightened her grip on little Chiltepín's hand. She had to get bread for these hungry mouths even if it meant going to High Mass. Everyone would be dressed to the teeth *y iban a hacer malas caras* at her rundown shoes, which she had cleaned with water, and her common dress. Everyone would look down their noses at her. Well, they could eat shit, *que coman caca*, she reasoned. Bread was bread, and the children had to eat.

When they got there, the church was already crowded, the men lining up behind the pews in back. No, *se iban a morir de calor* if they stayed there. It was too hot so she pushed her three children ahead and squeezed them into an already full pew near the front. The boys immediately saw that the Sisters were all sitting across the aisle. They could see the hooked nose of "La Mala" poking out from her habit. She would be glaring knives at them if they said one word, and to heck with that! So right away they said, "Ma, we want to sit in back." "*Cállense!*" Shut up! said Abuelita and made them sit down. They wriggled and sat on Chiltepín until they pushed her out and got the aisle space, where there was a little more room for themselves. Chiltepín hated it up front because everybody acted like she could sit down on one inch just because she was little, and she couldn't see anything either. She tried to squat down behind the footrest, but Abuelita told her to cover her *calzones* and sit up like a girl.

This was not only *el día de pan para los pobres* but also the archbishop was visiting, so all the Sisters would have ants in their pants and find ways to punish them at school for how they acted in church. Already, the mean one had noticed them. Her eyes were glued to them and her stiff pale face was glowing in anticipation of slamming a yardstick against their butts.

El Güero y El Prieto kneeled down and stared at their dirty knuckles, gritting their teeth so they wouldn't start laughing or La Mala would drag them out from the pew in front of everybody. Chiltepín jammed herself in between Abuelita and a *gorda*, a big fat woman with red nails and rings on her fingers, who ignored the child and took up all the kneeling space.

The High Mass was longer than ordinary mass, and it looked like they put in more stuff because of the archbishop. There were four Fathers at the altar with him dressed in their gold robes. Everybody was wound tight from pride that they were having communion on this important day, and from fear that they wouldn't get through the mass without mishap because it was so hot and crowded and they were starving. Getting up and down and kneeling and sitting, back and forth, with rapidly beating hearts and dry mouths, *la gente* tried hard to concentrate on the holy mass. Their stomachs rumbled like freight trains and they coughed to cover up that noise so the whole church sounded like they had tuberculosis.

The hunger of the cathedral full of *gente* was tangible. It quickly made itself into a giant, straining entity reaching out to engulf the altar and finish the mass so it could get at the bread. The attending Padres felt it and glared out at *la gente* with narrowed eyes, daring them to be inattentive. So they shifted each guilty *nalga* gingerly one at a time, hanging from the edge of their seats and staring at their *libros de misa* with serious faces but not seeing a thing. Ruffling the pages for no reason, they gazed around at the walls during the reading of the epistle, unable to understand the archbishop's fractured pronunciation. Then they mumbled along with the Latin parts. There was a sudden wakeful silence when they heard the priest say, "And those are the words of the Holy Gospel, amen." After that, the Padres went through the offering of the Chalice, the Pater Noster, and the passing out of the Host with swift determination.

The people receiving communion had not drunk even a drop of water since the night before, and the Host stuck to the roofs of their mouths. To the innocent, there was always the possibility of panic, wondering if they were going to choke on the body of Our Lord and fall down and crack their heads on the marble floor. Trying in vain to swallow, and not daring to bite down on it, the boys contorted their faces and finally got their tongues to roll the wafer into a little ball, which they balanced while clasping their hands and scurrying back to their seats. They then worked the little balls of dough around in their mouths until they found the saliva from somewhere to swallow them. They were in a hurry for the mass to be over so they could eat the bread; the sooner the better.

With grand authority, the archbishop shouted out the prayers following communion and the people, chastised, beat their breasts with fervor, especially the children, because this was a chance to redeem themselves and feel sorry for all their greedy feelings. But all of them were secretly inching toward the end of their pews, getting into position for the charge to the altar rail for the bread.

From under lowered eyelids and squinted eyes, they observed the helpers bringing out the huge cardboard boxes from the sacristy. After one taut second of forced decorum, the entire mob surged forward, pushing and pulling the little ones in front so the number of hungry mouths could be counted. Those who got their loaves fought their way outside, skipping down the wide steps and barely dashing around the corner before ripping open the soft, fragrant tantalizing *pan birote*. This was a moment for all stomachs to expand. But Abuelita was strict with her ideas—she wouldn't let them start eating in the street. To stop their *chillando*, she told the boys they would have the responsibility of carrying the *pan birote* home safely.

It must be said, to their credit, that the family was more than halfway home before the two boys started to drift behind. *Los dos gallitos, un güero y un prieto, pero los dos de sangre de jalapeño*, roosters with jalapeño juice for blood, were grinning for one reason only: the *pan birote* felt like a captured warm-breasted chickadee in their little hands.

Ya venían mugrosos. They were filthy from the hot sun and the desert *remolinos* that showered them with dust more than once, but the thrill of inspiration was making their hearts beat faster. They were hungry *now*, and besides, a little dirty area, which no one would want to eat anyway, had appeared on one end of the *pan*. So El Güero, with the authority of the oldest, pinched and twisted off one end of the *pan birote*, along with the surrounding area, and popped it into his mouth. El Prieto followed with his loaf. The crisp, golden end appeared for one instant only between his shining, white teeth.

Flushed with the success of their initial acts, and with stomachs alert and pleading for more, it was a foregone conclusion that the soft, luminescent, innermost center of the *pan birote* swiftly appeared. The contrast of pure white against the brown of their hands and the dark fabric of their coats had the power of a beautiful painting.

This is what Chiltepín saw when she twisted her head around to check on the continued existence of the *pan*. Just as she turned, the boys tore off large chunks and, giggling and shoving each other in encouragement, stuffed it into their mouths. Seeing this scandalous activity taking place a few feet behind, and aware that she was still a vast distance from the kitchen table and the just apportionment of the *pan birote*, Chiltepín yanked hard on Abuelita's hand, crying, "Ma! Ma! the *pan birote*, they're *eating* it!" But to her dismay and complete incomprehension, Abuelita did not even turn around. She merely responded with an angry voice, "*Anden cabrones! No les pagues atención!*" Those jerks! Don't look at them! Nearly frantic over the rapidly diminishing *pan birote*, Chiltepín tried to get free of the hand keeping her from the bread, but Abuelita wouldn't let go. She was forced to gallop along in anger and despair, hearing behind her the guilty but triumphant laughter and the sound of chomping teeth. She could not understand why Abuelita wasn't doing anything about it, why she was told to play the part of the hungry and proud, but these things were nothing compared with the desire to get her share. In spite of being younger and a girl, deep in her blood she knew the meaning of equality. *She* was hungry and *she* had a right to eat too. And this had nothing to do with who was bigger or better.

The sun beating down on the long walk to and from church, the fasting ordeal already endured, and the insult to her stomach from the long-awaited *pan birote* that was in danger of never arriving—the bitter injustice of these things—was too much, and she finally twisted her hand free.

"You better give me some," she said, barely keeping the quiver from her voice.

"Oh yeah? And what are you going to do about it if I don't?" mocked the oldest. The other one, ashamed but a conspirator, said nothing.

They kept walking, holding the *pan birote* aloft and tearing off pieces with predator teeth.

"If you don't, I'll spit on it!" She was advancing while walking backward.

"You do and you won't have a mouth left," the oldest said.

"Maaa!" she wailed. "They're eating all the bread."

With a stiff back, Abuelita repeated, "*Déjalos cabrones.*" Forget it. "*Ya que lo manaciaron todo, que se lo coman!*" Now that they got it all dirty, they can have it!

"Why do they get to eat it and I don't?"

"*Porque así son los hombres.*" That's how men are. She walked faster. Chiltepín had to run to keep up.

"I don't care. You said we could eat it when we got home!"

"*Pues, ya ves, así es el mundo.*" That's life.

"No!" She ran back. Her tormentors committed the final sacrilege of tossing what was left of the bread back and forth between them, out of her reach. Facing them and planting her feet, she screamed, "I want it! I want it! Give it to me!" demanding more from the world than just bread.

"Here, you stupid crybaby," said the oldest. Tearing off a hunk, he threw it at her. She was picking it up when he shoved her.

"Leave her alone," El Prieto said then. "Let her eat it."

She ran to Abuelita, happily dividing her piece. "Here, Ma," she held up the fragment.

"*No. No quiero.*" Then kindly, "*Cómetelo tú, mi'jita.*" You eat it.

"Come on, Ma, it's for you."

Abuelita looked down and then carefully took the offered crust and bit off a tiny piece. "*Ya, no necesito más.*" That's all I want.

So straggling behind, *los dos jalapeños* ate the remainder of their *pan birote* down to the last crumbs on their identical blue suits. And Chiltepín, rejoicing in the fruits of her struggle, nibbled the wonderful *pan birote* with her strong baby teeth all the rest of the way home.

Somewhere Outside Duc Pho

Daniel Cano

The night we heard that our good friend Jesse Peña was missing, we decided to get a search party together and check the bars in Duc Pho, an old city in Vietnam's central highlands. We were in the rear area for a short rest before beginning the next operation, and we knew that under stress, sometimes guys who reached the limit and could not go on another day ended up AWOL, lost in the delirium of booze and chaos. But our orders came through and we were restricted to base camp, forced to disband our posse.

Two days later a long line of double-propped Chinook helicopters with 105 howitzers and nets full of ammunition dangling beneath them choppered us into the mountains, about a half hour outside our base camp. They lifted us to the top of a mountain that was scattered with light vegetation. Below and all around us, the jungle landscape was immense. Mountain ranges stretched in every direction.

We began knocking down trees, clearing away brush, unloading tools, equipment, packs, and ammunition. On our bare shoulders we lugged 55-pound projectiles into the ammo dump...long lines of shirtless men, bodies shining with sweat. The sledgehammers clanged against metal stakes and echoed as the gun crews dug in their howitzers. We filled and stacked hundreds of sandbags, which formed long crooked walls, some semi-circular, others round or rectangular—all protecting the battery just like the walls of a castle. And above the shouting voices, the striking metal, and the popping smoke grenades roared the engines of the helicopters as they landed, dropped their cargo, and quickly lifted away.

Once the battery was settled in, I took up my position on the outpost. There were three of us. We dug a four-foot deep bunker for ourselves and stacked three rows of sandbags around the front and sides, protection from incoming rounds and something we didn't like to think about: human assaults on our position.

One night, after a week of wind and cold, a trip flare erupted, lighting up the jungle in front of us. We waited, then saw a shadow move across the perimeter. Instinctively we threw hand grenades and set off the claymores. Later, from another outpost, a machine gun burst into a steady stream of fire. The howitzers exploded, sending bright lights into the sky. I gripped my rifle tightly and watched the shadowy treeline as the flares descended and a cold silence filled the air. As always the flares burned out. Once the darkness hit, again the world rumbled around us.

An explosion sent a blast of light across our field of vision, the ground vibrated, my ears buzzed . . . and moments later, my left arm felt warm. I slid my fingers over the wet skin and touched a hole of punctured flesh, just below the shoulder. I told the others that I was wounded, and they got on the field telephone and called for a medic. The firing stopped. The jungle reverted back to an eerie blackness. Doc Langley, the battery medic, walked me back to our small infirmary and gave me some antibiotics, bandaged my left arm, and told me to get some sleep.

The next morning I was choppered to the field hospital at Pleiku. Doc Langley, who was also a good friend, went with me to take care of the paperwork and refill his supply of Darvon. The doctors sewed me up and I slept the whole day.

When I woke up, Doc Langley was sitting on my bunk. I caught most of his talk, even though I felt dizzy from the anesthetic. He told me that Jesse Peña had been spotted. Some men from the Tiger Force, a reconnaissance outfit, had been on a listening post in the jungle. They'd been observing a squad of Vietcong. As the enemy moved along the trail, there, right in the middle of the VC column, they saw Peña, or a chubby Mexican-looking guy in American fatigues. The Tigers claimed that Peña carried an M-16 and walked right along with the VC squad, not like he was a prisoner but like he was a part of them.

When Doc Langley left, I sat up in my bunk. There was no way I could believe that Peña was in the jungle with the VC. It was just too ridiculous, and I knew that none of our friends would believe it either. I started to think about Peña and the last time any of the guys or I had seen him.

Peña was part of a small group of friends. There were about ten of us when everybody showed up, but usually five or six regulars. Since most of us were assigned to different units of the 101st Airborne Division, we'd split up during the operations, but always get back together when we were in the rear area. Each night, we would meet at an isolated spot somewhere in the brigade area—behind a sandbag wall or trash dump—for what we called our sessions. We would drink beer, joke, and talk about hometowns and friends.

Peña, who could hold our attention for what seemed like hours, hadn't said much that last night he was with us. He'd been a bit removed, sitting slightly in the shadows, and he refused to drink any beer. Still, he had smiled a lot, as if nothing was wrong, and had eaten a couple of cans of peaches and just watched and listened. Someone had asked if he was all right, and he'd just answered, "Yeah, I'm o.k." While it was still early in the evening, he got up and said that he was tired—carrying the radio during the last operation had kicked his ass. He straightened his fingers into a mock salute, touched the tip of his cap, and said, "Time to go."

"So early? How come?" Little Rod had asked.

"I'm getting short . . . only three months. Gotta save all my energy so when I get back home, I'll have everything ready for you guys. Sabes?" said Jesse, his words confusing us.

"Come on, have a beer," Little Rod persisted.

"Can't, gotta keep my mind clear. Me voy."

Jesse turned, walked into the darkness of the brigade area, and that was the last we saw of him.

Jesse Peña was short, rotund, and always smiling, like one of those happy little Buddha statues. Although overweight, he was handsome. There was a childlike quality about him, a certain innocence and purity that made him immediately likeable. Two large dimples, one on each chubby cheek, brought a glow to his face.

After each operation, we'd look forward to our sessions, so we could hear more of his jokes and stories. His humor wasn't slapstick or silly, but intelligent, and always with a point or moral. Sometimes he'd reminisce about family and friends back home in Texas, like his cousin Bernie who was so much against the war that he had traveled down to Eagle's Pass, Texas, pretended to be a bracero, and was picked up by the U.S. immigration. According to Jesse, Bernie, who was American and fluent in English, spoke only Spanish to the INS agents. He was deported and went to live with relatives in Piedras Negras. All this, Peña said, just to beat the draft. In this way, Bernie could say that he hadn't dodged the draft; it was the U.S. that had rejected him.

His stories led to questions and analyses, and all of us participated, pulling out every piece of information and insight that we could. Peña always seemed to have the right answers, but he was never overly egotistical. Always he came across as sincere and gracious.

I envied his ability to switch from English to Spanish in mid-sentence. His words moved with a natural musical rhythm, a blend of talk-laugh, where even tragic stories took on an element of lightness. He didn't present himself as an intellectual. His speech had a sophistication that didn't come with schooling but with breeding. Someplace is his family's background of poverty, there must have been an honest appreciation of language.

And he loved his Texas. To hear him talk, one would think that San Antonio was San Francisco, New York, or Paris. In his mind, San Anto', as he called it, had culture and personality. When it came to music, no one could come close to the talents of Willie Nelson or Little Joe Y La Familia. Those of us from California didn't even know who they were. He'd play their music on his little tape recorder and we'd laugh and call him a goddamn cowboy, a redneck Mexican out of step with the times, and then we'd slip into arguing about our states and which was best, and how the city was better than the country... and on and on until we'd drained ourselves.

I placed my hands behind my head and looked at the wounded men around me. I didn't really see them, though, because I was thinking too much about Jesse Peña. It didn't make sense that he had suddenly shown up on his unit's duty roster as missing. Why would he go AWOL?

Three weeks later, the operation ended, the scab on my arm had hardened, and we were all back at our front area base camp. I wasn't the only one who'd heard the rumor. All of the guys knew about it. Big Rod, who was about six inches taller than Little Rod, knew some guys in the Tiger Force who confirmed the sighting.

Feeling superstitious about the whole thing, we decided to move the location of our next session. Two of the guys found an isolated spot near the edge of the brigade area. On one side it was separated from the rest of the brigade by a decaying sandbag wall about four feet high. Many of the bags were torn, but the heat and moisture of the tropical valley air had hardened the sand as if it were cement. Empty wooden ammo boxes, some broken and black with mildew, were scattered around the area. Twenty-five yards to our front was the jungle—not as thick as the field, but dense enough to hide someone or something. As the night moved in, the foliage darkened and the only protection from the wilderness beyond was a gun tower manned by two fellow paratroopers.

It didn't take long before the guys, and some interested new ones, started arriving. We discussed the possibilities that Jesse was either kidnapped or had deserted. Kidnap seemed impossible because our base camp was a fortress: guards securing the perimeter in gun towers, M.P.'s patrolling in gun Jeeps, units posting watches throughout the night; it just didn't seem possible. Besides, I argued, what interest would the VC have in a PFC radio operator from San Antonio, who only cared about getting home to his wife and child?

Alex Martínez, a surly Californian from the San Fernando Valley, stuck to the argument that Peña had just gone AWOL. "Old Peña split, man—just got tired of the shit. He's probably shacked up with some old lady downtown. Tiger Force probably saw some fat gook dressed in fatigues and thought it was him, man. He'll be back. Give him a few days."

We kicked the idea around. It wasn't absurd. We were reminded of Michael Oberson, a cook who had gone AWOL, changed his name, and lived with a Vietnamese waitress in Saigon for fourteen months. He'd gotten himself a job with an American insurance company and a nice apartment in the Chalon district. He finally turned himself in, and while he waited for his court martial, he was assigned to our unit. We remembered how he had laughed when he told us that the U.S. government subsidized a portion of the salaries of all the employees who worked for the insurance company. "So," he would say, "Uncle Sam was paying me to stay AWOL. How could I give it up?"

Danny Ríos argued that Jesse was too short. Nobody went AWOL with only three months left. It didn't make sense, any of it. Besides, he reminded us, Peña was so committed to his wife that he wouldn't even look at other women. Although he admitted he'd seen a change in Peña's personality over the past couple of months. Like everybody else, Danny took it as a mood swing. He shook his head, more confused than anything else.

Big Rod said that he suspected more. "I've been thinking, you know," Big Rod began. "Not too long ago Peña told me something was wrong . . . inside. I asked him like if it was his old lady or kid, but he said no, it wasn't like that. He said it was more of a feeling, like something that grabs at your stomach and twists and twists and doesn't let go. Not too much a pain, you know, more like a chunk of metal glued to your stomach, something that hangs and pulls until it feels like your insides are falling, and he said it wouldn't go away. Every day he woke up feeling like that."

After a few hours, many of the newer guys went back to their units. The night thickened and the five of us who were Peña's closest friends remained.

We sat in a circle. In the middle was a used C-ration can filled with lighted heat tablets that gave some relief from the darkness of the jungle—a darkness that loomed silently around us. Every once in a while, we heard the whispers of the perimeter guards who were positioned in the jungle . . . human alarms against a possible attack.

Little Rod, who was from Brownsville, Texas—"Right down in the corner of the goddamn country," he once told us—pulled out his Camels, slowly tapped the bottom of the pack, and placed a cigarette to his lips. He sat on an empty wood ammo crate and leaned back against the sandbag wall. After a long silence, Little Rod leaned over, stuck his cigarette into the heat tablet, and sucked on the tobacco until the tip swelled in an orange glow.

"I seen him start to change," said Little Rod, whose English was heavily accented. He wore his cap down low on his forehead so that the shadow from the brim buried his eyes.

"When Peña volunteered to carry the radio, I told him not to do it. He never saw much action—not until he started humping that radio. I saw how he kept laughing, real nervous, when he came to the sessions, but I saw that he was trying to hide it. I could tell, man, that he was scared, too, something in his eyes. He tried to not show it . . . but I seen it. I seen it."

"Sure he was scared, man," responded level-headed Danny Ríos, a Northern Californian who always tried to find a balance in every situation . . . a cause for every effect . . . a good reason for every tragedy. He wore his cap high on his head, like a star baseball player, so that his whole face was visible. He continued: "Peña didn't know what he was getting himself into. He said he wanted to see some action, said he was tired of filling sandbags and carrying ammo. Yep, he got his transfer all right, and I think he hated it out in the bush. That's Charlie's country. That's his backyard. You go messing around out there and you best be scared. Common sense, man . . . common sense."

Little Rod didn't turn to face Danny. He spoke, his back against the dirty sandbags and his voice came out of the darkness: a somber tone exploring, probing, "It ain't what I mean. Peña's a nice kinda guy, you know? He got his vieja and kid. Every time the priest comes out to the bush, Peña goes to communion. Something bad had to of happen to him. Maybe he learned that God ain't out there. Maybe he learned that God ain't here either. The first time he carried that radio was when his platoon went in to help out C Company. You remember, C Company got ambushed . . . bodies tore up into thousands of pieces. Peña smelt the burnt meat, bodies that belonged to his friends. He saw those dead, nasty eyes."

"So what are you saying?" argued Alex. "You believe it was Peña the Tiger Force saw out there, that Peña is out there fighting with the Cong, that death is going to make him run off with the gooks? It don't make sense, man, no sense at all."

Little Rod continued, "I remember one time his squad come in from the bush, must a been right after his transfer; he's carrying that radio. Remember, Ríos? You was there. We was set up someplace outside of Tuy Hoa.

"Rain come down in chorros. Everything was like a sponge. Peña come out of that jungle into our battery area . . . his eyes big . . . like two big ol' hard boiled eggs. That ain't a regular scared. He's soaked, dirty, smelly, and he's talkin' a hundred miles an hour. You had to slow him down. Hundred miles an hour, ese. That ain't regular scared. Something happen to Peña, man. I seen it. That ain't no shit; I seen it."

"Little Rod's right. Peña was panicked. His face was stretched, his skin white . . . cold, like a ghost." Danny Ríos confirmed Rod's words. "He talked like a machine gun and moved with quick jerks. I felt sorry for him. His lieutenant let him stay with us a couple of hours. We made him some hot chocolate and warmed him up. He just kept talking, man. He couldn't stop. Two hours later, when his squad moved out, Peña went. No questions asked, didn't complain, didn't fight it; just like the other guys in the squad. He walked back into the bush like a zombie, and that jungle, with rain still coming down, swallowed him right up. They said they had to find cover before dark. Little Rod's right. That wasn't no regular scared. Hell, made me thank God I was in the artillery. But it's just common sense, man. Put a dude in a situation like that and . . . hey."

"Then it's still not logical. If he's scared," I asked, "why's he going to take off with the Cong? He wouldn't even know how to find them. And if he did, they'd probably shoot him first. Alex is right, man. It doesn't make sense.

"Yup. Don't fucking sound like Peña to me," Alex said, the light shining against his square jaw and pitted skin. "He's probably in town right now, hung over and wanting to come back."

Finally, Big Rod, who was like a brother to Peña, went through jump school with him, and had met his family while they were both on leave in San Antonio, spoke up, his voice more serious than I'd ever heard: "I think he went. I think he took off into that jungle and went with them. I don't know how he did it, why, or where he went, but he's out there looking for something . . . maybe looking for us . . . maybe looking for hisself. Remember his last words, 'I'll have everything ready for you guys.' He was trying to tell us something."

〜〜〜

The battery commanders from A and B batteries called each of us in to find out what they could. It was clear that they thought Jesse was AWOL and somewhere in Duc Pho. That's what most of the guys in the brigade thought, too. Jesse would come back, get court martialed, and that would be the end of it. But Jesse had never been in trouble before. He was the one who kept us out of trouble, making sure we'd get back to camp after a crazy day in town or calming us down after a run-in with an NCO or officer.

A month passed before a new rumor started. We were still operating somewhere outside of Duc Pho. A squad of grunts had made contact with a group of VC. They swore that a guy who looked like a Mexican, wearing GI camouflaged fatigues, had been walking point for the communists. It was no mistaken identity. One of the guys said he stared right into the pointman's eyes and that the Mexican just looked at him and smiled. Guns and grenades started going off, but Peña and his squad slipped back into the jungle.

Everybody in the brigade was talking about it. The guys who saw Jesse swore that it was "a Mexican-American" they'd seen out there. "The guy looked me right in the eyes. He coulda' shot me if he wanted. I was froze shitless" were the words of one grunt. It was strange how the words flew and the story built, but then, after a short time, the story transformed itself into a legend.

The story of an American leading a Vietcong squad was not uncommon. Everyone had heard it one time or another during his tour. Usually, the American was blond, tall, and thin. No one who told the story had ever seen the guy. The story was always distanced by two or three narrators, and it was more of a fable or myth, our own type of antiwar protest, I guess. What made this thing about Jesse so different was that the guys reporting it claimed personally to have seen him. Still, not many guys really believed it, except Big Rod, Little Rod, and the grunts who said they'd seen Jesse.

"Things are so crazy 'round this place guys'll make up anything fer 'musement," said Josh Spenser, an Oklahoman, who added, "I just don't know, man. I just don't know."

Two weeks passed before the next sighting. "Saw Peña, man." The guys who were now reporting the sightings started using his name, as if they personally knew him. One evening, when we were in the front area base camp, Big Rod, Little Rod, Alex, and I walked across the brigade area to talk to one of the soldiers who said he'd seen Jesse.

At first he didn't believe we were Jesse's friends. The guy didn't trust anybody because, as he put it, guys were saying that he was making the whole thing up, but after we explained our relationship to Jesse, he began to talk.

"It's the shits, man. Captain tol' me he didn't want me spreadin' no rumors," his voice lowered, "but I saw 'em. Big as shit, I saw."

The guy's name was Conklin. He seemed wired, like he was high on speed, sincere . . . yet nervous. He told us his story like someone who had been trying to convince people that he'd seen a UFO. Conklin said that he and his squad were on an ambush. They had the whole thing set up by nightfall: claymores out, good cover, M-16s, grenades, and an M-60 at the ready. He said that it was quiet out there, no noise, no animal sounds, nothing. But, as he told it, the VC never showed.

Since there had been no contact, the choppers came out to pick them up the next morning. He described how he bent down low and made his way out to retrieve the claymores. He disconnected the cap, and squatting down low, started to wrap the wire around the curved, green device. As he wrapped, he kept his eyes on the trail, looking both ways and also checking the jungle to his front. And then he saw Peña. Just like that, Conklin said, using Jesse's last name.

"Peña," pronouncing it Peenya, "was down in the bush, a Thompson submachine gun pointed right at me. I was gonna reach for my rifle but he just nods, cool-like, slow . . . and I know he means for me to not go for it so's I jes' set there and stare at him, and all he does is stare back. I couldn't talk, man. I couldn't yell. It was like . . . like one of them nightmares where you feel suffocated and can't nobody help you. Then he moves back, real slowlike, still squatting, like gooks do, an' then I see two other gooks, one on each side of him. He stands up and the gooks stand up and they move backward into the brush, just like that, fuckin'-A, man, and he's gone."

"What's he look like?" asked Alex.

"Got on gook clothes, man. Pajamas—a black top and black bottoms, cut off just above the knees . . . light complexion, 'bout like you," he says pointing to Big Rod. "I guess he's close to 5'7" or 8," not too tall . . . probably 145 or 150 pounds."

"Peña's closer to 175, maybe 180," Alex tells Conklin.

"Not no more he ain't. Guy I saw wasn't no 180. And when he

smiled, he made me feel O.K., you know. Even though I was scared and he could'a blown a hole through me, still . . . made me feel like . . . O.K. Maybe had something to do with those dimples. Big mothers . . . one on each cheek."

Big Rod and I looked at each other.

"Kinda made him look like a kid. But he wasn't bullshitting, man. It wasn't no joke. If I'd a gone for my weapon, he'd a blowed my ass clean away. I can't figure it out, man. Gone, just like that . . . disappeared with those gooks right into the jungle. And nobody else seen it, only me."

Three months had passed since Jesse disappeared. His ETS date came and went. Maybe we expected a miracle, as if Jesse was going to walk into the base camp, say "hi," and tell us about his days with the VC as he packed his bags and prepared to catch a hop to Cam Ranh Bay where he'd DEROS home. But nothing. It was just another day; besides, by this time we were in Phan Rhang, our rear area base camp, and a long way from where Peña had last been seen.

That night, the night of Peña's ETS, we held a "session," more of a funeral, over by the training course, which was at the perimeter of the brigade area. Even some of the nonbelievers showed up.

We met in front of the mess hall, one of many in the brigade area. It was located on a hill at the east end of the base camp, where we could look out over the entire airborne complex.

The sun had descended and the work day completed. We could see GIs slowly walking the dirt roads, some going to the Enlisted Men's or Officers' Clubs, others to the USO, and still others strolling as if they were out for an evening in some country town. In an hour or so it would be dark and carefully rationed lights would bring a different life to the area. There would be drinking and card games, laughter and yells, tales about families and girlfriends, stories of heroics in the field with a few guys displaying the macabre trophies. Some guys would listen to records in their tents and wonder what their buddies back home were doing. At the USO, they'd be talking to the donut dollies, playing Monopoly, Scrabble, dominoes, and other games, while in their minds they'd be making love to the American women who sat at the opposite side of the gameboards.

We turned away and headed toward the obstacle course. A range of jungle-covered mountains formed the camp's eastern perimeter.

We followed a dirt trail down a hill and gathered in a clearing that was used for a map reading course. It was off-limits at night so we had to be quiet.

As the two Rods and I approached, we saw that Alex and Danny, with C-ration cans and heat tablets, had designed a church-like atmosphere. The small blue flames, much like candles, were spread out in a circle to our front, lifting the darkness so that our faces were barely recognizable. The jungle surrounded us with a heaviness that leaned more toward enigma than fear. After a short while, the shuffling of feet along the trail stopped, the whispering voices were silent, and about twenty of us sat on logs formed into a semi-circle.

Big Rod said that there would be no drinking, not yet, anyway. Doc Langley handed him a stack of joints. Big Rod passed them around and said to light up. Not everyone liked to smoke, but this night they all breathed in the stinging herb. It didn't take long for the weed to take effect. The jungle moved in closer. The trees came down over our heads like thick spider webs and the plants weighed against our backs. The joints moved around the circle until the air and smoke mingled into a kind of anesthetized gas.

Big Rod pulled a paper from his pocket, unfolded it, and began to read. It was from Margaret, Peña's wife. The army had told her that Jesse was listed as AWOL because it couldn't be determined when he officially had been lost. In her letter, which made Big Rod pause many times as he read, she wanted to know what happened to her husband. She trusted that Rod would tell her the truth since it seemed nobody else would. Was Jesse dead? That's what she really wanted to know.

"Please answer soon," were her last words. Rod wanted to know how he should respond, then, frustrated, he gave me the letter. He said that since I was the one with some college, I should answer.

Johnny Sabia, an infantryman from Sevilla, New Mexico, and a guy who didn't come around much, said that we shouldn't be moping but that we should be celebrating. "Write her," he said to me. "Tell her the truth. Her old man split. The dude's the only one with any balls. I don't know how, but this guy Peña understands that everything here means nothing. I've never met the guy, but I've been thinking about him and I've heard the stories. Everybody's talking about him. I heard that

Peña lives in San Antonio, in some rat hole that he can't afford to buy because the bank won't lend him the money. I heard that in the summer when it hits a hundred, him and his neighbors fry like goddamn chickens because they can't afford air conditioning. So now they send him here to fight for his country! What a joke, man."

None of us ever talked about it. Peña never talked about it. Sabia was the first one who raised the issue. All we wanted to do was fight the war, get to the rear area, drink, joke, and never think about why we were here or what the truth was about our lives back home.

An argument started. Someone said that whatever we have it's better than what other people have. Even if we work in the fields in the states, it's better than working the fields in Mexico. An angry voice said, "Bullshit! We don't live in Mexico. We live in the U.S. Our parents worked to make the U.S. what it is; our fathers fought and died in WWII. We got rights just like anybody else."

Someone else wanted to know how come we get the worst duties. Whether it's pulling the shittiest hours on guard duty or going into dangerous situations, if there's a Chicano around, he's the one who gets it.

"Because we don't say shit, man. Whatever they want to push on us, we just take it. Like pendejos . . . we do whatever nobody else wants to do. We don't want to be crybabies. Well, maybe we should start crying."

"That's right," someone else said. "Gonzales got himself shot up because nobody else wanted to take their turn at the point. He walked the point for his squad almost every operation. What good did it do? He's dead now. Pobre Gonzales, man; talk about poor, he showed me a picture of his family who lived in someplace called Livingston, in Califas. His house looked like a damn chicken coop."

Then Alex stood up. He told how he was raised in the middle-class San Fernando Valley and remembered teachers who insulted him in front of his Anglo classmates, but only now, tonight, did he understand that it was because he was Mexican. Lamely, he said, "It never hit me. I just thought I was the only fuck-up in that school. There were a lot of white dudes who screwed up, but I don't ever remember the teachers jumping on them like they jumped on me."

Johnny Sabia talked some more, about tennis clubs built over fields where the townspeople of Sevilla had once grown corn and vegetables, about schoolhouses with holes in the roofs, streets still unpaved in 1967, primitive electrical systems for lighting. And he and others went on and on until they worked themselves into a fury.

Someone pulled out the beer. As the alcohol hit, the voices got louder and belligerent. Before long, the whiskey bottles started to make the rounds and nobody was talking about Peña any longer. Everyone talked about their friends back home, their girlfriends, or good places to find prostitutes in Phan Rhang. The session was over. Somebody kicked out the heat tabs, and the jungle, once again, distanced itself from us.

We marched over to the Enlisted Men's Club, toasted Jesse Peña several times, honoring him and wishing him well, and drank until they threw us out. Then we staggered along the roads, falling into ditches, staring at the stars splattered against the sky, and vomiting as we worked our way back to our units. We finally found our bunks and sank into a dizzying sleep.

The next morning when we woke up, most of us were hungover. We went through our usual routines, cleaning weapons and resupplying our units. A few days later, we flew out in C-130 transport planes to the next operation, somewhere outside of Chu Lai. There were a few rumors that Peña was still traveling with the VC, but no one would swear to the sightings. His memory became painful for those of us who knew him. When I left Vietnam, the new guys joining the Division heard about the Mexican who ran off to join the VC, and they kept the story alive, building on Peña's adventures. One squad reported that they saw his dead body after the ambush of a VC unit, but nobody believed that story either.

The Closet

Rosalie Otero

Every day I am suddenly aware of something taught to me long ago—of some certainty and self-awareness that grew out of conflict in my youth. When I was a child there had been many places available to me—for play, for daydreams, for imagination. I could talk to myself, spread out my toys, and escape to wonderful imaginary places. But, as the years went along, the family grew and encroached into my space until there was only my room and the garden. One day, when I was thirteen, my room went too.

It began when my little brother, Mikey, came upon me braiding the corn silk in the garden, running like the devil was behind him. I was engrossed in separating the corn silk into three even sections, the beginning of a prize-winning hairdo on my make-believe model. I let him know I didn't like his interruption, but he paid no attention to me, and just blurted out, "Tía Rufina is coming to live with us."

That Saturday Tía Rufina arrived. She was old. Her skull shone pink and speckled within a mere haze of hair. She wore orange-brown stockings on her contourless legs and a lavender coat with enormous buttons running down the front. As she rummaged through her purse, she complained about her hat, a gray flannel with tiny purple flowers around the band.

"Mariquita should know better. Mira, she bought me this gray hat to match my canas. Pa' más canas. I told her to take it back pero ya sabes estas muchachas. So you can match, Tía, mire las florecitas. Que match, ni match." She pulled out from her purse cough drops, which she considered a confection both tasty and salubrious, and gave two each to Mikey and me.

She had been delivered to us by two of her maiden nieces, Manuelita and Susana. She continued to think of them as young and would often refer to them as "las muchachas de tu Tía Mage." They were ten or twelve years younger than she was. They both had blue hair and black dresses with black beads on the bodice. They were, though maiden ladies, of a buxomly maternal appearance that contrasted oddly with their brusque, unpracticed pats and kisses.

As we dutifully kissed and hugged all around, Doña Maclovia Carson burst into the room in brilliant color and bustle. She was a portly woman with large breasts and skinny legs that made her look like a chicken. She had red hair which she dyed and always wore stacked on top of her head in a donut shape. Large glass earrings dangled furiously as she gestured with her head.

"Cómo estás, Rufina? Hace tanto tiempo that you've been here." She embraced my aunt who winced. Mikey giggled and I pinched him.

"I was hanging out the sheets and saw a car. I thought it might be you and I couldn't let you get away again without saying hello." My mother patiently explained that Tía Rufina had come to live with us.

"Oh, how marvelous! We'll be vecinas, comadre." Then in her usual style, sometimes subtle, sometimes brusque, Doña Maclovia began asking a series of questions, the answers of which she would later embellish as she gossiped with the other neighbors.

"Did you sell your house? Qué lástima, such a nice little house. You have arthritis? I have just the cure." Doña Maclovia considered herself a curandera claiming she had learned the art from her mother, Doña Dominga Sandoval. Mi Minga, as everyone knew her, had a good reputation and people from the community and even from faraway places came to her for help. She was too old and feeble now and needed constant care herself, but still every now and then she would wrap herself in her black shawl and place her hands on someone's pain. Doña Maclovia went about the neighborhood handling out remedies for everything from cancer to common colds. The people placed little faith in her cures and would say, "Esta no sabe nada. Nunca aprendió, nomás pa' mitotear y componerse la cara."

"Rufina, just mix some methanol and cinnamon and rub it in. Then cover up with a warm blanket and the next day you can do the varsoviana." She let out a raucous laugh and the donut on top of her head shook loose a few red strands.

"Maclovia, can you cure Fleabit? He's been limping all day," Mikey broke in with a pleading expression. He had really done it this time. Not only had he interrupted an adult conversation, equated Tía Rufina's ailments with the dog's, but he had broken the social rule. All adults had to be addressed as Don, Doña, Mano, Mana, Aunt, Cousin, Uncle . . . and a thousand other appellations indicating familial relationship and the lowliness of the addressor. My mother looked hard at him and then at me. I grabbed Mikey's hand and dragged him into the kitchen. Mikey's puzzled look became a mischievous grin when I scoldingly explained what he had done.

"Well, you didn't have to squeeze my hand so hard."

I shushed Mikey and listened to the cacophonous conversation in the other room. It was perfectly audible because Doña Maclovia was obstreperous and the three tías were hard of hearing. Only intermittently did we hear the mellifluent voice of my mother.

"No, that was Pablita, daughter of Pablo and María. Tú sabes, vivían en Cheyenne," Tía Susana was explaining.

"Hermana de la Josephina tu vecina?"

"No, no. Cousin to Josephina. She only had brothers."

"You remember, the oldest one was killed in the war and they never returned his body."

"Oh, si, she was the one who married her first cousin and they had that idiot son, cómo se llama?"

"Manuel."

"Sí, Manuel."

Mikey began to get fidgety. He wasn't interested in genealogies and neighborhood gossip.

"I'm hungry."

"Shshsh . . . I want to hear about the idiot."

"You're the idiot. I'm the hungry one."

I was torn between bopping Mikey and forever being ignorant

of the idiot, Manuel. "You always interrupt at the juicy parts. Go get an apple."

"I want a cookie."

"You brat!" I took a swing at him and missed. Mikey grabbed the package of Oreos and escaped to the TV room.

I missed the whole thing about Manuel. When I got back to listening, the women were on a different subject and I had missed the transition.

"Su vida fue muy triste, muy pesada. Siempre la tenían sembrando, escardando," Tía Manuelita was saying.

"Her father used to call us 'Carajas' especially when he felt we were keeping her from her work."

I wondered what that meant. I had learned a great deal of Spanish from being around grandpa before he died, not like Mikey who didn't know anything, but I did not know the meaning of "Carajas." I made a mental note to ask my friend, Mercy. She knew everything.

Late that afternoon the two tías readied themselves to leave and Doña Maclovia escorted them out acting as if she was sincerely going to miss them.

That night I went to bed in Mikey and Danny's room. Actually, Danny had moved into the room with David and so now that room was really mine and Mikey's, but it wasn't mine. I felt strange, out of place. I couldn't sleep and tried to read, but Mother said that I would have to turn out the lights because Mikey was sleeping. I wanted to protest, but it wouldn't have changed anything. I would just have to accept the fact that that's how things were and would remain. I cried softly into my pillow.

One evening I went out to the garden, the only place where I could sometimes be alone. The earth was pale clay yellow and the trees and plants were ripe, ordinary green and full of comfortable rustlings. As I knelt near the apple tree and heard the hollyhocks thump against the fence, I felt the breeze lift my hair playfully and watched the trees fill with wind. I felt a sharp loneliness. The kind of loneliness that makes clocks seem slow. I wondered if anyone could understand what I was feeling. There seemed to be no place for just me.

Our house was comfortable and quite large. Mother and Father had been very proud that they were able to purchase their own home soon after they were married. It had been a two bedroom, one bath house, but Father had built additions seemingly with every new child. He converted the garage into a large den complete with paneled walls and a built-in entertainment center. Later he enlarged the kitchen and added a bedroom and bath. When Mikey was born, he divided the den into two rooms; the smaller portion became David's bedroom and the larger side remained the TV room. Still later, Father built a large laundry room for my mother which he also divided into two rooms. Half became a pantry-closet. Mother always mourned the fact that the large window was on the closet side and she had to rely on electric lights whenever she did the laundry. Soon after Dad finished that project, however, he surprised Mother with a freezer and the closet became the "catch-all" room. Mother no longer canned vegetables and fruits; she froze everything. I think that was about the same time the kitchen was enlarged with a space for the freezer and a small pantry.

Father loved building projects. When there was no more room for add-ons and enlargements, he began with the yard. Every summer he would feign a fight with the lawn, pull out his wheelbarrow, and begin mixing cement. Every summer the lawn became smaller and smaller and flagstone spread in all directions. I was relieved that Mother had insisted that the backyard remain green with space for trees and flowers and a large garden. The grass in the backyard grew wild for the most part and much of the area had been left bald by strenuous play with the neighborhood boys. But even in the back, Father had made a large flagstone patio and walks leading to the garden and the small orchard.

I smiled as I recalled the determination and pleasure with which Father always seemed to work. He'd expect the whole family to inspect and approve all of his projects, which we did dutifully because they were always done well. My mother used to say that when Father nailed something, it would remain that way for all eternity. I walked back to the house comfortable with my thoughts. As I neared the door, I heard Doña Maclovia's ringing voice. I stole silently into the kitchen where the adults sat talking.

"Mano Mon is dying. I just went to take him some té de oshá. Anda, Maclovia, see what you can do, me mandó mamá. Pero what can I do? He just coughs and coughs."

"Is Tiófila with them?"

"Sí, pero esa uñas largas comes to see him con interés. She already took some of Pablita's, God rest her soul, best china. And poor Ramona ya tiene los ojos rotos de tanto llorar. I keep telling her that her brother hasn't died yet, but you know." She shook her head and her earrings went into a frenzy.

I knew Mano Mon. We called him "chipmunk" because he always had both cheeks filled with tobacco wads which he gummed down to a fine pulp and spit brown and rich on the street. I'd also never seen such a bald head. It glistened and the boys would say he buffed it every morning, first thing.

He died later that winter and we all went to the wake and funeral. Velorios were always festive times for children; there was good food to eat, the adults were busy, and we could run around unsupervised. Sometimes we would steal into the room with the coffin, peak at the dead person, and run outside to tell the others the horrors we had discovered.

"Mano Mon moved. Really!"

"He's gonna come and get you tonight."

"As long as he's not buried, his ghost is still around."

"You lie."

"I don't lie. My Dad told me that Mano Mon's spirit had gone to our house to say goodbye. The salt shaker fell off the table and nobody was moving it."

"Yes, that really happens. Doña Maclovia Carson swears she heard Mano Mon calling her. Right outside her window."

"She wished." This from one of the bigger boys who grinned lasciviously. "Yeah, she probably hasn't ever had anybody call her." Everyone giggled as if they had some great secret among them. I giggled too, but I felt a sadness for her. She dressed in loud colors and bohemian styles and talked friendly to everyone, but nobody loved her. She didn't have any friends, any real friends. I think my mother was the only person who really felt sorry for her and tried to be her friend.

"Whaddya think about Doña Maclovia and Inocencito?" The whole group went into hysterics. The boys jostled each other and the girls giggled into their hands.

"A match made in heaven." Floyd, one of the older boys, folded his hands as if in prayer. The rest of us just laughed harder. Inocencito, not his real name, although I don't know if anyone remembered his real name anymore, was a short squatty man with coarse black hair that fell unevenly around his head. He often wore a baseball cap sideways and since he rarely shaved, his wrinkled, weathered face looked dirty. He collected old newspapers and sold them along with the current ones. As if conjured up by our laughter, Inocencito approached timidly. He headed toward some of the men standing near the doorway. He removed the baseball hat and stuffed it into his jacket.

"Se murió."

"Sí Inocencito, se murió." That was my father's voice.

"Sí, he was killed. With a gun."

"No, he was sick. He just died a natural death."

"Read about it here." He pointed to the newspapers under his arm.

"Quién? Who died?"

"Pues, era el mero de Washingtón. El Presidente. The best we ever had."

The men stood straighter and listened more intently. The President had died? We listened too. My father took the newspaper from Inocencito. The edges were yellowed with age. The front page bore pictures and the story of President Kennedy's assassination. Everyone breathed as if in unison.

"Sí, Inocencito, President Kennedy was killed, but that was almost ten years ago. Where did you find this paper?"

"Ten years ago?" He shook his head not comprehending. He threw his head back in quick jerks in an effort to remove the hair from his eyes.

"Ten years ago?" He stepped through the men and into the house.

"I wonder if he thinks Mano Mon is the President?" Mikey asked.

"He just found that old newspaper. That's what I call being behind the times!"

"Hey, it could be worth lots of money."

The economics of the old newspaper were left to another day; the adults were gathering their children and leaving. Neither Mikey nor I slept very well. Our minds were filled with death and ghosts.

"Lucy, is it true what they said?"

"No, Mikey, they just wanted to scare you. Go to sleep."

"I don't want to die."

"You won't for a very long time. Now go to sleep."

"Is Tía Rufina going to die?"

"Yes, someday. We're all going to die. Someday."

If Tía Rufina died I could have my room back. I shuddered that I could even think such a thought. I prayed hard that she wouldn't die. "Oh, God, oh, Mary, sweet mother of Jesus, I didn't mean that I wanted her to die. Please don't let her die." I felt that by my mere thinking of the possibility, it could happen; it would be my fault.

"Lucy, are you praying? Are you scared?"

"Sh, Mikey, go to sleep. Everything will be okay."

Mikey finally fell asleep, but I lay awake a long time trying very hard to hear Tía Rufina's breathing in the next room.

On Saturday morning Mikey ran into our room squealing, "Lucy, Lucy, it snowed. It snowed. Will you help me build a snowman?"

"Good grief, Mikey, it's only six o'clock. Why aren't you watching cartoons?"

"Please, please. I'll go away if you promise."

"I promise."

How beautiful the white field in its blur of fallen snow, with delicate black pencil strokes of trees and bushes seen through it. I stood in front of the kitchen window for a long time. The snow silence becomes hypnotic if one stops to listen. I looked out on the patio and saw the charming lacing loop and circle lacing of Fleabit's tracks through the snow. The dog was racing around, waving his tail.

David and Danny appeared in the kitchen at the same time. They looked so much alike—tall, wiry, with thin lips and large brown eyes. It was hard to believe sometimes that they could be so different. David was seventeen, intelligent, quiet. He hardly ever talked, usually just gestured or grunted. He preferred to read or listen to music, especially jazz. Danny was fifteen. He was energetic and boisterous, more like Mikey. He loved to tease me, but he didn't get rough with me like he did with David or Mikey.

"What's for breakfast, little mama?" he drawled as he sneaked up behind and tickled me. I squealed. Mother, who had already started heating the comal for pancakes, frowned at us.

"Lucinda, get the bacon from the refrigerator. David, go take the cereal box away from Mikey. Danny, get your coat on and help your father sweep the front walk."

Danny groaned, but he was soon outside throwing snowballs at the windows and the dog. Mother shook her head, but I noticed a small grin.

"You kids, I swear. I should have sold you when I had the chance." She smiled at me and I felt happy to be in the kitchen with her. Mother was a flame that warmed and lit everything around her. Yet she was often, I feel sure, close to exhaustion. She swallowed the unacceptable because it made life so much easier. Hers was a life spent all in giving, spent for others, as the beloved queen of a tiny kingdom. She was a magisterial woman, not because of her height, she was only five feet tall, but because of her bearing and her upbringing. Her love for her children was utter and equal, her government of them generous and absolute.

That afternoon, Mikey and I bundled up needlessly since the sun was bright and hot and went out in the field to build a snowman. We put one big ball on top of another and carved them down with kitchen spoons till we had made a figure of a man in voluminous trousers, his arms folded. While Mikey knelt and whittled folds into the pants and shaped the bottom to look like oversized shoes, I stood on a wooden crate and molded his chin and nose and his hair. It happened that Mikey swept his pants a little back from his hip, and that his arms were folded high on his chest. We didn't do it on purpose—the snow was firmer here and softer there, and in some places we had to pat clean snow to make a stronger shape. When we were finished, he seemed crude and lopsided, but still suggested a corpulent man standing in a cold wind. We hoped the man would stand long enough to freeze, but in fact while we were stamping the snow smooth round him, his head pitched forward and smashed on the ground. This accident cost him a forearm. We made a new snowball for a head, but it crushed his eaten neck, and under the weight of it a shoulder dropped away. We went inside for a snack, and when we came out again, he was a dog-yellowed stump in which neither of us would admit any interest. During the winter there were other snowpeople that took the fat man's place. Some actually turned out symmetrical and jovial and stood for several days.

It was a long winter and there were rare days when I could escape by myself to some corner of the house. At least in the other seasons I could still visit the garden, but during the winter, I would get cold quickly and couldn't retreat into flights of imagination for chattering and thinking about the chill.

One day spring arrived. The garden had been full of surprises as the spring flowers blossomed, one by one. One morning Tía Rufina wanted to go out with me. She wrapped a wool shawl around her shoulders and leaned on my skinny arm.

"Que jardín tan lindo." She admired the lilacs that were out in profusion.

I felt a sadness about Tía Rufino. She was going from us, little by little. She seemed distracted or absent-minded, but I think that, in fact, she was aware of too many things, having no principle for selecting the more from the less important. She was in the final flowering and meaning of her life, but she would not be dragged into it, protesting, resisting, crying out. She was able to do less, enjoy everything in the present like a child.

"Tan lindo. Tan lindo." I felt helpless and sometimes terribly irritated by her repeating the same phrase over and over as she did. And she had death in the back of her consciousness much of the time. She would often say to my father, "Y que me muero y no me muero y allí estoy."

"Y esa ventanita?"

"That's the broom closet."

"It looks right out here. Such a pretty view. Such a pretty view."

The inspiration came slowly, but then, there it was. I jumped up, my heart thumping, my brain conjuring the perfect plan. I rushed to my aunt, danced around her, hugged her, kissed her wrinkled forehead shouting at her, "Oh, Tía, thank you. Thank you. That's it!"

She looked pleased. Did she know? Did she understand what I'd been feeling, needing, wanting, all these months? I galloped toward the house leaving Tía alone in the garden. Flushed, blustering, I deluged my mother with every logical and illogical reason I could contemplate. I made promises, resolves. I pleaded until she succumbed.

I finally got moved into the broom closet. It was a tedious affair what with all the junk that had been accumulated in there. Not only did I remove the brooms and mops, but hundreds of paper sacks, plastic bags, old newspapers, rotting potatoes, forgotten boxes, and rags, hundreds of rags—old, dirty, small, and large. The closet had also become the permanent residence of several microscopic creatures. I winced as I cleaned out sticky cobwebs and minuscule furry nests.

But I was determined to have my own space, so I had pulled down my sleeves—I couldn't bear the feel of cobwebs on my skin—and got to work. All day long the family paraded by.

"What are you doing, Luz?"

"Why are you in there? Are you being punished? What did you do?"

"Hey, Lucy, you found my old T-shirt?"

"Hey, Luz, are you gonna give these newspapers to Inocencito?"

"Lucinda, you are making a mess."

"Luz, can I have this neato albino spider for my collection?" and on and on and on.

I tried to ignore everyone. I had too much to do to engage in lengthy conversations or explanations. Besides, they wouldn't understand.

"You can't live in a closet," Mikey stated emphatically on his twentieth trip past the closet door. He crossed his arms over his slight chest and stood pouting.

"I can so," I shouted back. "Go away and leave me alone."

His eyes misted and he ran off to keep from crying. I felt badly that I had yelled at him. He was the funniest and most enjoyable of the whole family. He had shared his room with me eagerly, happily. He was always ready to talk and eager to learn. Every day since he started school, he would come home with a new word:

"What are piojos?"

"What's a lombriz?"

"Tomás said Doña Maclovia had almorranas. What's that?"

"What's a pecoso mocoso?"

Each time, mother would cringe or blush, look at Tía Rufina and either explain or dismiss him abruptly. One day he ran into the kitchen slamming the door behind him and asked, "What is chingado?" Mother turned redder than I had ever seen her. The color started at her neck and raced to her forehead as if she were being submerged in cherry Kool-Aid. Before Tía could even get a gasp out, Mother grabbed Mikey and dragged him to her bedroom. Mikey wouldn't say what she had done or said, but I know it had to have been very very serious and he was careful what he asked after that.

On his twenty-first trip past the door I apologized and tried to explain that since I was a girl I needed my own room.

"Besides, now you can have your room all to yourself and you can spread out your toys and play without my bothering you."

"You didn't bother me, Lucy. Don't you like me?"

"Of course I like you. Besides, now we can visit each other. I'll invite you to my room and you can invite me to yours." I tickled him and he ran off to "spread out" in his own room.

The broom closet was small, but it was mine. I arranged my bed under the window, my small dresser at the foot, and my father helped me put up a pole for hanging clothes. My mother made ruffled curtains that matched my bedspread, one for the window and a large one to act as a closet wall. I arranged and rearranged my belongings and looked out the window at the garden every few minutes. Tía Rufina shuffled in to admire my new room. She brought a large bouquet of lilacs.

"Pa' tu cuartito." She winked at me.

Enero

Mary Helen Ponce

"The baby," *la doctora* said, her wide hands pressing lightly on Constancia's protruding belly, "will be born in January. Uh, *Ineerio?*"

"*Sí, enero.*" Constancia smiled up into the pleasant face of *la doctora* Greene, then slowly raised her thick body to an upright position. In the clean, uncluttered bedroom the window curtains danced in the morning breeze and cooled Constancia's warm brow. She adjusted her underclothes, smoothed the bedsheet, then sat quietly on a chair, waiting for Doctor Greene to leave.

Constancia felt tired, lethargic. But my day is only half over, she told herself, smoothing down her dark hair. She sat, watching Doctor Greene, who with her customary efficiency, packed the worn stethoscope into her scruffy black bag, jammed a brown felt hat atop her head, and then, in her sensible brown shoes with the wide heels hurried down the porch steps and to her car. Her crisp cotton dress crinkling at the waist, Constancia stood watching the dusty 1938 Dodge as it went past, Doctor Greene at the wheel. On sudden impulse she leaned over the porch railing, her swollen stomach straining, to snap off a pink rambling rose from a nearby bush. She held the dewy soft flower to her nose and inhaled. The sweet fragrance made her dizzy, yet happy. She thought back to what *la doctora* had predicted. *Enero.* It would be a winter baby after all! The first of her ten children to be born in January, during cold weather. The others, born in spring, summer, and early fall, she remembered, had had a chance to thrive before the mild California weather turned cold. She sighed: *enero*, the first month of the New Year—a month full of promise. *Enero*, the month when winter roses bloomed.

Across the street Constancia spotted a neighbor and waved, the flower clutched in her hand. At thirty-eight Constancia was still a pretty woman. Her olive face was unlined, the black, wavy hair slightly gray. She, like other women in the Mexican neighborhood, spent her days cooking, cleaning, and caring for a large family. She washed on Mondays, ironed on Tuesdays, and each Sunday cooked a pot of stew for supper. Unlike some of her friends, Constancia was not overly religious, although she made certain the children attended catechism and Sunday Mass, and, during Lent, took part in the *Via Crucis*.

She took pride in her clean appearance, knowing that Americans looked down on "dirty" Mexicans who lived in the barrio. She never left the house without first washing her face and combing her hair. She seldom wore an apron without washing it and wore cotton stockings all year round, even in summer. She disliked wearing the maternity smocks stored in a box under the bed. Throughout her pregnancies she wore starched cotton dresses until her expanded waist literally burst the seams; then she retrieved the cardboard box under the bed, dusted the full-blown cotton smocks, and rinsed and ironed them. They hung in the small closet until the last months.

Constancia no longer tried to guess her unborn child's birth date—or sex. After the first two—a boy and a girl—it no longer mattered, or so she told herself. What did matter was that this baby be healthy, she conceded—healthy and strong enough to fight disease. She leaned against the railing, took a deep breath of the cool October air, pushed a lock of hair off her face, then went indoors.

In the roomy kitchen, Constancia pulled open a drawer where aprons lay next to snowy dish towels, took one, then slowly tied the flowered apron around her extended belly and began to work. She felt sleepy. The night before, the stirrings of the unborn baby, the rain that hit against the window, and thoughts of Apollonia, her eldest daughter, had kept her awake. Try as she might, she could not close her eyes without seeing the thin, pale face of her tubercular daughter.

The day before, a warm Sunday of blue skies and white clouds, had been busy. Getting the children washed, fed, and then dressed in their good clothes for the short walk to church was a chore. Gabriela, the baby, had fussed at being left behind by the older kids and had to be held for a time. Aware of the children's disapproval, a stubborn Constancia had forgone Sunday Mass. I'm not in a mood to pray to alabaster saints or sing hymns of hope and praise, she decided. Nor do I want to squeeze myself into my "good" maternity dress (bought at J.C. Penney). While Gabriel napped, Constancia prepared for the visit to Apollonia. Once the children returned she fed them the usual Sunday fare: *cocido*, stewing beef with carrots, potatoes, and onions. While the older girls washed and rinsed dishes, she packed a bar of Palmolive soap, chewing gum, and lemon drops into a small carton; then, with Justo at her side and Felicitas in the back seat, they drove to visit Apollonia. Later that evening, when they returned, Constancia felt tired and depressed.

But today is another day, she sighed, pushing aside the kitchen curtains to stare out the window, and I must finish my work. She rinsed the breakfast dishes left soaking in the sink, dried them, and put them away in the cupboard above the linoleum-covered counter. *Enero.* Three months left to visit at will the sanatorium where Apollonia, now almost eighteen, lay dying of tuberculosis. Three months to cope with the pain of knowing Apollonia would not live past Easter Sunday. Three months to make arrangements for the inevitable funeral—and to prepare for the child that was coming.

Apollonia, the serious, sulky child born to them in Mexico, had been in the sanatorium close to three years. When in elementary school she was diagnosed with pleurisy, then later with tuberculosis. Soon after, she was sent to a nearby sanatorium. At first, her condition had improved. Her youth, and the daily rest and medication, had arrested the fever, but the raspy, dry cough remained. The experimental surgery and the latest drugs have not helped my daughter, Constancia often thought, trying not to be bitter. Last month Apollonia had been moved to the infirmary reserved for critical cases. Two operations had failed to cure her; her weight had recently dropped. She was close to death.

The visit on Sunday had been especially trying. Constancia shivered as she remembered holding Apollonia's thin hands, squeezing fingers too weak to squeeze back. Long past visiting hours she had sat next to the sullen Apollonia, plying an embossed ivory comb through Apollonia's limp, curly hair, hoping to cheer her dispirited, pale daughter. But Apollonia, a bright and studious girl, knew she was not getting better, but worse. She refused to smile or eat the oatmeal cookies baked by Felicitas. Her dark eyes, like those of Constancia, shone bright, a sign not of good health but of the fever that was consuming her. When they left the sanatorium, which was surrounded by a grove of lemon trees, the sun was no longer visible. By the time they got home, a light rain was falling. Now, as she wiped the kitchen counter, Constancia thought once more about Doctor Greene's visit that morning. She sighed, thinking: I must prepare for life . . . and death.

Constancia hitched up her dress, then picked up the wicker basket near the zinc tubs in the washroom, *el lavadero*. The small cluttered room adjacent to the kitchen was a repository for dented tubs and empty glass jars. She walked outdoors, her steps slow yet firm, to the clothesline, where *calzones*, shirts, and pants flapped on the line. She laid the basket on the ground, pulled the clothespin bag toward her, then began to take down the clothes. Back and forth between the lines she moved, strong arms glistening in the sunlight. Constancia glanced up at the sky, never so blue, and at the birds darting here and there. With minimum effort she pulled, folded, and stacked the clean dry clothes inside the basket. Her pliant fingers released the wooden clothespins, then placed them in the faded cotton bag. The sun felt warm on her round face, in which the dark eyes, so like Apollonia's, blinked, then focused on a white cloud floating in the cobalt blue sky. *Enero.* In three months the clothesline would hold cotton diapers, and the *zapetas* would be folded in the trunk, Constancia knew. Once more I'll have a child and be forced to stay in bed for a month. One month without seeing Apollonia! How will I bear it? Constancia felt familiar tears sting her eyes. She took a handkerchief from her apron pocket, wiped her troubled eyes, then continued with her work.

It seemed to Constancia that most of her life had been spent caring for children. As a girl in Mexico, she had helped care for Rito and José, her mischievous younger brothers, a job she hated. The boys outshouted and outran her, slung mud and sticks at each other, and chased after the newborn calves. They refused to obey her and, during harvest time, hid in the haystacks piled along the road. She liked best to sit indoors embroidering linens, or to work in the rose garden that was her mother Martina's pride and joy, but she dared not disobey her parents. And now here

I am, she thought, pulling at the clothesline, still caring for children, still chasing after boisterous boys who play with sticks and mud. Still, still. Except that unlike my mother, I have nine children who depend on me and, come January, one more baby to care for.

Constancia lingered by the clothesline, resisting the urge to reenter the confines of the house. She stood on tiptoe, her stomach straining from the effort, to inhale the pungent scent of the green leaves on the walnut tree. The tree, planted when they first moved to the roomy house, was as old as Apollonia. Unlike the sickly, pale girl, the walnut tree had taken root in the rich California soil. It now stood tall, with a thick, gnarled trunk and large branches that sprouted glossy, gray green leaves. Around its base small shoots were beginning to show.

By next year the tree would bear fruit, Constancia knew. Round, meaty walnuts for the children to roast and for the Christmas cookies baked by Felicitas. She inspected the tree, her strong hands caressing the veined leaves, unmindful of the laundry in the basket: socks rolled tight as baseballs, undershirts folded in three equal parts, khaki pants turned inside out—clothes ready for the hot iron. She stood silhouetted against the walnut tree, her stomach round as a watermelon, brown eyes fastened on the fluffy white clouds that drifted across the pale sky.

It was during fall that Constancia most missed her family in Mexico. She vividly remembered the sudden change in weather with the arrival of the harvest months, when she and her sisters worked alongside their mother. During the peak days of the *cosecha*, they cooked *cocido* in the huge cauldrons set atop open fires and piled high the large wooden tables with steaming platters of frijoles, *sopa*, and baskets of hot tortillas. Each table held an enamel coffeepot which Constancia kept filled with *café*, the strong chicory-flavored coffee preferred by the ranchhands. Providing for the workers in Mexico was hard work, Constancia remembered, frowning slightly, as is caring for a large family. She sighed, looking up at the sky once more. And having to appear cheerful when I feel like crying is most difficult. But, I must persevere, like all the women in my family. At least until *enero*. I must be strong, for the new baby . . . and for Apollonia.

Don Pedro, her father, was often on Constancia's mind. As *gerente* of a large hacienda in Leon, Guanajuato, his job was to see that all went smoothly on the ranch. An intelligent, hardworking man, Don Pedro was responsible for the hiring (and firing) of workers, the harvesting of crops, and the replenishing of stock. More importantly, he kept all the business records and submitted monthly reports to the hacienda owner.

As Constancia folded a worn shirt into the laundry basket, she thought of her father and the many evenings he sat hunched over the kitchen table to enter numbers into the old, dusty ledgers kept on a shelf. With painstaking care he had dipped a quill pen in ink, then entered each transaction into the record. An astute, honest man, Don Pedro was known throughout the area for his kindness and integrity. Constancia sighed, her thoughts on the ranch in Mexico, then slowly picked a clothespin off the ground and put it inside the pin bag.

My mother, too, worked hard, Constancia recalled, pulling at her sweater—very hard. As the ranch manager's wife, Doña Martina kept the large house allocated to the manager in perfect order; there was never panic or confusion in that busy household. In addition to caring for a family of seven, her mother, an expert with medicinal herbs, often assisted ranch women during childbirth. Doña Martina also supervised the women at numerous chores connected to the ranch: hauling water, making soap, and wrapping goat cheese in muslin squares. During harvest time when the ranch teemed with men, wagons, and oxen, she was at her best.

When older, Constancia was allowed to deliver lunch baskets to the workers in the fields, where the warm sun and clean air beckoned. She enjoyed being outdoors with girls her own age, aware that the young men in the fields were potential *novios*. The older girls who already had beaus hid extra tortillas in the baskets for their men. Once lunch was delivered the girls, flushed from the long walk—and from being around the young men—were free to walk around at their leisure. Constancia had roamed the lima bean fields, staring up at the sky and clouds, wondering when Justo would return, when they would marry. She envied her sisters whose *novios* lived nearby, and who chided her for choosing to marry a man who wanted to live *en el otro lado*—a man who would take her far from her family, her roots.

Yes, we women on the ranch worked hard. Constancia groaned, shaking a creamy yellow towel, and so do women in America. But at least I don't have to make stacks of tortillas every day, although Justo would certainly like that. Still, there's nothing wrong with white bread. The

Americanas buy it, so why shouldn't I? And besides, she sighed, I've cooked enough in my lifetime. She pulled the laundry basket close, then yanked down a pair of socks with bunched toes, rolled them tight, and tossed them into the wicker basket, her mind still on Mexico.

Harvest time was fun too, Constancia remembered, folding a pillowcase into a perfect square. Large wooden tables were set beneath the cottonwoods that stood like sentinels next to the ranchhouse. There the workers were fed a tasty stew garnished with chiles grown on the ranch. Constancia and her sisters, giggling and smiling, had helped their mother prepare the food. She enjoyed the camaraderie among the workers; both the men and women relished hard work and the knowledge that they would be well paid. She recalled how the men attacked the food with gusto...and smiles of appreciation. She especially liked being assigned to serve the younger men, many of whom shyly looked away when *la hija del patrón* approached. But once Justo asked for her hand—and she accepted his proposal—she stayed behind to help her mother in the kitchen, trying not to pine over the tall, handsome boy she was to marry.

At eighteen, Constancia had married Justo de Paz, a man two years her senior. When seventeen, Justo had emigrated with an uncle to California, where for three years he worked the lemon groves that flourished in the damp, cold town of Ventura. He saved money, spending it only for room and board and an occasional sack of tobacco. His plan was to return to Mexico, marry, then return to *el norte* accompanied by his bride. He often worked on Saturdays, too. Now and then he went to town with his uncle, but for the most part Justo remained at the ranch to read the Spanish newspaper. Soon he taught himself to write. He wrote to Constancia, the crude letters smudged across the lined paper bought at the five-and-dime. He regaled her with stories of the wonders of her soon-to-be adopted country.

Everyone here owns property, Justo wrote: land, a house . . . and an automobile! I earn more money in the lemon groves than I ever dreamed of. He also described what he perceived as "strange American habits." Here everyone brings their lunch to work, he wrote, unlike in Mexico where a rancher feeds his workers. In this country they only give you water, and at times, very little of that. He told of buying a *lonchera* for his cold tacos. *Aquí todo es diferente*, he noted. Everything is different. This strange custom, of not feeding workers, was to Constancia appalling; her parents, she knew, took pains to feed the ranchhands. But, Justo insisted, in America each man provides his own work gloves and his own lunch. He posted the letters, counting the days until his return.

When it was agreed she and Justo would marry, Constancia began to make preparations. She accompanied her mother to Silao, a nearby town, to buy a bolt of muslin for the linens she would take to the new country. She and her sisters sewed tablecloths, *servilletas*, and a simple trousseau. Each afternoon they sat beneath the cottonwoods, assorted pins and needles at their sides, to embroider as a flushed Constancia read Justo's letters aloud. Her sisters were impressed with the reports written in large, round letters. Once read, the letters were stored in a cedar chest. The women all agreed: Justo de Paz was indeed a young man with a future. But that was long ago, Constancia now told herself . . . long ago.

Inside the house Constancia removed her sweater, then arranged the folded sheets inside the *petaquilla* that years before had accompanied her from Mexico and now stood at the foot of her bed. In it, between sacks of potpourri, dried rose petals wrapped in faded lace, were sheets, doilies, and assorted baby clothes. At the bottom, wrapped in faded tissue paper, was Apollonia's baptism gown, now thin and worn but with the lace intact. Constancia bent down, took out the potpourri, and brought it to her face. The aroma of dusky roses filled the room. She sighed, thinking back to Sunday's visit to Apollonia.

That day, as a surprise for her sister, Felicitas had wrapped dried flowers in a muslin square, sprinkled it with eau de cologne, then tied a bright ribbon around it. When given the packet, Apollonia had plunged her nose into the fragrant flowers, then smiled happily at her mother, who smiled back. But Apollonia will never return to this house, Constancia reminded herself, nor will she walk in the rose garden. She stood, closed the trunk lid, then returned to the kitchen, the smell of roses in her hair.

On warm summer evenings while the older girls washed the supper dishes, Constancia retreated to the rose garden to snip roses and carnations left to dry outdoors next to bay and mint leaves. When ready, the mixture was crushed, then wrapped in pieces of muslin and stored in the linen closet. But, thought Constancia, as she retied her apron, come next year, when carnations bloom once more, Apollonia will be dead.

Now, as she set up the ironing board in the kitchen, Constancia felt the baby kick. She sat down, held a hand to her stomach, and waited, but the baby was quiet. She continued to sit, hoping once more to feel the child inside her. She pulled at her stockings, then slowly stood, spread a starched pillowcase across the board, and began to iron. As she worked, she thought again of what was uppermost in her mind: Apollonia and, to a lesser degree, the baby due in *enero*.

As she ironed Justo's shirt, Constancia recalled how upset she had been to discover, early in May, she was once more pregnant. One time *la doctora* had cautioned her and other neighborhood women not to have so many children. "*No es* good for you!" the good doctor had said, her face agitated. "*No es* good!" And now here I am, Constancia sighed, pregnant with my tenth child. As she grew heavier, and the summer sun became unbearable, the visits to Apollonia tired her more and more. The drive to the sanatorium was neither bumpy nor long and, under different circumstances, it would have been pleasant, what with the orange groves and flowering oleanders along the highway. But Constancia feared catching tuberculosis, the highly contagious disease prevalent among Mexican families. Early on, the public health nurse had instructed her on what precautions to take when visiting Apollonia so as not to endanger the other children—and the unborn baby. Thereafter, upon returning from the sanatorium, Constancia quickly changed her dress and stockings, washed herself carefully, then, prior to cooking, rinsed her hands with alcohol in a tin basin.

After this baby comes I must remain in bed for six weeks, sighed Constancia, spreading a checkered tablecloth across the ironing board, or at least for a month. And I must try to get someone to help with the children. Justo does his share, and the older girls help with the cooking, but I do not want to burden them with my work. Never will I keep Felicitas home from school to do housework. Never. Yet with each baby I feel more tired, and it takes longer to heal. But until *enero* I'll visit Apollonia every Sunday and take her lemonade and cookies.

Once the baby is born, Constancia swore, the iron steady in her hand, Justo and I will have to sleep apart again. It will be difficult for him, she admitted, as she slid the iron across the shirt yoke, but it has to be done. She often heard the neighbor women comment on Justo's slim form, his unwrinkled skin. But, she grumbled, bending to retrieve a fallen handkerchief, I shall insist. Surely Justo will understand how weary I am of childbearing.

Soon after Gabriela's difficult birth, Constancia had claimed the sunny bedroom that looked onto the rose garden as her own. Justo now slept alongside his sons in an adjoining room. In Mexico, Constancia knew, couples who wanted to limit their children followed this custom, one more difficult for men than for women, a thing that created strife in a marriage. And Constancia loved her kind husband, keenly aware that at forty, Justo was still a handsome, virile man.

As the afternoon wore on, Constancia continued with her housework; the pressed clothes covered the kitchen table. She looked out the window, thinking of her mother, and of the subject of birth control. It was rarely discussed on the ranch, even among married women. Her mother had made brief references to couples who slept apart, as did she and her husband. According to *la Iglesia*, Doña Martina had intoned, her face a bright pink, any kind of birth control is a mortal sin. However, she concluded, one can always sleep apart. *That* the Church will condone. Constancia had heard her mother proudly note that her children, like those of her own mother, were born three years apart. Anything else was said to be *muy ranchero*.

Now, as she buttoned Justo's shirts, Constancia felt the baby kick again. She sat, waiting for the incessant kicking that often irritated her. She pressed down on her stomach, but the baby refused to move. With a weary sigh Constancia walked to the stove to stir the beans in the blue enamel pot, then returned to the iron. As she worked she thought back to her cousin Amador's last visit, a visit she sensed had contributed to her pregnancy.

Justo was not a drinking man, although he now and then bought a jug of dago red at an Italian market. The wine was stored in the pantry for company, or special occasions. Constancia hated the taste of alcohol and stuck the jug behind the oatmeal. Like her mother before her, Constancia feared *el vicio*, the alcoholism said to afflict even the best of families. She remembered well her parents' pain when Lucas, her brother, moved to the city and took to the bottle. The shame still rankled. She knew her father approved of her husband because Justo, an anomaly among his friends, rarely drank. He drank only when her cousin, that rascal Amador, visited.

Amador was Constancia's first cousin, a well-built, fair-skinned, vain man who wore a white Panama hat in summer and a gray fedora in winter. He visited often, accompanied by his sour (and homely) wife and three robust sons. Amador liked to drink. He also liked for everyone else to drink. When he visited in his shiny Ford (with a rumble seat) he brought two things: a jug of wine and roses for his cousin Constancia. As much as she protested his drinking, Constancia's eyes lit up at the sight of Amador, her handsome, flirtatious cousin who throughout the visit chided Justo for having married the boss's daughter. Within minutes of Amador's arrival, Constancia took to the kitchen to prepare his favorite dish of chicken *mole* while the men sat to talk—and drink dago red. By suppertime Amador's fair skin was flushed red, his caramel brown eyes slightly glazed. After the meal, if the weather was warm, the men sat in the small patio covered with palm fronds to eat *capirotada* and drink hot coffee. While Justo and Amador ate dessert and drank coffee from the flowered cups given free with Rinso soap powder, Constancia hid the wine in the pantry, a clear sign that all drinking had come to an end.

In early April Amador had visited and, as usual, polished off a jug of wine. Unable to drive, he asked to remain overnight. Much to Constancia's chagrin, he was given her husband's bed. A smiling Justo returned to the double bed. Soon after Constancia knew she was in the family way. A contrite Justo returned to his solitary bed. His loud snores, he carefully explained, made sleep impossible for his pregnant wife.

Inside the large kitchen, a flushed Constancia stirred the beans cooking on the stove. By the time the famished children arrived home from school, she knew, the rosy plump beans would be ready. The bean soup garnished with tomatoes and onions was especially tasty with hot tortillas, and was a favorite of the children, except Gabriela, who hated onions.

Although she worked hard, Constancia knew enough to pamper herself. She napped most afternoons and, whenever possible, slept in. She no longer cooked tortillas for each meal. She knew the younger children preferred Weber's bread, bought at the corner store. Lately she was too tired to cook even a few tortillas; Justo now ate bread, too. As she added a limp onion to the beans, Constancia stopped to gaze out the window at the graying sky. It will be cold in *enero*, she sighed, cold and wet.

She was surprised to see birds darting back and forth outside, small twigs in their beaks. The birds are preparing for winter, Constancia thought—securing nests and storing food. Arms folded across her swollen stomach, she leaned on the window frame, gazing at the clouds.

Her habit of watching cloud formations often irritated Justo.

"*Qué tanto miras en las nubes?*" he often asked.

"*Nada. Sólo me gusta ver para afuera.*"

The clouds remind me of the ranch in Mexico, she longed to say, and of the lazy summers when I played on the open meadows . . . of when I was free. On sudden impulse, she pushed aside the curtain. The sky above, she noted, was almost as blue as the Mexican sky that long ago hovered over her sisters and her as they walked across grassy meadows, kicking at dirt clods. Evenings at the ranch were spent telling stories, while the overhead sky turned a deep, purplish blue. When of late Constancia gazed at the sky, Justo said nothing.

Inside the large kitchen Constancia slowly moved, aware of the baby pushing against her ribs. She wandered outdoors, to the rosebush that bloomed from early summer to late fall, adjusted her cotton dress, then squatted on her bare knees. The soil felt cold and damp against her warm skin. She pulled the dry leaves off the rose plant, then bent low to get at the shoots sprouting at the base. This bush cannot grow with these small suckers, she grumbled, her hands coated with mud. They take the nourishment needed by the plant to grow. If I get rid of them the roses will bloom much bigger and prettier. Still, I must cover them at night, or the frost will kill them. She remained in the quiet garden, her round form bent low, until Gabriela, in need of a bottle, called her; then she reluctantly went indoors.

Later that evening, as she cleared the crude table made years ago by Justo, Constancia noted the household repairs she wanted done before January. New linoleum would be nice, she murmured: blue with a red border. Two more clotheslines would help too. And, while it was not a priority, a yellow rose plant would be nice. She smoothed her crumpled apron, thinking of the one task she had so far ignored: the sorting of the baby clothes in the trunk, a job she found depressing. Still, I must do it while I have the time, Constancia reasoned, pushing back her dark hair—before Apollonia gets worse . . . and before *enero*, while I have the strength. She rinsed her hands, then walked to the bedroom that over-looked the rosebushes.

With each pregnancy Constancia added and discarded baby clothes: undershirts, flannel nightgowns, embroidered sweaters of soft, light colors. The worn diapers were used as cleaning rags and, when handy, by Justo to wipe oil off his hands. But Apollonia's clothes, worn by no one else, lay intact at the bottom of the trunk, between yellowed sheets of tissue paper: smocked dresses trimmed in lace, crocheted caps braided with pink ribbons—each item too precious to discard. Each piece had been stitched by her mother and sisters in Mexico. Each buttonhole had been sewn when life had held such promise, such happiness! But now Apollonia is dying, Constancia sighed, fighting back tears. I have no reason to keep them.

In the dim bedroom Constancia pulled close the rocking chair. She heaved her ample body into the chair, then slowly pulled the dented trunk to her feet. She rummaged through the clothes that smelled of dust and roses; her fingers clutched a faded bonnet, then came to rest on a tiny gossamer dress. Constancia's eyes brightened at the sight of the silky dress, now a faded rose color. She pressed the tiny gown to her breast, then brought it to her face. Apollonia. *Hija mía*, she sighed, as warm tears streamed down her face to land on her breasts and stomach. I cannot bear to lose you.

In the evening shadows the rose plants visible through the windows shone a deep green, the blossoms closed tight for the night. Constancia sat lost in thought, the baby dress clutched in her hands. Perhaps the baby can wear Apollonia's dress, she decided, wiping her swollen eyes. Perhaps. She held the baptismal dress against her beating heart, leaned back in the rocker, and closed her eyes. She remained motionless for a time. Suddenly, Constancia stood up, smoothed her dress, and took a deep breath. I *will* dress the coming baby in Apollonia's clothes, she vowed—in the dresses, booties, and crocheted jackets. I'll wash the baptismal dress and come next Sunday, I'll show it to Apollonia. Knowing her new brother—or sister—will be christened in this gown will make her happy, make her smile. She shook the clothes free of dust and closed tight the metal trunk; then, baby dress clutched in her hands, Constancia went out of the dark room and into the warm kitchen.

Smeltertown

Carlos Flores

"Your mother says we won't be able to have the *carne asada*."

"Why not?"

"She had a fight with your sister. Your brothers have gone out with their friends, and your father may not be back until late."

Disheartened, Américo laid the razor on the washbasin's rim, then lowered the toilet seat and sat down.

"I told you there would be no point in having a *carne asada* with my people," he said.

Jovita's gaze fell. The *carne asada* had been her idea, a family cook-out like those they had so often enjoyed at home with her family.

"*Ni modo*," she said, resting her sad face against the doorjamb.

Américo pulled his socks from out of his cowboy boots, crossed his legs, and dusted off the bottom of his foot. He was not accustomed to boots but wore them to please Jovita, who had grown up close to the ranch life of South Texas. She enjoyed seeing him dress like the men from Escandón. He did not particularly like the boots, although the riding heels did give him a bit of height, an illusion of stature, and another illusion—that he belonged with Jovita, with her relatives, and with the other Mexicans in Escandón who looked upon him as an outsider. He slipped on his socks, put on his boots, and looked up at Jovita.

"What do you want to do?" he asked.

"We could go eat in Juárez."

"Too much traffic on the bridge. Remember, it's Sunday. Besides, I don't want to touch another drink."

"What about a movie?"

"*Chula*," he said, wanting to reach for her and hold her so he wouldn't hurt her feelings, "I didn't drive six hundred miles to El Paso just to see a movie. Maybe we could go for a ride."

"But where?"

"Anywhere," he said.

They were silent for a moment. Américo thought about the lake. He decided against it when he remembered its muddy waters and gangs of shirtless Mexican men, beer cans in hand. Then he thought about a ride out to his father's acreage down the valley. No, he didn't want to go there either, having been there with his father several times, politely listening to his impractical dream about how one day the whole family might move there, build their homes, and live happily ever after. Then the image of a cross atop a peak popped into Américo's mind.

"How about Smeltertown?" he said.

"Smeltertown? What's that? An oil refinery?"

Américo laughed.

"No *mi'jita*," he said. "It's where my mother was born. A little Mexican village upriver."

"That place you pointed out when we were coming back from New Mexico on our honeymoon?"

"Did I?"

"Don't you remember, Américo? It was the first time you brought me to El Paso to meet your parents. We drove up to New Mexico and got stuck in the snow."

"I didn't get stuck. The car just skidded all over the place, that's all."

"Well, whatever. When we drove back, you said, 'Look, that's where my mother was born,' and then we went to eat at that restaurant nearby."

"La Hacienda?"

"Yes."

"Would you like to eat there again?"

Américo loved to see Jovita happy, the delight in her dark eyes. Américo got up and kissed her cheek.

"I'll be ready in a minute," he said, stepping to the washbasin.

Américo turned to the mirror and saw a Mexican face the color and shape of a chunk of adobe, his black hair unmanageably aflame. With his fingers he spread the aerosol spurt of white cream against the *tierra-café* of his skin. As he shaved, he decided that their three-day visit to El Paso had not been as unpleasant as others. Still, he knew that if Jovita had not insisted upon these yearly visits since the beginning of their marriage, he would never have set foot in El Paso again. He rinsed the razor and his hands and put the shaving things away. After combing his hair, he slipped on gold-rimmed, green-tinted glasses. Dressed in dark blue pants and a white *guayabera* embroidered with blue and black pyramids, Américo prepared himself to face his mother in the kitchen.

~~~~~~

"Look how handsome my son looks!" said Señora Izquierdo.

"Good morning," he said.

"Good morning?" responded Señora Izquierdo. "You mean good afternoon."

"What time is it?"

"There's a clock on the wall."

It was already past one in the afternoon.

"Señora," said Américo, inhaling self-consciously, "I'm on vacation. It's Sunday." Américo never said "Mom."

"At home," Jovita said, her eyes gliding on a smile from Américo to his mother, "he never gets up earlier than twelve on weekends."

"You don't go to church on Sunday?" asked Señora Izquierdo. Her eyes widened in feigned shock at what she had always known to be Américo's indifference toward church. She attended when she could, by herself.

Américo rolled his eyes.

"Too much of this," said Señora Izquierdo, cocking her hand so that her thumb almost touched her lips and her pinky stuck out like an upended bottle.

"Nonsense," said Américo. He smiled. "It's just that Jovita never lets me out of bed in the morning."

"You lie, Américo!" said Jovita, embarrassed.

"It's true, Señora," he said. "What else can a man who wakes up with a beautiful woman do except stay in bed?"

"Américo, *te sales!*" said Jovita, ready to spring at him.

"Jovita, why are you so mean with my son?" said Señora Izquierdo, chuckling. "Why don't you let him out of bed in the morning?"

"Señora, it's your son," said Jovita. "The Izquierdo men are terrible."

Señora Izquierdo blinked. "You can say that again," she said to Jovita.

"Is there any coffee?" said Américo.

Señora Izquierdo's face changed. "Sí, mi'jito," she said, bundling toward the stove. "Do you want any breakfast?"

"No, thanks," said Américo.

He took a chair at the table next to Jovita. As his mother poured the coffee into the cup, it steamed. Señora Izquierdo returned the coffeepot to the stove, walked to her place by the kitchen sink, and began peeling potatoes. She had been a maid before she married. Her short, pudgy body was at home in cheap cotton dresses and flat sandals. Her fingers were stubby from housework.

"*Bueno*," she said, talking seriously now, though with a mischievous sideways grin, her eyes upon the blade sliding beneath the potato's skin, "since both of you have such a difficult time getting out of bed, when, I would like to know, are you going to give me"—she looked up— "a grandson?"

"First, we need to buy a house," said Américo. "We want to travel too, maybe Europe."

"Naw," said Señora Izquierdo irritably, "that'll take too long. I may die before I see my first grandson."

"You're not that old, Señora," said Américo.

"You never know."

"Tonight," said Jovita. Américo looked at Jovita with a what-are-you-talking-about frown.

"That's better!" said Señora Izquierdo. "Did you hear that Américo?"

"Well," Américo said, an earnest tone in his voice now, "we have been thinking about a child. We just don't know when or how soon."

He took out a cigarette. When he looked around for a place to dump the match, his mother found an ashtray hidden in one of the kitchen cabinets. White-edged streams of smoke filled the bright kitchen. Américo knew what she thought about his smoking, but he couldn't put off the cigarette much longer. Besides, his father wasn't home.

"You and Jovita are going to eat here, no?" asked Señora Izquierdo, her eyes on Américo.

"We are going out to dinner," said Américo.

"Ooooooo!" Señora Izquierdo stopped peeling potatoes.

"I want to take Jovita to see Smeltertown."

Señora Izquierdo's face registered dismay.

"Smeltertown? What are you going to do in Smeltertown? There is nothing there."

"Américo wants to show me where you were born," Jovita said.

Señora Izquierdo's eyes flared at her son.

"Américo," she demanded, one arm akimbo, "when was I born in Smeltertown?"

"I meant to say that you were raised there," Américo apologized.

"Your father put that idea in your head. He thinks I was born in Mexico. No señor—I know where I was born. It was not Mexico. It was not Smeltertown. I was born in Williams, Arizona."

No one in the family knew anything about Williams, Arizona, not even his mother, as far as Américo could tell, but Señora Izquierdo had always made it a point to say that she had been born there. Not El Paso, not Ciudad Juárez across the river, where most of her surviving family lived in a three-room adobe hovel. Not Smeltertown, where she had been raised from early childhood by La Abuela and Tía Rosaura.

"Ay qué Américo," sighed Señora Izquierdo, "you don't even know where your mother was born." Her eyes flashed at him again. "Do you know who your mother is?"

"No, I don't," he said. He loved the banter. It brought him close to his mother.

"Américo!" Her black hair shook in every direction. "I'm your mother."

Jovita laughed. "Are you *sure*, Señora Izquierdo?" she said.

"What?" Señora Izquierdo said indignantly, though a smile glimmered. "I know my children like the palm of my hand. I should. I cleaned them enough times with it!"

Américo grinned and shook his head.

"I can prove I'm from Williams, Arizona," insisted Señora Izquierdo.

"It's your father I worry about. He's such a liar I wonder sometimes if he's really from where he says he's from."

But Américo knew better. Señor Izquierdo was not born in El Paso either. He was from Puerto Rico, a potato-shaped island in the Caribbean Sea. Américo had visited it once in a disappointing attempt to find out more about the old man. Señor Izquierdo hated El Paso, an empty desert surrounded by arid mountains, so unlike the lush green of Puerto Rico, *la perla de los mares*. He sometimes talked of abandoning his family and returning to his *Borinquen querido*. With that threat and others, he reminded them that he was no Mexican.

They heard a car in the carport. Its engine died abruptly and someone got out. Señora Izquierdo peeped outside the kitchen door.

"It's Papi," she said, running back to her place. Her knife whipped around the fresh potato she took from the kitchen counter, and her face became self-absorbed.

Américo put out his cigarette and sat upright in his chair. Beneath the table, one of his legs began to bounce nervously. He raised his eyebrows at Jovita, who reclined in her chair with her hands together on her lap.

The door cracked open, then slammed shut. Señor Izquierdo wore a fedora on his frizzy head and carried a brown grocery bag in his arms. He was a short man in his sixties. His sharp, restless gaze alighted upon Américo and Jovita: he ignored Señora Izquierdo at the sink.

"Hello, Américo," he said in a level voice.

"Hello, Pop."

"*Buenas tardes*," Señor Izquierdo said to Jovita.

"*Buenas tardes*."

One at a time, Señor Izquierdo's muscular arms reached inside the grocery bag and retrieved fistfuls of apples and oranges. "I brought you these," he said to Américo, a boyish smile parting on his mustachioed mouth.

"Thanks, Pop."

"Do you want one?"

"No, thank you."

Jovita declined too.

Señor Izquierdo, momentarily unsettled, put the fruit inside the bag and moved it to the kitchen counter. Without looking at his wife, he strolled to the stove where he poured himself some coffee. His squat, rural hands were unsteady as he stirred the cream and sugar into it. He wore an old, unfashionable shirt and once dressy pants exhausted by repeated laundering and daily wear. It was part of his refusal to waste his "children's money" on new clothes for himself, though he needed them for his public image as a furniture salesman. He stood in shoes swollen by hours of vigilant work.

"I understand you are leaving tomorrow," said Señor Izquierdo.

"Yes, sir," replied Américo.

"Do you need any money?"

"No, sir. Thank you very much."

"You know that you can always count on me if you need anything."

"Yes—I understand."

Señor Izquierdo's eyes wandered toward Jovita, who sat quietly next to Américo. Américo knew she wouldn't speak to his father if she could avoid it, but Señor Izquierdo thought he had gotten her attention.

"My children," he said to her, "come before anything else in the world. They are not like so many children I see in the streets—filthy, hungry, no one to tell them what's wrong or right. My children have a man for a father!"

Américo hated what his father said and the manner in which he said it, the tone of his voice as impudent as the ridiculous fedora askew on his head.

"Have you eaten?" Señor Izquierdo's attention returned to Américo.

"No, sir. We are going out to eat. We were going to have a *carne asada*," Américo said, "but everybody left, and we didn't know when you'd get back."

"You can have a *carne asada* without me."

"We want the family together."

"Yes." He sipped his coffee, nodded his head thoughtfully. "A family should always be together, should always work together. A family is a source of strength. Of course," he raised his eyebrows, "it's not easy. There are always people in the family who oppose the family's unity, people who plot against the father, who refuse to serve him a decent meal . . ."

Américo tensed at the obvious insult to his mother. It was an old conflict, this business of the food, and it turned his stomach.

"Have you died of hunger?" shouted Señora Izquierdo. She kept her back toward them.

"Do you know Américo," the old man continued, "that half the food in this house is wasted because it is not cooked properly? Do you think that is right?"

Señora Izquierdo turned and glared at the back of her husband's head.

"If you don't eat," she shouted, "it's because you are an old man who cannot eat with your false teeth!"

Américo glanced at Jovita. She swallowed a smile. He focused his eyes on the clock on the wall.

"Américo," his mother said, taking a position at Señor Izquierdo's side, her face drawn, "ask your father who showed him how to use a bathroom. Ask him who told him he could sit on a toilet bowl, that he didn't have to crouch on it as if he were in some outhouse in Puerto Rico. You should have seen him. For years he perched like a *gallo* on the toilet bowl. When your father arrived in El Paso, he was nothing but a *jíbaro* and it was me"—she pointed the knife at herself—"who educated *him*"—she pointed the blade at her husband.

She remained where she stood, eyes, ears, and mouth alert for whatever else he might say.

"All my life," Señor Izquierdo said to Américo, "I have worked to provide this house with everything it needs. My children have had everything they needed. Your mother has never had to work."

"And who has washed your filthy underwear?" Señora Izquierdo eyed her husband with the tusk-keenness of an embattled *javalina*.

"Yet, this is all I get," said Señor Izquierdo, regarding his wife with contempt. "A filthy mouth, ingratitude, disrespect."

Señor Izquierdo shook his head. He turned to Américo and in a confidential tone said, "I'll be in my room. I am working on some big plans I'd like for you to know about. I am thinking about opening a store."

He prepared himself another cup of coffee and then disappeared as abruptly as he had arrived, sliding the kitchen door shut behind him.

"Good," said Señora Izquierdo, relaxing her grip on the knife and turning toward Américo and Jovita. "He's gone."

Américo's leg stopped bouncing beneath the table. He felt he could breathe at last. Jovita leaned forward, put her arm on the table, and smiled at Américo, though it was a smile contrived out of bewilderment.

"Every day he comes home like that," Señora Izquierdo said, her face engrossed in the knife's slightly erratic movement through the potato in her hand. "I never do anything right. He says he has never been able to eat a decent meal since he left Puerto Rico."

"Is it true he's thinking about opening a store?" Américo asked.

"When hasn't your father been up to something that was going to make him a millionaire? I let him talk about his big plans. What you don't do when you are young, you won't do when you are old. It won't be long before both of us are dead."

"Ay señora," said Jovita, "you are just like my grandmother. Every Christmas she says farewell to everybody because she thinks she has less than a year to live. She's been saying that since I was a little girl. Look at her. She's buried my grandfather and is in her eighties. You're very young."

Señora Izquierdo's eyes brightened. "Thank you, thank you." She glanced at Américo. "I've been told I look like your father's daughter."

Jovita laughed, "Ay, Señora Izquierdo."

Américo looked at the clock again. "We have to go," he said.

"So soon?" Señora Izquierdo said. "We didn't even have a chance to talk."

"Why don't you go with us?" asked Jovita.

"Yeah, why don't you come with us?" said Américo with a smile. "You could give us a guided tour of Smeltertown. After that, you could eat all you wanted at the Hacienda Restaurant."

Señora Izquierdo liked the idea. She said, "Mmmmm," and then acted as if she was gobbling food. She laughed loudly and warmly, her white teeth beaming in her round face, an older and weathered version of Américo's own. She followed Américo and Jovita to the door.

"No," she said. She whirled her forefinger about her temple, an allusion to her husband's mental condition. "I have to stay here and feed the *deschavetado*."

~~~~~

América drove up the sloped street away from his parent's white stuccoed house, which had been built on the escarpment at the foot of the Franklin Mountains.

"I'm glad we were able to get away," said Américo, glancing at Jovita, who reclined comfortably in her seat. "I can't breathe in that house."

He turned onto the street that would take them downtown.

"Your mother is so funny," said Jovita.

Curious and agitated, he glanced at her. "What do you mean?" he said.

She sat there with a smile, shaking her head at the thought of his mother. "I don't know," she said. "She's a real character. One minute she's laughing and joking, the next minute she's battling your father, then she is laughing again as if everything had been one big joke."

"Well, it hasn't always been one big joke," said Américo, staring morosely out the window. He stopped at an intersection by a lush green park.

"Let's take the mountain road," said Jovita.

He veered onto Scenic Drive, the popular road that zigzagged across the southernmost extension of the Franklin Mountains. Its curves snaked in and out of the crevasses. As they gained altitude, the vast cityscape spread out below, offering them a view of an American metropolis glittering in the desert sun under an immense sky.

"El Paso is very beautiful," Américo said, "but I could never live here again."

"My mother came here to visit many years ago. She fell in love with it. She even wanted to come and live here."

"I'm glad she didn't."

"Why?"

"I would never have met you."

They exchanged smiles.

Américo reached the look-out area, the highest point on the road. Atop a pole an American flag flapped sporadically. The Mexican mountains, dark and remote, rose beyond the urban valley. To the west appeared the smokestacks. The road curved sharply into the mountain, and the descent to the valley began.

Américo shifted into low gear and stopped riding the brake pedal. He maneuvered through the familiar curves gracefully.

"Your family is strange," said Jovita thoughtfully. "They treat us well. The refrigerator is full of food. Your father brings sacks of fruit and offers you money. Compared to my family, they have everything, but they cannot eat a meal together. Your family seems like a family of strangers."

Américo sighed. "That's the way we were brought up. My father has always said that you don't have any friends but your own family. Yet he has never been a friend to any of us. It's impossible to talk to him."

She shifted in her seat. He felt her eyes settle on the side of his face. "What I meant to say," she said, "is that they're good people, despite everything. You can't go on hating them all your life."

He kept his eyes on the winding road. "It was here in El Paso that I learned to live with the assumption that I have no family."

"That's what's so frightening about you sometimes," said Jovita softly. "Sometimes I feel you owe allegiance to nothing, to no one, perhaps not even to me one day."

He looked over at her brown eyes. "Don't say that. I've never loved anybody as much as I love you, and I never will." He said slowly, "I would hate to see us become what my parents are. But then you never know. This business of living is so tricky. Some families are cursed for generations."

"Still, curses can be lifted, no?" Jovita smiled.

"No," Américo said, returning the smile.

They came off the mountain road. They took the avenue that sloped down to the heart of El Paso. Cars glittered like luminous insects in the bright sunlight. They idled past San Jacinto Plaza, once a station on the Spanish king's highway, now the city's main plaza where city buses disgorged riders. Clusters of people, most of them Mexicans, walked in the shadows of the tall buildings that enclosed the downtown area. Américo turned west when they reached Paisano Drive.

"Paisano connects with the old highway at the train depot," said Américo. "I like this route because it runs along the Rio Grande."

"I'd get lost if I had to drive here," said Jovita.

"You get used to it."

They drove past the train depot, which resembled a Spanish cathedral, and onto the old highway.

"There's Mexico," said Américo, nodding at the low-lying hills clustered with adobe huts beyond the sandy river. As usual, the stark contrast between the two sides of the river struck him. It reminded him that his mother and her family were originally from Mexico, despite her denials.

"You can walk across," said Jovita.

"I know. The river isn't very deep here."

"What river?" joked Jovita. "The *arroyos* in Escandón have more water in them than that."

Américo smiled. Jovita loved to tease him about the Rio Grande. It was not as large in El Paso as it was in Escandón, but it linked him to her nonetheless. He drove on, passing under a concrete bridge; beyond, the Hacienda Restaurant appeared against a mountain backdrop.

"Look, there's Mount Cristo Rey!" cried Américo, pointing to a small basalt peak in the distance, a tiny cross at its pinnacle. It looked like a small, perfectly shaped volcano set against the enormous Texas sky. "Every time I see Mount Cristo Rey, I imagine the Holy Land. My mother once told me she and La Abuela made annual pilgrimages to the top of Mount Cristo Rey."

They were approaching Smeltertown. To the right of the highway, Américo saw the ASARCO smokestacks—the short one and the two long thin ones.

"Smeltertown is across the highway from the smelter," said Américo. "It should be somewhere around here."

They looked around as they passed a slag-covered ridge beyond which rose the complex of metal buildings overshadowed by smokestacks. They did not see any signs of life. No wooden shacks, no grocery store, no cars or people, no church.

As they drove on, they passed under a black metal bridge on which the trains from the smelter crossed over the highway.

"Jovita, I'm sure it's not past this bridge. We missed it."

Américo turned back. As they approached the smelter again, they slowed down and pulled off the highway, stopping in front of a bright sign: For Sale, Coronado Realty 566-3965. They got out of the car.

"The smokestacks are there, so Smeltertown should be here," he said, standing at the edge of an empty field.

"Look, across the field, isn't that a church?"

Seeing the remains—white walls, no roof, debris—he asked, "So this is it?"

"Your mother was right," said Jovita. "There's nothing here."

Américo gazed at the empty field. Though he had driven along this highway several times before he left El Paso and later when he took Jovita to New Mexico on one of their honeymoons, Américo had never paid much attention to Smeltertown. It had merely been the wretched town where his mother had grown up with La Abuela, his great-grandmother, and Tía Rosaura, his great aunt.

"I want to look around," said Américo. "Do you mind?"

"No, it's early. I'll join you later. I want to look at the church."

He wandered across the field. There was none of the billowy sand he remembered trudging through every time his mother brought him and his brothers and sisters to visit La Abuela and Tía Rosaura. The dirt felt compact; severed roots showed that it had been planed recently.

There had once been candles burning inside La Abuela's wood frame house. Sulfur and incense mingled with the smell of food. She was a very old woman, short and frail, with a wrinkled face and green eyes. She wore a *chongo* at the back of her head, gold-rimmed glasses, and a black shawl wrapped around her shoulders. He could recall nothing of her temperament. He remembered the other woman, Tía Rosaura, a short woman with a square head on neckless shoulders, a woman who seemed to have been smelted from the igneous rock of this land. Their hearts lay buried somewhere in this soil that had poisoned his, and he felt like a ghost crossing an immense desert in search of their blessings.

Unable to find where his abuela's house had stood, Américo attempted to reconstruct the earlier scene from memory—a picket fence; an outhouse that smelled and had spiders that scared him; a lanky, yellow-eyed dog in the dirt yard; and a dark wooden house with a corrugated aluminum roof. Once on a visit here his mother sent him to the store a block away. It had been a short walk; the store had been on a street facing the highway. If he could locate where it had been, he might find Abuela's property. To his left Américo spotted a curbstone, a few yards from the highway, where there had once been a street corner. As he walked toward it, he came across a prominent mound of dirt and stopped.

When he stepped onto the mound, the soil grated beneath his foot. He hit the ground with the heel of his boot. It sounded hollow. He crouched down. Clearing some of the dirt aside, he found a slab of wood, and when he lifted it, he saw the hole. It had been hastily and incompletely filled in—it looked as if it might have been a hole for a cesspool. He studied the distance between the mound and curbstone and church; if his estimates were correct, he might be standing on top of La Abuela's cesspool.

He wanted to tell Jovita about his discovery, but she sat on a wooden beam in the shadow of the church walls. He crossed the field and sat down next to her.

"Did you see where I was standing?" he asked.

"Yes."

"There's a mound of dirt there. I think it's a cesspool. A block away, there used to be a store on the corner. La Abuela's house would have been where that mound of dirt is. I am almost certain it was her cesspool I was standing on."

They sat quietly for a moment.

"Where's the Rio Grande?" asked Jovita.

Américo glanced at the church walls. "Behind the church. We can't see it from here."

"Is Mexico on the other side?"

"I don't think so. Somewhere around here the river turns and stops being the border."

"What was your abuela's name?"

"Just La Abuela."

"Didn't your mother tell you her name?"

Américo paused. He sifted through the assortment of memories he had about his childhood: Smeltertown, his mother, the sulfur fumes— all links to La Abuela—but he could not remember her name. His mind seemed as empty as the field at his feet.

He shook his head. "My mother told me her name, but I can't remember." He paused and then added, "My mother often said she grew up like an orphan, alone. I suppose she meant she grew up without her mother and her brothers and sisters. Her father was murdered in Mexico."

"Did you come to visit La Abuela and Tía Rosaura often?"

"Maybe once or twice a year. My father objected to our seeing my mother's family. Whenever we came here, my mother would say 'Shhhhh, don't tell your father we're going to see La Abuela.' We'd come on the bus frightened to death my father would find out, and there would be another fight."

"That's very sad," said Jovita. "We grew up with all of our relatives, and when our grandparents died, they died at our house."

"I've always wanted to have a family like that," Américo said. "To be able to speak to my father, to respect him."

"Well, my father isn't a saint. He's never laid a hand on my mother or any of us, but he's made my mother's life miserable. At least your father has provided for your family." Jovita looked at her watch. "It's three o'clock."

"Are you hungry?"

"Not yet."

Américo looked at the church. He had not been inside a church for years. He wondered if this was where La Abuela had been brought when she died. He got up and walked to the front of the church's entrance and found a doorless passageway through which he could see the blue walls inside. Piles of smashed wood, brick, and glass blocked his way to the front steps, but he saw a thin path.

"Let's climb inside," he said to Jovita.

"No, it's dangerous."

"I'm going inside," he said. "It won't be long before all of this is torn down."

"Be careful. There are nails all over the place."

Américo took the path and climbed the steps. He sat on the door sill and stared inside at the blue walls smouldering in sunlight. He pushed himself over and landed on the dirt floor several feet below. Somehow he had expected to see some vestiges of the original church still intact—a pulpit, an altar, a cross, anything. All he saw were the marks on the walls where the floor had once been and piles of broken wood on the dirt floor. Up front, where the altar must have been, rose a stack of tattered linoleumlike roofing. Set high in the walls was a series of broken windows and, beyond the roofless walls, the sky.

He walked amid the debris to the center of the church floor, which was bisected by shadow and sunlight. Finding a wooden box, which he pulled to a clearing, he sat down and lit a cigarette. Américo imagined two old women leading a young girl down the center aisle for communion, and the people in the pews listening to the choir as a priest poised white wafers on the tongues of the communicants. He imagined an old woman lying dead in a coffin.

The images were interrupted by the memory of a story his mother had once told him. During the years of the war, it had been here, in Smeltertown, where his father, a soldier then, had come to look for his mother at La Abuela's house. It was one night, months after they had been married and Américo had been conceived. He had come drunk. She would not open the door even after he stopped beating on it and began to thrash about on the ground, crying and threatening to kill himself if she did not return to him. It had been La Abuela who scolded his mother, telling her that she was now a woman, wife, and mother-to-be, and that unless he abandoned her, she must never leave him, regardless of how unhappy she might be. His mother had opened the door.

In a few years his father had moved the family from a decrepit *barrio* in south El Paso to a nice neighborhood near Five Points and then to the suburb at the foot of the mountains. Whatever else Américo may have detested about his father, he had always admired his father's capacity for hard work and making money. In his prosperity he thought he could return to Puerto Rico and change everything he had left. The thatched-roof hut he grew up in with his many brothers and sisters, the poverty and misery of his saintly mother, and tyranny of his tall, red-headed, machete-wielding drunken father. He sent money instead. The times he visited Puerto Rico, he went with his wife's blessing and the knowledge that he didn't have to return. But to his Texas family's relief, he always came back to Texas. In his drunken rages he cursed the desert, the mountains, his wife, the Mexicans, and his fate.

Américo could never forgive, then or now, his father's humiliation of his mother and rejection of her family. In his isolation, Américo turned to books. And, when they weren't enough, to Mexican cantinas and abandoned women. When his long pent-up desire to leave El Paso forever—to destroy it by his absence—was satisfied by an opportunity to teach in Escandón, he found refuge. He found Jovita.

And every time he returned to El Paso, zipping along the elaborate highway from the south, Américo felt an immense weight settle upon his shoulders. At first it was gentle, then it would begin to push down upon him so hard that he felt the mountains were crushing him. At his parents' home and everywhere else he went, everything seemed devastated—until Jovita and he escaped to the other side of the Rio Grande, where he drank excessively at the Kentucky Club. That is where they had been the previous night and why he had gotten up so late. It had been a wonderful time, alive with Mexican music, polite waiters in white shirts, and superbly rendered Scotch and sodas. But this time, he felt unusually weak, as if something that had driven him along all those years was beginning to fail him. The sensation frightened him. Was it Jovita's and his desire to have a child and settle down? Perhaps Jovita's wish to get away from the nightlife whose warmth and charm had sustained him for so long among strangers? Whatever change was afoot, he was certain of one thing—he would still have to travel a long distance, years, before he could turn around, look at El Paso, and feel free of it.

When he finished his cigarette, Américo stood up and looked around, wondering if he had missed something. No. All of it was dead—Smeltertown, La Abuela, Tía Rosaura, and even his mother, the little girl who, with La Abuela, had washed clothes in the Rio Grande and climbed Mount Cristo Rey in religious processions. Then, as his eyes scaled the church walls, a glint of yellow caught his attention. It was a window, stained blue and yellow, resting high on the church walls, still intact.

He picked up several pieces of brick and tossed them. He missed several times. At last he lobbed a chunk squarely at the base of the window so the pieces cascaded backward into the church and landed on a pile of wood armed with splinters and nails. The face of a madonna, with drooping eyes and a silver halo around her head survived in a triangle of glass. He imagined the madonna shining inside the church where La Abuela and his mother must have seen it years ago. He stepped forward, marvelling, Jovita should see this, he thought.

Américo got as close as he could. He did not see the nail when he reached for the madonna, just felt it. A thin, rusted nail like a rattlesnake fang curved out of the stick of wood, striking the side of his hand. He cried out, and his feet blundered on the pile of wood, upsetting the madonna. She fell and burst.

He climbed to the outside, paused, and caught his breath. He turned and began to run back around to the front of the church, then stopped.

"Américo!" Jovita called.

As he dashed around the corner of the church, she saw the handkerchief wrapped around his hand.

"What happened to you? I heard a window crash."

"I just wanted something to take home with us. It was a piece of glass with the face of a madonna. It was beautiful, but it broke."

His eyes embraced the graveyard of his Mexican past.

"Come on, we'd better go," he said.

Together they crossed the field.

"How does your hand feel?" asked Jovita.

"All right."

"Maybe you should get a shot."

"It'll be too much trouble. I'd have to go to a hospital."

They stopped between their car and the elongated shadow of the real estate sign. Américo looked at everything once more—the ASARCO smelter and its smokestacks across the highway, the curbstone, the empty field, the church walls, and Mount Cristo Rey.

"There will be nothing left," he said.

Jovita, who had been gazing at the church walls, turned to Américo and said, "There will be your father and mother."

Summer League

Danny Romero

That first Saturday after school had been let out, the three met by a baseball field in the park. With their fingers in the holes of the fence behind the backstop and their faces pressed up against the wire, the boys discussed their plans for the summer. On the field, the Pop Warner League played hardball.

"I'm signing up for the softball league on Monday," said Antonio. He stuck another long piece of sour grape bubble gum into his mouth, a small river of purple drool creeping out from the corner. He listened to the slap of the ball against the catcher's mitt, the sound reminding him of his brother being whipped with a belt by his father on his bare ass the night before. The fast ball slapped into the mitt once again.

"So am I," said Paul. The boys turned to see the black man who was there every Saturday dressed all in khaki with a rumpled hat on his white head. He rode a bicycle with a front basket and yelled, "*Cacahuates! Cacahuates!* Get your *cacahuates* here . . ."

"My mother said she'd even buy me cleats," Paul went on, the three craning their necks, following the bicycle rolling in a circle on the grass by the restrooms. The man drove back over to the bleachers, tossing a bag of peanuts to a father and son and easily catching the quarter thrown to him. Some of the players waved him over to their dugouts, sticking their money through the holes in the fence, exchanging their coins for bags of nuts.

"Play ball!" was yelled, a hush falling over the crowd, the only sound heard: shells cracked and discarded.

"How 'bout you, Michael?" whispered Antonio to his friend.

Michael stared at the batter on deck putting weights on the end of his bat and warming up his swing. "I don't know yet," he answered, turning to watch the black man on the bicycle rolling off to another field.

"Heeeeeeey," said Paul, and Michael looked back at the sound of the crack of the bat and the crowd, too late though to see the hit heading over the fence and out of the ballpark.

"Pheeew. You see that one?" said Antonio. "He cleared the fence easy."

The crowd jumped up in the stands as the runner ran past third and headed for home. "Wow!" said Michael, as if he had seen it. "Man, that was bad!" said Paul. The three boys left to buy some ice cream.

They walked over to the parking spaces across from the railroad tracks. There a Dipsey Doodle truck sat, its stereo tinkling out "Twinkle Twinkle Little Star" and a large group of black children milling around it, laughing and yelling, "I was here first." "No you weren't, blood." "Yeah I was, man!" "Forget you, man."

Antonio and the others stood on the outskirts of the crowd, some of the black children turning to look at them with hard stares and sneers.

"Say hey—gimme one of those hot tamales you got there," said a black teenage boy.

The man in the truck said, "All I got is ice cream, candy, and soda."

The boy went on, "Man, what kind of a honky-ass truck you got here anyway?" The crowd laughed and jeered. "Honky-ass, honky-ass!" they said.

"Now get the hell away from my truck!" the man said. "Just get the hell away, you rotten bunch of jungle bunnies. Get the hell away!"

"Yo' mama honky-ass," said that first teenage boy. Some of the crowd threw rocks at the truck as it drove away.

And when Michael came home from the park he told his family he wanted to join a baseball team and that all it would cost would be two dollars. "And they even give everybody a trophy too," he said to his mother and sister. "And we get to keep our caps too, I think."

"But you don't have a glove," said the mother.

"I know that mama," said Michael, "but I'm sure I can borrow one when it's my turn to play. Antonio says that's what everyone does and it's alright. Paul said his mother was gonna buy him cleats, but no one really needs those either." He stopped and caught his breath. "And I heard the coach takes the team to McDonald's after every game they win. And . . ."

"Alright now Michael, that's enough," the mother said. "You can join if you want to. I'll give you the money on Monday."

Michael smiled and said, "Thanks, mama."

"So you're joining the little league," said the older sister. "You must think you're big stuff now, huh?" she said.

"I am big stuff," said Michael, "and it's not the little league I'm join-ing. They call this one the tiny league."

So his sister cooed at him and said, "Hoooooowwwww cuuuutttteeee, the tiny league," beginning to laugh and ending up smiling at him as if he were four years old and not the eight that he was. And Michael wished he hadn't told her that, feeling like slugging her in her pretty smile and saying, It's not cute, you stupid dog.

A couple of days later the boys were in the park, with their two dollars in their hands and great expectations. "Where's Paul?" Antonio said, not knowing that Paul was now in Tijuana.

"He was supposed to show up and he's not here yet. They're gonna start choosing the teams," said Michael.

Antonio and Michael stood side by side in a sea of some sixty other boys. The coaches were in front trying to look official. The boys had heard of some of them. There was Mr. Patterson, a red-faced white man with cowboy boots and Levi's hanging onto his hips, and Mr. Parker, the coach of the last two years' league championship teams, a muscular-looking black man wearing sweat pants and a T-shirt, a whistle around his neck. And there was Mr. García. He was a dark and sweating man with an accent, thick mustache, bloodshot eyes, and a silver tooth in the front of his face.

Mr. García was Michael's coach. They were the Red Sox, though the caps the man handed out that practice were maroon. "You can keep these for your very own," he said to the boys all sitting down or kneel-ing on one knee in a circle around him. He smiled his silver-toothed smile and shook all the boys' hands with beer on his breath.

The group did a few jumping jacks, the coach's son, David, leading the others. "Now go run a couple of laps around the field," said Mr. García. "And I'll tell you when to stop." He then went over to his car in the parking lot and had himself a few more beers. Some of the boys grumbled as they ran, complaining of an ache in their side. They would stop and walk a ways until the son, David, told them to keep on going, saying, "Eh, what are you—a bunch of sissies or what?"

But after a while even David grew tired, slowing down and holding his side, walking with a look of pain on his face. "Hey, Dad," he yelled over to the car. Mr. García poked his head out of the window. "What do you want?" he said.

"Can we stop now?" asked David. "I'm getting tired."

"Alright then, why don't you bring it on in," said the man.

He stepped out of his car, a few empty cans falling onto the parking lot surface, and hiked up his pants. The boys all collapsed onto the grass, catching their breath, eyes closed, and chests heaving. "Alright, alright. You boys done good. We're gonna have a great team this year that's for sure." The boys all grunted at most for a response. "Alright, alright. Now I want to see you all tomorrow. Three-thirty sharp and we'll start a little ball playing. And one more thing boys . . ." said Mr. García. "The Fourth of July is coming up and I got a few things you might want. Cherry bombs. Firecrackers. Some rockets too, for sale. So let me know if you want any. So . . . the first game's in ten days, but we'll be ready. Alright, alright. I'll see you all tomorrow. Come on now, David, let's go." And then so ended the first day of practice.

The season wore on. Whenever Michael played he spent his time in the outfield. Center field, right field, left field, nothing much ever happened out there. He was good at running after the ball, but not at catching it. He had to throw his mitt off, it being right-handed and him being left-handed. Sometimes he could make it to bat before the inning or game was over. A few times he was walked and even got lucky once or twice with a hit. The ball would roll by the pitcher's mound, the pitcher scooping it up and throwing it to first base before Michael's bony legs, pumping as fast as they could, ever reached the bag.

When the Red Sox played Antonio's Pirates it was a close game,

Michael's team losing by only three. Mr. Parker asked Antonio after the game if he was going to McDonald's with the team. Antonio said, "Nah, that's okay. I'm getting kinda' tired of going there every Saturday. And anyway my friend's coming over to my house for lunch."

The family drove the few blocks to their house in their big and shiny new car with power windows. Michael sat in the back with Antonio and his brother, the sister Martha sitting up front with the parents. At the house they all gathered in the dining room, around the table all set with dishes and silverware. "Can I use the bathroom?" asked Michael. "Of course," said the mother. "It's right through those doors." He stood and walked down a corridor noticing and looking at the pictures on the walls of Antonio and his family all smiles and good cheer at the beach and Disneyland, the circus and mountain snow.

They had tomato soup and hot dogs for lunch, Michael eating three. The family talked about the game and especially Antonio's two home runs.

"Actually, I think you got a raw deal there," the father said to Michael. "That umpire must have been drunk or something. 'Cause I know for a fact some of those pitches thrown at you weren't strikes."

Michael smiled and said, "I guess so," taking another spoonful of soup, and blowing on it before putting it in his mouth. The father took a drink of his beer, then patted Michael on the shoulder, causing the boy to almost burn his tongue, and saying, "You're alright, Michael. I like that. You got real heart. I like that. Heh, heh, heh."

When lunch was over Antonio and Michael went outside and played a little catch in the backyard, trying to decide who was the better pitcher, Koufax or Drysdale. Michael said he thought it was Koufax for the simple reason that he had read a book about the man. Antonio didn't think so. "Drysdale's the man I'd put my money on any old day," he said, "and that's for sure."

They stopped and stood around, Antonio throwing the ball absentmindedly against the fence. "Eh, Michael," he said, "if we ever got into a fight who do you think would win?" Michael said he would, but Antonio disagreed. So they tried, wrestling with each other while standing and banging into and off the fence in their efforts, then rolling onto the ground and into the dirt and finally stopping when the mother called,

"Antonio, you better come in now. We're going to the movies." The two got up and dusted themselves off. "We'll see you later, Michael," said the mother. "Thanks for coming over."

"Thank you, Mrs. Trujillo," said Michael, starting down the street, not bothering to see if they offered him a ride home.

"Come on, Michael," said his mother just before the season ended. "Get in the car." Michael knew it had been payday from the smile on the woman's face. The two drove over to South Gate, stopping in front of the Big Five Sporting Goods Store. They walked in on that Thursday afternoon, Michael all excited and the mother not really knowing how to go about buying a mitt for the boy, being polite and slightly nervous when addressing the clerk.

"We have a fine selection of baseball mitts in the store, ma'am," said the clerk. "And yes, indeed, we even have left-handed models." He led them over to an aisle in the back of the store, passing the sets of weights and basketball equipment, the tents for camping and skis for skiing.

"Thank you," said the mother as the clerk left them alone. Michael began trying on the mitts, it seeming awkward for a moment because they fit. His mother eyed the price tags, handing the boy the less expensive ones and seeing if they fit.

"Good choice," said the clerk, ringing up the purchase. "That'll be $15.56," he said.

"Alright," said the mother, digging in her purse for change.

At home the boy played catch with his sister. The glove was stiff and her boyfriend said to him that he should oil it to soften up the leather. He took the mitt from Michael, placed a hardball in the pocket of it, and tied rubber bands around it, holding it in that position as if it were a ball being caught. He used the large rubber bands he sometimes brought over from the post office. He said this method would help break the mitt in.

Michael thought for sure the coach would play him the Saturday coming up, now that he had his own mitt. And so the coach did, placing him in center field, like so many times before, but this time at least Michael knew he could skip the charade of dropping the mitt while he ran for the ball and throwing toward home plate with his left hand. This Saturday, Michael knew, he wouldn't have to feel like a fool.

The inning dragged on. Michael watched the pitcher walk ten batters in a row and he was getting tired of being out there in the hot sun and bored as the runs kept adding up. He thought to himself that those batters were so stupid they wouldn't even swing. The heat was getting unbearable as that inning seemed like it was never going to end. He shielded his eyes with his new mitt and shifted his weight from his left leg to his right, then back again and over. Why won't they swing? he thought. That last pitch sure looked good to me.

In the end the damage was twenty-three to zero, the game being called off after the third inning. All the boys looked gloomily at the winners as they spelled out their name in a cheer. Bloodshot-eyed Mr. García told the boys they weren't so bad really.

"And next year we'll get those guys. You'll see," he went on. "And by the way I still have some cherry bombs and things for sale, if any of you boys still want some. And drop by and see me sometime. Football season is just around the corner and I hope to see you boys coming out to the park and playing some. And, well, anyway, I'll see you all at the awards banquet on Tuesday night. At seven in the gym. There'll be food and drinks for everyone, so be sure to bring your family."

All the boys shook the man's hand and each others and said goodbye. Mr. García went up to Michael, saying, "I hope to see you out here next summer too. That new glove of yours should be all broken in and working fine." He tipped his cap and winked at the boy. "I'll see you Tuesday night," he said.

"Alright," said Michael, turning and heading away through the park toward home, knowing he wouldn't show up on Tuesday, but thinking that maybe, just maybe, he would see him next season. Maybe he would. Michael read the name written in the center of his new glove: some left-handed ball player whose name no one recognized. Much like himself, he thought. Maybe he would, next season.

Hollywood!

Dagoberto Gilb

Santa Monica beach was clean and quiet. The sand was moist, the air cool, the ocean as gentle as a bay, and Luís was happy that he didn't have to pay for the parking.

"The sun's out," he said. "Just look what a pretty day it is."

"It's still *cold*," Marta told him, making sure he didn't get away with it. She was trying to wrap her sweater around their son Ramón, who wasn't about to cooperate and was about to cry because his mommy wouldn't leave him alone.

"He'll be alright," Luís said to ease her worry. "It's good for him just to get out."

"It's not good for him to catch a cold!" Marta was mad at Luís for insisting that Ramón wouldn't need any more than shorts and a T-shirt at the beach.

"He won't. Look at how happy he is." That was the kind of reasoning Luís liked to use.

Ramón was, in fact, happy. His plastic grader tore through the sand, slicing out a smooth road for his Matchbox cars. He didn't seem the least bit cold.

Marta had learned long ago that she couldn't fight with Luís's logic. She lay down on the old blanket she'd never convince him to replace, draped the sweater over herself, and looped her arm over her eyes. The sun *was* out. She felt pained.

Fishing boats bobbed on the near horizon. Helicopters battered the air. Joggers came and went along the wet part of the shore.

"If they worked like us they wouldn't have to run," Luís said of the joggers.

"At least they move to keep warm," Marta shot back.

"We've got the whole beach to ourselves. Think of what memories he'll have."

She scoffed. Ramón's cars vroomed and squealed and crashed into themselves and mounds of sand.

"The beach is just great," Marta shivered. "I can't wait to tell everybody at home what a great experience our first vacation ever was." It was Luís's idea to visit California in the winter because the motels were said to be cheaper and everyone said it was warm anyway.

"He's gonna remember this forever," Luís said. Just to make sure, he went over to his son. "You wanna go see the ocean up close?"

Ramón looked over to his mommy. He seemed to know, even at his very young age, that his daddy didn't always have the best ideas.

Luís picked Ramón up and carried him to the breakwater. "Now those boats out there—they look like the ones you have for your bath, don't they?" Luís felt pretty clever thinking of that. It was always better to describe things to a child in a way he could understand. "Those boats go around and catch fish so that people can eat. It's just like at home at the groves. Except instead of nuts it's fish, like sardines. You know, those fish from those cans your mommy puts in my lunch sometimes."

Ramón seemed to listen and Luís was sure he was getting through to him. He was determined to not lose the momentum.

"And the seagulls, those birds that are flying around out there, see? See how big they are? Those are called seagulls and they go around and catch fish too, just like those boats, and that's how they live."

Ramón was listening. He was watching the birds.

"The ocean's just like the land. Animals live in it. Men make a living on it the same way I do working in the groves for Mr. Oakes." Luís thought this over and realized he didn't know how to explain himself any better. "The only important thing in life is hard work." That was somehow what he was getting at, and in any case he loved these kinds of statements, and he always sincerely believed them.

Ramón started fidgeting.

"You wanna get down? O.K. You should get your feet wet. These are nice waves . . ."

Now Ramón was crying. The water was very cold and the little waves scared him. He ran up the sand to his mommy.

"Why can't we go to Disneyland?" Marta implored Luís back at the blanket. "It can't cost that much. He would have such a good time, even if it is expensive. I could pay with that money I saved . . ."

"It's not the money."

"Or we could leave a day or two earlier and with the money we save by leaving . . ."

"No."

Marta rolled her eyes and shook her head. It was no use. Even though every little boy and girl dreams of going to Disneyland at least once, Luís had his ideas and this was one of them: it was better for his son to learn the important things first. What would a place like Disneyland teach him besides cartoons? Of course Marta didn't believe him for a second. She knew he was just being cheap.

A couple came wearing bathing suits and left with warmer clothes on. They didn't stay long. A teenage couple came carting a portable stereo with a cassette player. They listened to a tape of Tierra and felt each other up. Luís finally couldn't stand it and told them to turn it down and to make their sex private. They left, but once he got a safe distance away the boy yelled something obscene at Luís about his mother. Marta laughed. Ramón wanted a hot dog because the day before Luís had promised him one.

"They do too sell hot dogs up on that pier," Marta told him. "I saw that man coming down the stairs eating one."

"No, they don't," Luís insisted. "Besides, we brought these sandwiches."

"You already told him you would!"

"Hey, look at all the birds landing around us," Luís said to his son, changing the subject.

Ramón stopped whining and looked. They were seagulls and pigeons. They waited in segregated clumps.

"Let's feed them! We can feed them some of the bread!" Luís

pinched off chunks of the white bread from his sandwich and threw them at the birds. They squawked and flapped their wings and moved in closer. Ramón watched ecstatically. Seagulls hovered in the air and Luís tossed the balled-up crumbs so they'd catch them there. More gulls flew in from the ocean and more pigeons from the pier and then Ramón threw the pieces of his sandwich too.

Luís tried to show Ramón how to tear little pieces off the bread so he wouldn't go through the sandwiches too quickly, but the boy had already lost control. Pigeons were almost crawling on the blanket, and it seemed all the ocean's gulls waited by him while he talked and laughed, letting the pigeons eat from his hand and making sure each and every seagull got something.

Pleased as he was, Luís was also relieved when the last sandwiches were spared by three high-pitched beeps, and then music and song, which distracted Ramón from the feeding.

"Look!" Marta pointed. "They're making a movie over there on the pier. See the camera?"

Ramón went back to the birds. Luís looked at the filming area skeptically. Marta demanded that they go see it up close. Luís, watching his son take out another sandwich from a plastic bag, gave in to Marta's wish and waved the birds away.

It was a commercial for A&W root beer but Marta didn't care. This was Hollywood! There were film people everywhere, standing by electronic machines and under wire cables. There was a fat director, dressed in a casual velour suit, arranging scenes with waving hands and arms. There was a cameraman, who wore a cowboy hat, sitting on a rolling lift. And there were handsome young actors and beautiful young actresses and a punk-style woman dabbing them with makeup.

"They're all blonds," remarked Luís cynically.

"Those two men on the roller skates have dark hair," Marta corrected him. "And there's a black man."

"Boys. Those are all boys."

First came the beeps, then the music, and then the action: cute, barelegged actresses drank from a can of the soda and expressed amazement and pretended to sing the jingle that screamed out of a speaker in front of them. Other actresses jogged to a stop and one of the actors twirled on his roller skates. They all moved toward a park bench while the camera aimed down and away from the crowded park bench.

They watched the actors do this several times before Luís made them move to another area behind the rope. He didn't like standing near the shirtless blond longhairs with tattoos who, according to Luís, didn't do anything more than smoke marijuana and drink beer.

After a while Luís stopped paying attention. He watched a man below him driving a tractor across the sand. He watched a truck collect the trash from the barrels on the beach. Then a uniformed guard was standing next to him telling him something in English. Luís noticed that the fat director was glaring at him, and when he looked to his side for a translation he realized that Marta and Ramón had left him alone. He stiffened until the guard put his hand on his shoulder and slowly drew out the word "move" and pushed Luís farther down the rope.

"It's because you were in the picture," Marta explained to him.

Luís still felt like everyone was looking at him. "The boy should be playing on the beach. Maybe he'll want to get wet in the ocean."

Marta frowned. "I want to see this a few more times. He's hungry. Buy him a hot dog."

"There's still two sandwiches," he reminded her.

"He wants a *hot dog*."

Luís wanted to argue, but once Ramón had heard his mommy mention hot dogs, he started whining again. Luís knew it was hopeless. He took his son to the nearby stand.

"One hot dog," Luís told the fry cook.

"The long or the short?" the man said in a hoarse foreign accent. "The sauerkraut, the chili, the cheese?"

Luís stared at him mystified. "I want one hot dog," he said in English.

The man stared back at Luís. "You wannit the long dog or the regular? You wannit the chili or the sauerkraut or the cheese? You wannit the plain or the mustard and relish?"

Luís looked down at Ramón in defeat. The fry cook, irritated, started to go over the options again, but before he finished, Ramón, in clear English, told him he would have a regular hot dog with ketchup only.

Luís returned to Marta with the news.

"He watches television, and a lot of his friends talk to him in English," she said unimpressed. "And when I baby sit for Mr. and Mrs. Oakes, the children speak English to him. The Oakes speak Spanish to you, but not to their children."

~~~~~

Luís wished he could talk to either Ramón or Marta on the way back home, but a sore throat and fever kept his son whimpering the whole way and made Marta mad at him. So he drove fourteen straight hours, secretly not unhappy that they were getting back from expensive California two days earlier than they'd planned.

Late the next night, Ramón was tossing and turning on the bed between his mommy and daddy, who had been trying everything to get him to stop his crying.

"He used to go to sleep when you sang to him," Luís reminded Marta.

"Well, you see it hasn't been working this time," she said, tired. "Maybe you should tell him one of your stories. Tell him how much money we saved not going to Disneyland."

Luís, as always, ignored her sarcasm. But he liked the idea. He liked to tell what Marta called his stories, and he believed Ramón liked them too, because many times he did go to sleep hearing about the men Luís worked with or the animals they raised or the plants they grew. And, according to Luís, this was good for him since they would help him in the future, especially since Ramón went to sleep with them. He considered talking about the wild burros he saw in the Mojave Desert, or those saguaros near Picacho Peak, or the piscadores in the chile fields near the Rio Grande. Any of these could have worked too.

"Remember when we were at the ocean, where the waves ran up your legs? And the helicopters, and those fishing boats?"

Ramón stopped whimpering.

"Remember those birds that flew around those boats, and how they all flew onto the beach when you and I started feeding them bread?"

Ramón seemed to listen, was quiet. Already Luís felt a little like gloating to Marta, who'd rolled her head over to watch. "Those birds make their life there, mijo, and with their wings . . ."

But suddenly Ramón lost interest. He turned to his mommy and cried about the sore throat and how hot he was. Luís was sincerely disappointed.

Luís and Marta stared up at the darkness toward their small bedroom ceiling. There were crickets outside, and they could hear a hard breeze rustle the trees and bushes around their house, a tumbleweed scraping against the backdoor screen. A cat yowled louder than the boy and that was comforting to them both.

Marta hummed a few unmelodic notes. "How did that go?" she asked Luís softly. "A and double U . . ."

Luís didn't know the words, but he tried to remember the music to the jingle. They'd heard it a dozen times or more, but things like that didn't stay with him.

"A and double U root beer . . ." she whispered, hoping that maybe Ramón had finally fallen asleep because he wasn't crying.

Marta kept trying. Luís would tell her when she didn't have it, which was every time.

Then, Ramón, with his eyes barely open, sang the first words, just loud enough for them all to hear.

Luís couldn't believe it. Marta laughed. She sang: "A and double U tastes so fine, sends a thrill up my spine! Taste that frosty mug sensation—uuu!" And she laughed again, hummed the rest of it, laughing still more, and Ramón fell asleep as she sang it over and over to taunt Luís, who this night was happy to lose his battle.

Easy Time

Jack López

"Kick for the huevos and cover your face!" yelled Alex as he slowly shadowed Tony, his head slightly moving, tensed and deliberate, like a cat watching a bird.

Tony circled again. He stopped, planted his left leg and kicked for his uncle's crotch. His Uncle Alex turned slightly, taking the kick on his hip, spun, and kicked Tony hard in the ass. Tony swung around. All he saw was the hooded cobra on the back of Alex's hand coming at him. The cobra hit its mark, this time crisp, and Tony went down. His uncle stood over him, knees bent, fists clenched like an oriental warrior. The cuffs of Alex's slacks and his hard shoes were covered with dust. He wore no shirt, and his upper body rippled with tattooed life: the beautiful Mexicana with long black hair and the five black tears heaved in and out on Alex's chest as he stood over Tony. Black snakes on his arms vibrated, writhing and twisting as blood travelled through them.

"You want to be a man? C'mon, get up. You want to fuck up? C'mon," Alex taunted him.

Tony got to his feet. He moved slowly in a circle, stalking his uncle, looking for an opening.

"Close your mouth, stupid! Clench your teeth and keep your tongue back. Didn't your old man teach you nothing?"

Tony thought of his father. He thought of his brother and of the boxing gloves. He and Jimmy were supposed to spar but Jimmy would always hold his punches and their father would lose his temper, taking the gloves from Tony, and go at it with Jimmy, leaving him bleeding. Tony would unlace the boxing gloves for his brother, trying to stop the blood that should have been his.

Tony darted in at Alex, backed off, and came in quick, throwing the punch. Alex danced with him, forward and back, and when Tony delivered his blow, Alex blocked it and countered with his own. The cobra snapped out then stopped on Tony's face, just barely hitting so that no real damage was done but leaving a mark.

Tony dropped his hands to his sides. His face stung from different blows. His hair was dusty and his shirt was sweaty, caked with dirt. He looked to the sky and saw clouds moving sideways, pink with sunset.

"Look, Tony, if you're scared, I'll go in with you," said Alex. "I'll call my P.O. and tell him I can't find work, I might screw up. I'll go in with you."

"No. I'll take care of myself," Tony said.

"I'm going to be honest with you," Alex said. "Whatever happens, don't run. I don't care how many there are, *don't run.* If you need help, go to the brothers, they'll protect you. And remember, don't talk to the man. Another thing, don't wear those bun-huggers you wear. You got some boxer shorts? I'll bring you some in the morning."

"It's O.K., I have some. What time you coming?"

"I'll be here at eight." Alex walked to Tony and they embraced. "Hey, Tony," he said, walking out to his car, fanning himself with his sleeveless shirt, "you'll be alright. You're looking at easy time. It's nothing."

Tony walked to the front of the house. It was on a small mesa overlooking the ocean. Far off, the sun was a golden yellow coin fading into the sea. The clouds were coral in front and cold gray in back, the color of steel. October, the sky was chilled, the sand below was dark, wet, and the foam of breaking waves was lighting up the beach in small explosions. He sat on the lawn in front of the guest house. The guest house was his, his and his mother's now that his father had moved out. He thought of the old days when Jimmy was still alive, the autumns when the hunters would come and sometimes the big shots would drink too much and shoot pelicans and seagulls. But nobody cared about the gulls anyway. He had always thought it strange that the guest house faced the ocean and overlooked the tidal marsh, while the hunting lodge, which should have had the better view, faced the road. Tony watched the sky darken and felt the land breeze start to blow, cooling his drying sweat.

In the house, he turned on the lights. He climbed the stairs to the loft, and he bent his head as he entered the low-ceilinged room. It was the summer of the tenth grade when it became necessary for Tony to bend forward just to walk in his bedroom. At school the football coach used to come and get him out of class, bring him hot chocolate, and talk about the team, how they could use him at split-end. Tony liked missing class and talking with the coach; Jimmy had been on the very same team. But in those days he was in Asia, in those days he flew a helicopter. The reason behind Tony's refusal was a simple one—he spent his afternoons with Sylvia. Afternoons with Sylvia would then have to become afternoons with the team. Afternoons without Sylvia would drive him crazy. Finally the coach stopped coming to the door of his classroom. Tony smiled, thinking of high school, ducking his head.

He showered in the added-on bathroom, in the tiny metal stall with just room enough to soap yourself. Then he dressed and left a note to his mother. As he walked down the dirt road past the hunting lodge, he heard the dry cornstalks crinkling in the wind. They should be turned under by now, he thought. His father used to work the fields in that old red John Deere, turning the soil, turning the cornstalks in thick heavy furrows. Gradually, the field became smaller as tracts of houses crept up to the ocean, surrounding the hunting lodge. That was before Jimmy died, before his father had moved out with that woman. Then the stables up by the road were sold and so was the hunting lodge and all the surrounding land, but nothing had come of it. Once, about six months ago, a helicopter landed right in the strawberry fields. Men wearing suits got out and walked through the neat rows that were then filled with weeds. When they left, they flew over the marsh again and again and the rotor cutting the air with that whump whump sound upset Tony, and Sylvia put her blouse on as if the men could see through the roof.

Tony crossed the highway, heading toward the Colonia. It was only about a mile inland and was an old neighborhood completely surrounded by big expensive tract homes. There were still roosters and pigs in the Colonia, and on the big holidays they would make carnitas in the old copper vats. Tony walked on to his grandparents' house. Even though there was a chill in the air, his grandfather had all the windows and the front door open. He was sitting directly in front of the television set with the volume turned way up, watching wrestling on the Spanish station.

Tony came through the screen door and said, "Hello, grandfather." The old man smiled at him with his missing front teeth; the teeth on the sides looked like fangs. Then Tony went in the kitchen. His grandmother was washing dishes with the sleeves to her pink sweater rolled up. He bent down to hug her and she kissed him, and her smell of Chanel bath powder lingered on his face.

"Are you hungry?" she asked.

"Starving," he said.

It seemed comical to Tony how small his grandmother looked as she walked to the refrigerator and took out some chorizo. She shuffled back to the stove clapping her yellow house slippers that were too big. She cut off a large chunk of the orange sausage and took a small cast iron skillet from the oven and put them on the flame. Soon, the sausage was talking through the rising steam, spitting and cracking, filling the air with a spicy aroma.

"Have you seen your father?" she asked.

"No."

"You won't go and see him?"

"No. I'm not going to that house."

"And your mother?"

"She's alright. She's barely speaking to me."

His grandmother left the stove and stood in front of him at the dinette. "She's scared to lose you," she said, stroking his hair.

"I know," Tony said.

"What happened to your face?"

"Alex came by, showed me some moves."

"Alex?" she said, walking back to the stove, shaking her head. "I saw my son more when he was in." She warmed the homemade tortillas on the gas flame, flipping them quickly, then she rolled beans and chorizo into burritos with one end folded and tucked into itself and the other end open like a cone.

After Tony ate, he went into the living room and sat on the plastic-covered sofa, trying to watch wrestling. After an acceptable amount of time, he left. His grandmother cried when they hugged goodbye.

"Take it easy," his grandfather said in his deepest voice. He knew what it was all about—a long time ago, he too had spent time in jail.

Recrossing the highway, Tony walked back home, thinking of things to tell his mother. How after getting out, he would work, help her with the rent. And then after saving some money, he would go to junior college. He began walking faster to the house, and when he arrived, he burst in upon that lonely quiet.

There was a note on the back of his note. She didn't want to see him now. If he wanted to be like his father's family, fine. But she wasn't going to be a part of it any longer. Going to jail doesn't make you a man. She was sorry but she couldn't bear to see him in the morning, to see him leave. She would be at Virginia's.

Tony crumpled the letter, thinking of the big party Payaso's parents gave their son before he went in. Sylvia had let him undo her pants, after the party, when they were alone down in the hollows. And there was the party they had thrown for Alex, right here, when he got out, and he and Sylvia did it for the first time, but she wouldn't do it the way that made you pregnant, she would only do it the upside down way.

He threw the letter on the floor, took the white vase from the window sill and broke it over the letter. He knew that a party wasn't really in order for only thirty days, but he still felt hurt that there wasn't even one person to spend his last night with. Sylvia had changed, the same way his mother had changed. He hadn't even talked to her since the car thing. And that was why he had stolen it in the first place—to go and visit her up at college, to go and show her how he had tattooed her name on his bicep.

"I don't think we should see each other," she had said, standing in front of her dormitory. She always had to study now. And she had cut her long black hair that used to be down below her waist, without even asking him. "Stupid!" she called him for stealing the car, for putting her name on his body. That was the last time he saw her. He had driven around all night in the car, the white bathtub Porsche with the small roof that rolled back and let in the sky. But Tony's was the only car on the road. And early in the morning, he had the bad luck of being in a stolen sportscar speeding down the empty coast highway, just as it was getting light.

Leaving the house, walking toward the beach, he crossed the marsh on the old pontoon footbridge and slid down the small dune covered with ice plant, landing in the sand. The tide was high, so there wasn't much beach. The breeze was picking up, blowing off the tops of the waves. Tony looked up to the house and could see the dim lights of the guest house filter through the small windows and he could see the dark outline of the hunting lodge. How many Fourth of Julys had it been since he had thrown the sparkler that caught the roof of the hunting lodge on fire? Jimmy had climbed the roof and put out the smoldering shingles before a real fire erupted. His father was drunk, telling Navy stories—how they landed the Marines with their LCPVs, but they couldn't make it to the beach and some of the Marines drowned with all their gear, and the ones that didn't got gunned down anyway when they hit the sand at Tarawa. When his father had thought the lodge was catching fire, he stumbled for the garden hose and managed to douse the coals that were roasting the buried goat.

Now, the wind was drying up all the moisture, making the stars against the black sky seem even closer than they were. Tony sat in the sand and removed his jacket. The beach stretched for miles to the south where it stopped at the cliffs. To the north, the coastline was straight and then jutted out in a huge peninsula. Weak lights from the mansions on the peninsula twinkled as if they were stars that money could buy.

The wind felt warm and Tony removed his clothing. Entering the ocean, power-stroking through the small waves, he stopped past the breakers and treaded water on his back, letting the tops of breaking waves rain back on him. It was cold now that the summer waters had gone—the waves were not big, but at night they seemed bigger, and when the larger waves approached, you could never be ready for them. A wave broke on top of him, pushing him down. He relaxed, exhaled, and sprang off the bottom, the way Jimmy had taught him when they were young. Upon breaking the surface, another wave was in the same place, breaking directly above him. He dove again, pushed off the bottom, and swam to the surface. This time he took a huge gulp of air in case the ocean was serious, but she wasn't, so he swam into shore. The wind made his teeth chatter as he dressed.

He walked back to the house and stopped outside next to the porch and picked some of the green mint that grew wild there. Inside, he put water to boil and threw the note and larger pieces of glass into the trash. He added the mint to the pan and then swept the floor. He called Virginia's house. Her daughter answered the phone—no, they were not at home. They had been, but they went to get some coffee.

"Tell my mother I called," Tony said. In the bathroom, he towelled salt from his body. He ran warm water through his hair, warming his fingers, looking in the mirror, examining the face that sometimes didn't seem to be his. The scar on his chin from falling off his bike. The scar above his eyebrow from that fight after the football game when Payaso broke that guy's jaw. His wavy black hair that Sylvia used to love to run her hands through. He returned to the kitchen, removed the pan from the flame, letting the boil die down, the tea steep.

The wind was strong now, making the old house moan, making the tall palms outside rustle together and drop big fronds. Tony walked out to the back porch, with his cup of tea, and began rummaging over the sagging shelves his father had built. He brought in a tall wooden box covered with an old towel. Both his and Jimmy's yearbooks were in the box, and there were trophies, little golden men with big baseball gloves, and helmeted men catching passes. And his certificate for making the honor roll that one semester when Jimmy first went in the Army, framed and in glass. His mother had been proudest of that. He kept digging through the box, looking for the velvet bag. It was on the bottom, flattened with years. Taking it out, he felt its softness, its mystery, its strange authority. Opening it, he removed Jimmy's medal.

Tony left the house, walking through the cornfields behind the marsh toward the hollows, carrying Jimmy's Silver Star. The hollows were a series of man-made caves, connected and cut into the mesa, all cement, to act as stockpiles of ammunition for the war his father had fought. Now, they were empty and forgotten.

The wind was waving and bending the huge eucalyptus trees that served as windbreaks for the fields. The moon was big, but not full, and it hung directly overhead, the wind unable to displace it. At the first hollow, he walked down the cement grade and lit a match. The match went out quickly so he lit three at once. Gathering up some paper trash and lighting it, Tony thought how dirty and uncared for it seemed down here. He got the paper lit, then went back up and gathered some brush to start a fire.

We kept it cleaner, Tony thought. He thought of the nights here with Sylvia. The nights with Payaso and Joker and David and their girlfriends. Payaso was doing federal now. Joker too. Armed robbery. Who would have thought it? And now David in the service. He looked around the small sphere of visibility, seeing all that showed for so many years of his life. Broken bottles and trash leading out of the light.

Suddenly, there was a feeling of freedom that surprised him and made him want to do something spectacular. The worst that could have happened to him was already over; he was going in tomorrow. He took the medal from his pocket and thought of Jimmy. He had cried in the shower before the funeral and didn't think he could ever stop until the hot water ran out. The casket had been closed but Tony knew that Jimmy was lying in there, his nose bleeding and it wouldn't stop and he just wanted to unlace the gloves for him and stop the bleeding. And when the honor guard fired the salute, Tony cried in public, his dark sunglasses hiding his eyes. After that, he never tried to excel in school, the empty lost feeling never left. He used to carry on make-believe conversations with Jimmy in his head. Jimmy, you're a good soldier. Jimmy, you got good grades and you didn't hang around with the fuck-ups like I do. Fuck school, fuck the army, fuck that war. The only thing that helped the loneliness were the afternoons with Sylvia. It didn't seem so bad then.

Tony took a smoldering branch and walked to the cement wall, The heat burned his hand but he held the branch firm while he wrote his name huge on the wall and dated it with the charcoaled end. He then kicked apart the flames of the fire and walked back up into the wind.

~~~~~

Tony felt something grabbing his big toe. He kicked at it. It grabbed his toe again, harder, and wouldn't let go. He moaned and kicked at his toe with his free foot. Now, it had both big toes. He stretched and opened his eyes and saw his mother at the foot of the bed.

"I'll make you breakfast," his mother said.

Tony just looked at her.

"I took the morning off," she said, smiling. "C'mon, get up."

Tony looked out the small window below the peak of the roof. The wind storm had left a litter of tree trash all about the hunting lodge and guest house. Branches and leaves and even a few small junipers were completely down. But the sky was a crisp blue, a blue so strong you couldn't help but notice—it only happened a few times a year. Off in the distance, he could hear the rhythmic pattern of breaking waves.

Downstairs at breakfast, Tony asked, "Who's going to clean up here?" She had made fried potatoes and bacon and eggs and pancakes.

"You mean from the wind?" she asked him, sitting off to the side of the table, on her stool, smoking a cigarette. Her hair was black like Tony's and her face was still pretty, although Tony thought she was stunning, beautiful.

"Yeah, who's going to clean up the trash from the wind?"

"Don't worry about the trash, Tony. I want you to listen to me. I'm going to move in with Virginia. I can't be alone here. Please don't worry about the litter," she said exhaling smoke, reaching for her coffee. A car pulled into the gravel before the hunting lodge.

"Everything will be here when you get out," she said smiling, but looking hurt. Alex arrived at the screen door and knocked, then entered the kitchen, and with him came the overpowering smell of Mennen after-shave. He smiled at Tony's mother.

"You ready, Tony?" Alex said.

"Let him finish his breakfast," his mother said. "You want some coffee?"

"No. You have some orange juice?" he asked her, sitting next to Tony. Tony tried to eat, but his appetite just wasn't there.

After finishing breakfast, they drove out the dirt road next to the cornfields in separate cars. Tony was in a Chevy station wagon that belonged to Alex's girlfriend; his mother drove behind in the big battered luxury car with the hubcaps missing. She hadn't cried at the kitchen door. She simply said, "We'll talk when you come home." She had seen the vase, she had read the note.

At the highway the cars went in separate directions. His mother waved as she took off for the coast highway. Alex drove the road toward the mountains. The mountains were painfully visible, you could see the folds in the foothills, almost imagine the fir trees high up that surrounded the huge basin.

"Ophelia called her brother and they got word to Spider that you're coming in. Look for him when you get out of processing," Alex said. "Hey, c'mon Tony, you'll be okay."

Tony turned around and saw the blue of the ocean as he looked back and watched the lodge and the house get smaller and smaller.

"Everything's cool, Tony," Alex said. "Did you wear boxers?"

"I didn't wear anything underneath."

"Shit."

"What?"

"Nothing."

"No, what?"

"Just don't let them put you with the queers."

"I'll be alright."

They drove through the flats that used to be all farmland. They drove past shopping malls and past homes that they never could buy, no matter how many hours they worked. The streets, the shops, the stores, the people who were walking, everything seemed to be charged with electricity, seemed to have new life, as if the wind had rejuvenated the land and the people.

They drove up to the main entrance to the city within a city. Alex stopped the car right in front of the doors, left the ignition running, and got out, walking around to open the door for Tony. It was all cement gray with no windows, not one, and big, bigger up close than Tony could have ever imagined. On the very top, there was a high fence topped with barbed wire.

"Those are the handball courts," Alex said to Tony as they both cocked their heads to the sky. "You'll get good."

Tony got out of the car. Alex embraced him and said to be cool, not to back down from anybody. "If anything comes down, remember, you're from the South. Nothing that heavy will happen though," Alex said. He walked back around the car, got in, and just drove off, leaving Tony standing there.

Tony put his hand in his pocket and felt the medal he had forgotten to return to the box. He squeezed it and thought of Jimmy. How he flew back under fire to get his men. He simply did it. *Stupid* kept ringing in his ears, the stupid that Sylvia had called him, the stupid that hurt his mother. Tony walked in the glass doors, trying not to show how scared he was, trying to suppress that lump in his throat, trying to think of easy time.

La Loca Santa

Ana Castillo

La Loca was only three years old when she died. Her mother Sofi woke at midnight to the howling and neighing of the five dogs, six cats, and four horses, whose custom it was to go freely in and out of the house. Sofi got up and tiptoed out of her room. The animals were kicking and neighing and running back and forth with their ears back, fur standing on end, but Sofi couldn't make out what their agitation was about.

She checked the bedroom with the three older girls. Esperanza, the eldest, had her arms wrapped around the two smaller ones, Fe and Caridad, who were sleeping strangely undisturbed by the excitement of the animals.

Sofi went back into her own room, where her baby, the three-year-old, had slept ever since Sofi's husband disappeared. Sofi put the baseball bat back under the bed. She had taken it with her while checking the house just in case she encountered some *menso* who had gotten ideas about the woman who lived alone with her four little girls by the ditch at the end of the road.

It was then that she noticed the baby, although apparently asleep, jerking. Jerking, jerking the little body possessed by something unknown that caused her to thrash about violently until she finally fell off the bed. Sofi ran to pick her up, but was so frightened by her little daughter's seizure that she stopped short.

The baby continued to thrash about, banging her little arms and legs against the hard stone floor and white foam mixed with a little blood spilling from the corners of her mouth. Worst of all, her eyes were now open, rolled all the way to the top of her head.

Sofi screamed and called *Ave María purísimas* and her three other precious children came running, asking "Mami, Mami, what happened? Ahh!" Everyone was screaming and moaning because the baby had stopped moving and lay perfectly still, and they knew she was dead.

It was the saddest *velorio* in Los Lunas in years because it was so sad to bury a child. Fortunately, none had died since—well, if memory served right, Doña Dolores's last son. Poor woman. Eleven children and one after the next died on her until she was left with no one except for her drunken, foul-mouthed husband. They said all the babies were victims of a rare bone disease they inherited through the father's bloodline. What terrible misfortune for Doña Dolores, suffering the pangs of labor through eleven children all fated to die during infancy. Twelve years of marriage, eleven babies that did not survive, and to top it off, the husband drank up everything they owned. A sad, sad story.

The day after the wake, the neighbors all came out to accompany Sofi and the girls to the church at Tomé, where Sofi wanted the little baby's Mass to be given before they lay her in the cold ground. Everyone Sofi knew was there: the baby's godparents, all of Sofi's *comadres* and *compadres*, her sister from Phoenix, everyone except, of course, the baby's father, since no one had seen hide nor hair of him since he'd left Sofi and the girls.

It was 118 degrees that day and the two pallbearers, upon the instruction of Father Jerome, placed the small casket on the ground just in front of the church. No one was quite certain what Father Jerome had planned when he paused there in the hot sun. Maybe some last minute prayers or instructions for the mourners before entering the House of God. He wiped his brow with his handkerchief. He was a little concerned about the grieving mother, who at that point was trembling and nearly collapsing between two others. Father Jerome thought it a good idea to advise them all on funeral decorum. "As devoted followers of Christ," he began, "we must not show our lack of faith in Him at these times and in His, Our Father's fair judgment, Who alone knows why we are here on this earth and why He chooses to call us back home when He does..."

Why? Why? That's exactly what Sofi wanted to know at that moment—when all she had ever done was accept God's will. If it hadn't been punishment enough to be abandoned by her husband, then—for no apparent reason and without warning, save the horrible commotion of the animals that night—her baby was taken away! Oh, why? Why? That's all she wanted to know. "*Ay-yyy!*"

At that moment, as Sofi threw herself on the ground, pounding it with her small, rough fists, her *compadres* crying alongside her, saying "Please, please *comadre*, get up, the Lord alone knows what He does! Listen to the *padre* . . ." Esperanza let out a long and high-pitched shriek that started some dogs in the distance barking. Sofi stopped crying to see what was causing the girl's hysteria when suddenly the whole crowd began to scream and faint and move away from the direction of the priest, who soon stood alone next to the baby's coffin.

The lid had pushed all the way open and the little girl inside sat up, just as sweetly as if she had woken from a nap, rubbing her eyes and yawning. "Mami?" she called, looking around and squinting her eyes against the harsh light. Father Jerome got hold of himself and sprinkled holy water in the direction of the child, but for the moment was too stunned to utter so much as The Lord's Prayer. Then, as if all this were not amazing enough, as Father Jerome moved toward the child, she lifted herself up into the air and landed on the church roof. "Don't touch me, don't touch me!" she warned.

This was only the beginning of her lifelong phobia of people. She wasn't one of those afflicted with exaggerated fear of germs and contagion. For the rest of her life, however, she was to be repulsed by the smell of humans. She claimed that all humans bore an odor akin to that which she had smelled in the places she had passed through when she was dead. Where she had gone was the other thing that she revealed from the rooftop that day with the limited ability of a three-year-old's vocabulary, which though scant, was enhanced by her fluency in Spanish and English, so that what she didn't know to say in one language she said in the other *idioma.* Meanwhile, everyone below was genuflecting, paralyzed, or crossing themselves over and over as she spoke.

"*Hija, hija!*" Father Jerome called up to her, hands clenched in the air. "Is this an act of God or of Satan that brings you back to us, that has flown you up to the roof like a bird? Are you the devil's messenger or a winged angel?"

At that point, Sofi, despite her shock, rose from the ground unable to tolerate the mere suggestion by Father Jerome that her daughter, her blessed, sweet baby, could be the devil's own. "Don't you dare!" she screamed at the priest, charging at him and beating him with her fists. "Don't you dare start this about my baby! If our Lord in His heavens has sent *my* child back to me, don't you dare start this backward thinking against her. The devil doesn't produce miracles! And this is a miracle, an answer to the prayers of a broken-hearted mother. *Hombre necio, pendejo!*"

"Ay, watch what you say, *comadre!*" one of Sofi's *comadres* whispered, pulling Sofi off the priest, who had staved off her attack with his arms over his head, although she had only struck him on the back. "Oh, my God!" others uttered, crossing themselves at hearing Sofi call the priest a *pendejo*, which was equivalent to any blasphemy, crossing themselves all the more because the verdict was still in the air as to whether they were witnessing a true miracle or the work of the devil—and Sofi's behavior was giving proof to the latter—after all, calling the holy priest a *pendejo* and hitting him!

Finally, the crowd settled down, some still on their knees, palms together, all looking up at the little girl like the glittering angel placed at the top of a Christmas tree. She seemed serene and, though a little flushed, quite like she always did when she was alive. The fact was that she was alive, but no one at the moment seemed sure.

"Listen," she announced calmly to the crowd. "On my long trip I went to three places: hell . . ." Someone let out a loud scream at this. The child went on, "to purgatory . . . [she pronounced it "pugatory"] and to heaven. God sent me back to help you all, to pray for you all, *o si no . . . o si no . . .*"

"O si no, qué, *hija?*" Father Jerome begged.

"O si no, you, and others who doubt just like you, will never see our Father in heaven!"

The audience in unison gasped. Someone whispered, "That's the devil," but refrained from continuing when Sofi turned to see who it was.

"Come down, come down," the priest called to the child. "We'll all go in and pray for you. Yes, yes, maybe all this really is true. Maybe you did die, maybe you did see our Lord in His heavens, maybe He did send you back to give us guidance. Let's just go in together, and we'll all pray for you."

With the delicate and effortless motion of a monarch butterfly, the child brought herself back to the ground, landing gently on her bare feet, her ruffled chiffon nightdress bought for the occasion of her burial fluttering softly in the air. "No, *Padre*," she corrected him. "Remember, it is I who am here to pray for *you*." With that stated, she went into the church and those with faith followed.

When the baby was able to receive medical attention (Sofi took her child to a hospital in Albuquerque this time rather than rely on the doctor in Los Lunas who had so rashly declared her child dead) it was diagnosed that she was in all probability an epileptic.

Epilepsy notwithstanding, there was much left unexplained, and for this reason, Sofi's baby grew up at home, away from strangers who might be witness to her astonishing behavior, and she eventually earned the name around Los Lunas of La Loca Santa. For a brief period after her resurrection, people came from all over the state in hopes of receiving her blessing or her performance of some miracle for them. But because she hated being close to anyone and the best that strangers could expect was a glimpse of her from outside the gate, the "santa" was dropped from her name and she was soon forgotten by strangers.

She became known simply as La Loca. The funny thing was (but not so funny since it is the way of New Mexicans to call a spade a spade), even La Loca's mother and sisters called her that. Moreover, La Loca herself responded to the name and by the time she was twenty-one everyone had forgotten her Christian name.

Her sisters, Esperanza, Caridad, and Fe, all exactly three years apart from each other, had each gone out into the world and had all eventually returned to their mother's home. Esperanza had been the only one to get through college. She had gotten her B.A. in Chicano studies. During that time, she had lived with her boyfriend, Rubén (who, during the height of his Chicano Cosmic consciousness, renamed himself Cuauhtemoc) despite the opposition of her mother, who said of her eldest daughter's nonsanctified union: "Why should a man buy the cow when he can have the milk for free?" "*I am not a cow*," Esperanza responded, but despite this, right after graduation, Cuauhtemoc dumped her for a middle-class *gabacha* with a Corvette and they bought a house in Rio Rancho right after their wedding.

Esperanza always had a lot of "spunk," as they say, but she did have a bad year after Cuauhtemoc (who was Rubén again) before she recovered and decided to go back to the university for an M.A. in communications. Upon receiving her degree, she landed a job at the local TV station as a news broadcaster. (Eventually, Esperanza would go on to Washington D.C., where she would co-host a national news program and travel to such newsworthy places as Lebanon and Baghdad, but this would be much later after this story takes place and so what we have here are those transitional years.) But for a long time after their breakup, Esperanza felt like a woman with brains was as good as dead for all the happiness it brought her in the love department.

Caridad tried a year of college, but school was not for her. She was the sister of the porcelain complexion, not white, but impeccable. She had perfect teeth and round, apple-shaped breasts. Unlike the rest of the women in her family and despite her mother's insistence that they were *Spanish*, descendants of pure Spanish blood, but who all shared the flat butt of the Pueblo blood undeniably circulating through their veins from their mother's genes, Caridad had a somewhat pronounced ass that men just couldn't help notice everywhere she went.

She fell in love in high school with Memo, got pregnant, and they married the day after graduation. But two weeks had not passed before Caridad got wind that Memo was still seeing his ex-girlfriend, Domitila, who lived in Tomé, and Caridad went back home.

Since that time, Caridad had had three abortions, and La Loca performed each one. Their mother had only known about the first. They didn't tell anyone else about it but said to Memo and his family that Caridad had miscarried from being so upset about Memo's cheating on her. It was agreed by all that the marriage be annulled. It would have been a terrible thing to let anyone find out that La Loca had "cured" her sister of her pregnancy, a cause for excommunication for both, not to mention that someone would have had La Loca arrested. A crime against man, if not a sin against God.

The occasions when La Loca let people get close to her (only her mother and the animals were ever allowed touch her), when she permitted human contact at all, were few. But healing her sisters from the traumas and injustices they were dealt by the world—a world she herself never experienced firsthand—was never an issue.

Caridad kept seeing Memo for several years until he finally made his choice. It was not Domitila of Tomé and it wasn't Caridad of Los Lunas: It was the Marines. And off he went to be all that he never knew he was. For a while it was said that the Army made men, the Marines' motto, he was told, was that they only took men.

Three abortions and a weakness for tequila with beer chasers after work at the hospital where she was an orderly and Caridad no longer discriminated between giving her love to Memo and only to Memo, whenever he wanted it, and loving anyone she met at the bars who vaguely resembled Memo. At about the time that her sister Esperanza, who was definitely not prettier than her, but had more brains, was on the 10 o'clock nightly news, you could bet that Caridad was making it in a pickup off a dark road with some guy whose name the next day would be as insignificant to her as yesterday's headlines were to Esperanza the newscaster.

Fe, the third of Sofi's daughters, was fine. That is, at twenty-four, with a steady job at the bank, and a hard-working boyfriend whom she had known forever, she had just announced their engagement. Working the same job since high school graduation, she was a reliable friend to the "girls" at work. She was beyond reproach. Image was maintained above all—from the organized desk at work to weekly manicured fingernails and a neat coiffure. She and Tomás (Tom) Torres were the ideal couple in their social circle. He ran one of those Mini-Mart filling stations, sometimes working double shifts. He did not drink or even smoke cigarettes. They were putting their money away for their wedding, a small wedding, just for family and a few close friends because they were going to use their savings for their first house.

As it was, while Fe had a little something to talk to Esperanza about, she kept away from her other sisters, mother, and the animals, because she just didn't understand how they could all be so self-defeating, so unmotivated. Sometimes, when she came home and saw La Loca outside the stalls with the horses, always in the same dirty pair of jeans and never wearing shoes, even in winter, she was filled with deep compassion.

She had only been six years old when La Loca had had her first epileptic fit and her mother and the community, out of ignorance, had pronounced the child dead. She did not remember *"El Milagro"* as her mother referred to La Loca's resurrection that day in front of the church and highly doubted that such a thing as her little sister flying up to the church rooftop had ever happened.

Usually, Fe did not feel compassion for La Loca, but simply disappointment and disgust for her sister's obvious mental illness, the fact that her mother had encouraged it with her own superstitions, and finally, fear that it was, like her Indian flat butt, hereditary, despite everyone's protests to the contrary.

Fe couldn't wait until she got out—of her mother's home as well as Los Lunas—but she would get out properly, with a little style and class as none of the women in her family had, except for Esperanza, whose being on television every night was lending some prestige to Fe at the bank, although when Esperanza was in college being radical and living with that crazy Chicano who was always speeding on peyote or something, Fe hadn't known what to make of her older sister and certainly had no desire to assimilate Esperanza's La Raza politics.

She had just come back from Margie's Bridal Gowns, where she had just had herself fitted for her dress; and the three *gabachas* she had chosen from the bank as her bridesmaids (instead of her sisters) had met that Saturday to have their gowns fitted too, when La Loca pointed to the mail as soon as Fe came in.

"What? A letter for me?" Fe said cheerfully, recognizing Tom's neat, small print on the square envelope. She smiled and took it to the bathroom to get a little privacy. La Loca had that look like she was going to stick close to her. Sometimes she did that. She had this sixth sense when she suspected something was amiss in the house and wouldn't let up until she uncovered it.

Dear Baby Cakes, it began, a short note on yellow paper from a legal pad. This was a little unusual, since Tom always sent cards, cards with lovers kissing, with irises and roses, with beautiful little sayings to which he simply signed, "Your Tom." *Dear Baby Cakes* . . . Fe, stopped, heard a faint rap on the door. "Go away, Loca," she said. She heard her sister move away from the door. Fe read on: *I have been thinking about this for a long time, but I didn't have the nerve to tell you in person. It's not that I don't love you. I do. I always will. But I just don't think I'm ready to get married. Like I said, I thought about this a long time. Please don't call to try to change my mind. I hope you find happiness with someone who deserves you and can make you happy.* Tom.

When La Loca and Sofi—with the help of Fred and Wilma, the two Irish setters that immediately joined in the commotion of the women breaking down the bathroom door, and Fe's screaming and tearing the tiny bathroom apart—finally got to Fe, she was wrapped up in the shower curtain in the tub. "You're gonna suffocate, *hijita*, get outa there!" Sofi called, and with La Loca's help unwrapped the plastic from around Fe, who in her ravings had inadvertently made herself into a human tamale—all the while screaming at full pitch.

Sofi shook her daughter hard but when that didn't silence Fe, she gave her a good slap as she had seen people do on TV lots of times when-ever anyone got like that. But Fe didn't quiet down. In fact, Fe did not stop screaming even when Sofi announced that she was going to get Tom. She had to go personally to Tom's house when he did not return her calls.

"I got a daughter who won't stop screaming," she told Tom's mother, Mrs. Torres.

"I got a son who's got *susto*," Mrs. Torres replied.

"*Susto? Susto!*" Sofi shouted. "You think that cowardly son of yours without *pelos* on his *maracas* has *susto*? I'll show you *susto*! My daughter has been screaming at the top of her lungs for ten days and nights. She spent hundreds, maybe even a thousand dollars already on their wed-ding plans. She has people at work that she can't face anymore. And let me tell you something, Mrs. Torres, don't think that I don't know that your son has had her on the pill for a long time . . ."

"Wait, just a minute, *señora*," Mrs. Torres cut in, holding up her hand. The two mothers, believe it or not, had never met before. Fe had been too ashamed of her family to bring Mrs. Torres over to her house. "My son, my son is a good boy. He hasn't eaten for days, he's so upset about this breakup. But he said he had to do the honorable thing. He hasn't cost your daughter anything that he himself has not lost as well. What's money when in the long run he spared her an unhappy marriage?

I don't know why he changed his mind about marrying her. I keep out of my son's business. Just be glad he left your daughter when he did. You know how men are . . ."

"Ay!" Sofi moaned—because she knew full well that that last remark was meant to hit below the belt regarding her own marriage and she knew next to nothing about Mrs. Torres—thanks to Fe—to come back with a good rejoinder. But finally Tom came out of his room and she convinced him to come over so that he might make Fe stop screaming.

"What's that?" he asked, obviously spooked by Fe's shrill cries that were heard from outside the house. "Is that La Loca?" He had heard of her, but had never met Fe's "retarded" sister. "Are you crazy?" Sofi said, unlocking the door. "That's *your* girlfriend! Why do you think I brought you here? If I know Fe, she'll snap out of it—maybe by you talking to her. We'll see."

But Tom stopped at the threshold. "I can't go in," he said. He was pale. "I'm sorry, I just can't." And before Sofi could think of something to say to stop him, Tom was back in his car, smoking down the road. Damn, Sofi thought seeing him speed away, maybe he *does* have *susto*.

Unfortunately, nothing and no one could quiet Fe down. She wanted her Tom back. And even when Caridad managed to get some tranquilizers from her hospital friends, Fe would only shut up for an hour or two at a time when she slept. She even screamed while she was being fed (because now it was Sofi and her daughters who took turns feeding, cleaning, and dressing poor Fe, who was truly a mess, and who, if she were in any way capable of realizing it, would have been horrified at that thought).

Meanwhile, La Loca did what she could. She sewed a padded headband for Fe so that when she banged her head against the wall as she increasingly did while she screamed, she wouldn't hurt herself as bad. She also prayed for her, of course, since that was La Loca's principal reason for being alive as both her mother and she well knew.

Above all, however, she prayed for Tom, because like so many *nuevo mexicanos*—Hispanics, whatever he wanted to call himself, something about giving himself over to a woman was worse than having lunch with the devil. Yes, he had *susto*. And no tea and no incantations by the *curandera* his mother brought over to relieve him of it would ever cure him. The mere mention of Fe was enough to set him off into a cold sweat. So

La Loca prayed for him because in a few years he would no doubt find a new *novia* and marry her and no one, not even Mrs. Torres, not even himself, would know that he was still suffering from the inability to open his heart to anyone.

Fe and her screaming became part of the household's routine so that the animals didn't even jump or howl anymore whenever Fe, after a brief intermission when she dozed off, woke up abruptly at full pitch. But it was Caridad who, being a selfless being, would never have thought of becoming the center of attention, especially when her sister needed everyone's support as she did, but who ultimately caused the entire household, including animals, to leave Fe to herself when she came home one night mangled as a stray cat, having been left for dead by the side of the road. Too much blood to tell at the time, but after Caridad had been taken by ambulance to the hospital, treated and saved, just barely, Sofi was told that her daughter's nipples had been bitten off. She had also been scourged with something, branded like cattle. Worst of all, a tracheotomy was performed because she had also been stabbed in the throat.

When Esperanza finally managed to get her mother to come home to try to rest a bit, they found Fe dozing off in her room and La Loca nowhere around. They didn't find her in the closets, under the beds, not out in the stalls with the horses. The dogs would not reveal where she was, staring blankly at Sofi when she asked them about La Loca's whereabouts. Esperanza suggested calling the police. La Loca never left the house except to go to the backyard and out in the stalls and only with her mother did she take walks down to the *acequia*. Surely, the two women thought, after having been gone for more than twelve hours and seeing no reason to call Fe or La Loca, since neither really would understand or needed to know about Caridad's tragic condition, La Loca must've panicked and went walking by herself down the road to look for them.

But just as Esperanza was dialing the emergency number she heard a distinct "clunk" sound from inside the wood-burning stove in the living room. Sofi and the dogs heard it too and they all rushed at once to pull La Loca out. "Mami, is Caridad dead?" La Loca asked, soot-covered, arms around her mother's shoulders. She was crying. "No, *hija*" (Sofi preferred to call La Loca "*hija*" to her face). "Your sister is not dead. Thank God."

Just then Fe woke up and the walls began to vibrate with her screaming and since everyone, including the dogs and cats, had been concentrating on La Loca for a moment, in unison, they gave a start. La Loca began to cry harder and Sofi, who couldn't take the reality of a permanently traumatized daughter, another who was more ghost than of this world, and a third, who was the most beautiful child she had given birth to, cruelly mutilated, let herself sink into the couch and began to sob.

"Ma. Ma. Please, don't give up!" Esperanza called out, but did not come to put her arms around her mother's hunched shoulders. "Aw!" Esperanza said, clearly trying not to give in to it all herself. She said to no one in particular, since no one was paying attention to her: "I've been offered a job in Houston. I didn't know for sure if I should take it. But there's nothing for me here. This is all too much."

The next day, Esperanza went straight to her boss and gave her notice. The staff was pretty thrilled for her since the job in Houston was definitely a step up and things were looking good for Esperanza in the way of career opportunities.

As it turned out, she got a message before the end of that week from a certain Rubén out of her past. *Lunch tomorrow?* The message read. Sure, why not? Esperanza thought. Enough time had passed so that she could almost say she bore no hard feelings toward her college sweetheart. She was doing all right for herself and she was certain he had seen her on the nightly news so he must have known it too. Soon, she would be leaving New Mexico, broadening her horizons, freeing herself, as they say, from the provincialism of her upbringing, and Rubén with his blonde wife and their three-bedroom house, their coyote kid, their dog, and their mini-van could live happily ever after as far as she was concerned.

But, as it turned out, there was no more house in Rio Rancho and no more mini-van or sportscar. Rubén was driving an old clunker, and Donna had split with their kid to *Houston* (apparently she, too, was intent on starting a new life, broadening her horizons, freeing herself from her provincial upbringing, etc.).

"I have thought of calling you for a long time, Esperanza," Rubén told her. "Every time I go pray at a meeting or sweat, I think of us, and how it coulda been." He had put on a few pounds, well, let's say, more than a few, but to Esperanza, he still had that kind of animal magnetism she always felt toward him, what people call "chemistry."

"You remember, *vieja*, when we used to go to meetings together, when we sweated together back in the days when we were in college?" he asked, giving her a nudge with his elbow. He was holding a mug of beer in his hand and she saw as he waved his arms with great animation that he didn't spill any of it, but instead, chugged it right down and grinned at her. No, he wasn't drunk, just feeling good. It was good to see him again, to be back together and she ordered herself another beer too.

Esperanza didn't go back to work that day but ended up picking up where they left off, and to make a long story short, she didn't get to Houston that year, either. Every two weeks she was right there with Rubén, at the meetings of the Native American Church, Rubén singing and drumming, keeping the fire, watching the "door," teaching her the do's and don't's of his interpretation of indigenous spirituality and practices, lodge "etiquette," and finally the role of women and the role of men and how they were not to be questioned. And she, concluding as she had during their early days, why not?

After all, there was Rubén with his Native American and Chicano male friends always joking among themselves, always siding with each other and always agreeing to the order and reason of the universe, and since Esperanza had no Native women friends to verify any of what was being told to her by Rubén about women's part in what they were doing, she did not dare contradict him.

This was about the time that a virtual miracle occurred in Esperanza's house that eventually caused her to decide about her relationship with Rubén. Well, actually, she had been thinking about it for a while. Every time they went to a meeting, which was maybe once every two or three weeks, everything was good between them. They went to the meeting. Sometimes they also did a sweat. Afterward, they went home and made love all day. The problem was that then she would not hear from Rubén again until the next time there was a meeting. She was beginning to feel like part of a ritual in which she herself participated as an unsuspecting symbol, like a staff or a rattle or medicine.

For her, as the months went on, the distance between them between meetings and sweats had become unsettling. It completely separated her from her other life, the life to which Rubén referred rather derogatorily as "careerist," and she felt, for lack of a more sophisticated articulation of it, just plain sad and lonely about it. She wanted to share with him that part of her life. She needed to bring it all together, to consolidate the spiritual with the practical side of things. But whenever she suggested to Rubén that they have lunch again like they did that first time or to go out on a regular date between meetings, he simply declined with no apologies, regrets, or explanations.

What was left of Caridad had been brought home after three months in the hospital. In addition to caring for Fe, La Gritona (as her mother had begun to refer to her, although never to her face but just in the kitchen with her other daughters), it was Sofi's main job to care for Caridad, or as stated more accurately above, what was left of her.

La Loca took care of the horses and the animals, and of course, helped her mother prepare meals for her sisters. Both La Loca and her mother made sure they left enough chili and whatever else they prepared for Esperanza when she got home from work. She wasn't too picky about food and usually just microwaved whatever was put aside for her whenever she came in and went back out to do the nightly news.

It was right after one of La Loca's (fortunately not very frequent) fits that the miracle that Esperanza witnessed occurred. Sofi was tending to La Loca, who was on the living room floor, the tray with Fe's *carne adobada* and green chile all over her; Esperanza standing nearby as usual, not sure what to do and preferring not to do anything; and, of course, all the animals that had given their perfunctory warnings just beforehand standing nervously around as well, when movement in the dining room—which was adjacent to the living room—caught their eyes at once. Dogs, cats, and women, twenty-eight eyes in all saw *Caridad* walking soundlessly, without seeming to be aware of them, across that room. Before anyone could react, she was out of sight. Furthermore, it wasn't the Caridad that had been brought back from the hospital, but a whole and again beautiful Caridad, in what furthermore appeared to be Fe's wedding gown.

"Ma?" Esperanza said, hesitating, but still fixed on the empty space where Caridad had passed.

"*Dios mio*," Sofi gasped. "Caridad . . ."

"Mami," La Loca whispered, still on the floor, "I prayed for Caridad . . ."

"I know you did, *mi'jita*, I know," Sofi said, trembling, afraid to pull herself up, to go to the room, where she suspected Caridad's corpse was now waiting to be taken care of.

"I prayed real hard," La Loca added and started to cry.

The dogs and cats whimpered.

The three women huddled together went to the bedroom where Caridad was. Sofi stepped back when she saw, not what had been left of her daughter, half repaired by modern medical technology, tubes through her throat, bandages over skin that was gone, surgery piecing together flesh that was once her daughter's breasts, but Caridad as she was before.

Furthermore, a calm Fe was holding her sister, rocking her, stroking her forehead, humming softly to her. Caridad was whole. There was nothing, nothing that anyone could see, wrong with her, except for the fact that she was feverish. Her eyes were closed while she moved her head back and forth, not violently, but softly, as was Caridad's nature, mumbling unintelligibly all the while.

"Fe?" said Esperanza—who was equally taken aback by Fe's transformation. She had stopped screaming.

Sofi, sobbing, rushed over to embrace her two daughters.

"I prayed for you," La Loca told Fe. "Thank you, Loca," Fe said, almost smiling.

"Loca . . ." Esperanza reached over to place her hand on La Loca's shoulder. "Don't touch me!" La Loca said, moving away from her sister as she always did from anyone when she was not the one to initiate the contact.

"I'm going to call Rubén," Esperanza announced, probably to her mother since she was the only one who ever listened to her around there, but at that moment her mother was so overwhelmed by her two daughters' return to the living that she didn't hear Esperanza either.

"Rubén?" Esperanza said, when Rubén answered his phone.

"Yeah? Hey, how's it goin', kid?" he asked with a little chuckle. Esperanza paused. He talked to her on the phone like she was a casual friend. A casual friend whom he prayed with and whom he made love with but whom he could not call to ask on a given day if she was doing O.K. And when she was on her moon the estrangement between them idened since she was not permitted to go to the meeting or to sweat, nor did he like to make love to her. He, too, was a casual friend, one who accepted her gifts of groceries, the rides in *her* car with *her* gas, all up and down the Southwest to attend meetings, who took his collect calls the month he left on a "pilgrimage" to visit the Mayan ruins throughout Southern Mexico but who had not been invited to join him, who was always good to pick up the tab whenever they stopped someplace for a few beers and tacos just before she left him—after the meetings, sweats, lovemaking, on her way back home so she could get herself ready for that job for which he suspected her so much of selling out to white society, but which paid for all the food, gas, telephone calls, and even, let's admit it, the tens and twenties she discreetly left on his kitchen table or bedroom dresser whenever she went over, knowing he could use it and would take it, although he would never have asked her directly for it.

"It's my sisters," she started to say, but already something else was on her mind more pertinent than the recent recuperation of Fe and Caridad.

"Yeah, your sisters . . ." Rubén said. "Yeah, you got your hands full, huh, woman?"

"No." Esperanza responded with sudden aloofness. "As a matter of fact, they're taking good care of themselves. I just wanted to tell you that I'm accepting an offer in Washington. And that I think it's better if we just don't see each other anymore, Rubén."

"Well . . . uh . . ." Rubén was groping for a response that would reinstate his pride just demolished by Esperanza's abrupt rejection, when he was cut short by a click. Esperanza didn't mean to simply hang up on him but she had just caught sight of a man peering in through the kitchen window. What made it really eerie was that instead of barking, the dogs were waving their tails. Just then the man opened the door and stepped in. She recognized him right away since she was already going on twelve when he had left. "Papi?"

Yes. It was their father, Sofi's husband who had returned, "after all those years" as they would say around Los Lunas for a long time to come. Some say, *that* was the true miracle of that night. All kinds of stories circulated as to what had happened to him "all those years." Most of the rumors he would start himself, and when he would get tired of hearing them played back always with some new variation or detail of exaggeration added to them which did not quite suit his taste, he pretended to get angry about them, stopped them, and started a new story all over again.

With regards to his own adventures, he quickly realized he had considerable competition with La Loca's life, which she herself didn't relay but that he invariably heard from everyone else. When he tried to get her to fly to the roof or stick herself in the wood-burning stove, she simply stared at him, as if such suggestions were absurd. However, the one thing she did confirm was her repulsion with human contact whenever he came close to her, unless she was the one who initiated it, which, believe it or not, once in a while, she did.

She would approach him when he was eating or watching television and sniff him. Since he didn't want to scare her off, he'd remain still and pretend he didn't notice what she was doing.

"Hija," Sofi asked her daughter one day when they were alone. "What is it that you smell when you smell your father?"

"Mami," La Loca said. "I smell my papi. And he was in hell, too."

"Hell?" Sofi said, thinking her daughter, who had no sense of humor at all, was somehow after more than twenty years learning the art of irony.

But instead Loca replied quite soberly, "Mami, I been to hell. You never forget that smell. And my father . . . he was there, too."

"So you think I should forgive your father for leaving me, for leaving us all those years?" Sofi asked.

"Here we don't forgive, Mami," La Loca told her. And there was no question at that point in Sofi's mind that La Loca had no sense of humor. La Loca's throat was full with compassion. "Only in hell we learn to forgive, and you got to die first," La Loca said. "That's when we get to pluck out all the devils from our hearts that were put there when we were *here*. That's where we get rid of all the lies told to us. That's where we go and cry like rain. Mami, hell is where you go to see yourself. This father, out there, sitting watching TV, he was in hell a long time. He's like an onion. We will never know all of him—but he's not afraid anymore."

The Jumping Bean

Helena María Viramontes

He cocked his fisherman's face, seared and rumpled and buoyant in the sea of glass, combed the Tres Rosas pomade onto his hair, jamming three fingers to make a slick, shimmering wave. From where she stood, she caught a spark of the gold-plated crucifix, which hung around his neck like an anchor and flickered in the mirror until he buried it beneath his buttons. The young girl thought her papa pretty in his oversized salt-and-pepper suit jacket, the triangular lapels so wide they peaked to his padded shoulders.

He had no reason to see her. She was just one of the many children he labored for, carrying wet cement and grit on the bridge of his back, ignoring the Anglo plasterers. They called him "the jumping bean," because of his ability to scale a ladder towing more than his weight with the speed of a man half his age, as circles of sweat salt rung like the age of a tree on his work shirt. Even as the wooden poke of the hod stabbed against his belly like the spiked heat of midday, he had never thought to abandon them. Even when the thorny whiskey could no longer drown the sound of his own bones aching, he would never leave them. He reminded her mother constantly of his contributions and all of them were made to feel indebted to his relentless back and the two hands he rinsed with vinegar daily to relieve the burn of the abrasive, gray grit powder. He was a finch of a man, a sparrow of nerves, his fingers like swollen live wires too dangerous to touch.

He spotted her reflection and his smile made her feel as though it were permissible to approach him. He fished his hand into his deep pit pocket, jiggled loose change, reeled out a white coin. His head came forward to hers, his nose wide and flat and royal, his eyes, black as onyx beads, his teeth a tint of tobacco stain against his leathery skin. He handed her the coin, his thumb nail purple and bruised, and she stared at the disc, licked off the dust to discern that it was a nickel. She brushed his cheek with her lips, then disappeared into the kitchen voices of her family while he disappeared, the flask of Wild Turkey clinking against his crucifix.

~~~~~

She was the only one with patience to do it, break loose her mother's dandruff with long brush strokes, which hauled her mother back to sleep. So when her oldest sister, María de la Luz, woke her with, "Mama's not sleeping again," the young girl dragged her heavy feet to where Mama sat, an Avon brush by her side. The young girl's heart bucked wildly when she saw the prayer cards filed in a parade of saints on the kitchen table, as if readied by her mama for the pot banging miracles that never came.

"It's gonna be O.K.," María de la Luz said, but Mama had the look of cold sin in her eyes anyway. María gently rubbed the heated olive oil with concentrated effort on Mama's temples to ease and loosen the tumor of disappointment, then bent to thaw Mama's feet in warm, clear water while her own knees itched from the cool floor.

Reassured, the young girl began brushing the fall of Mama's hair. The white dandruff flakes drifted silently to the bones of her mama's shoulders. She leaned on one foot then the other to keep herself awake, but dreamed anyway, dreamed of snowcapped mountains, brown saintly faces that tumbled away like dead leaves in a rising wind.

A grayish phosphorescent stream flowing from the window was enough for the young girl to decipher a slithering form. She waited for María to say something about the long, green snake which S-ed its way under the table, its forked tongue savoring the cool autumn air, but María talked to her mama instead.

"You do what you have to do," said María when Mama broke out in quaking sobs because she'd kept her daughters up half the night. "That's what you taught us." Mama cried passionately, never realizing there was so much grief inside her.

"You're tired, Mama, is all." María replied matter of factly, too tired herself to speculate on the demons her mama was battling. She caught water in a pot, turned the faucet off, put it on the flames to boil.

The snake slipped under the murky gray morning like wet soap until the young girl felt the slithering tube slide over her bare feet, and the chilling sensation prompted her to drum her toes on the worn floor. She wanted to tell María, but was silenced by the snake, which spiraled itself around her ankles and tightened its grasp. She held her breath, felt her body swell with terror. She tried in vain to interrupt the exchange between María and her mama, but they had no reason to see her.

"Don't even think of it," María warned her mama, while she stirred the last of the Quaker Oats into the boiling water. It was the first day of school, and the children would get up hungry.

~~~~~

The foreman liked her papa. He felt this Spanish boy had heart. He nick-named him Zorro for his pencil-thin mustache and surname. But the plas-terers, carpenters, welders, bulldozer drivers resented his centaurlike ability to endure the work of three men and a mule, creating a standard to which they would inevitably be compared. In turn, they created their own standards and exiled him to exist only in their peripheral vision.

He worked in their oblivion. They denied the sweat that bled like torrents over his eyes when he climbed the scaffolds with 160 pounds of cement on his back, balancing himself on the thin planks, two stories, three stories high. They never imagined his rebelling bones collapsing like noisy spoons on the floor at the end of the day, the midnight whis-key that made him resentful and mean toward his children. They never imagined that his body had hit the canvas hard years ago and it was only from the monumental fear of going hungry that he rallied his strength, raised and buckled his knees, cast himself into the swelling heat, to draw or pull up what was necessary to yield another meal.

"What's the difference between a spic and a drunk?" Theodore, the one with three missing fingers, asked over coffee break as he sat on the step of his bulldozer. The other men sat around him on their haunches or stood and kicked gravel with their mustard construction boots, shrugged their shoulders.

"The difference is a drunk will sober up, but a spic will always be a spic, ain't that right, Zorro?" And the men would laugh too loud, slap Papa on his back too hard, causing him to spill his coffee.

Her papa missed the solitude of the sea and he felt no shame being insignificant against its immensity. There, without the pounding of jackhammers, pieces of sun glittered on the water. There, adrift, he would cast the net, not lose sight of the shore, feel the challenge of resistance in his hands whenever he pulled in the reins of his livelihood. He did not understand what this man Theodore was saying. He would memorize the joke, repeat it to María de la Luz, have her explain it to him. He turned to view the men clustered on the corner of Second and Main in downtown L.A., men like himself, scanning the oncoming traffic in hopes of some signal that would promise a day's work, a chance to prove their worth, carrying tools, working with iron, shovelling cement, any chance, any work. He did not understand, but forced a smile anyway.

Her papa screwed the cup of his thermos in place, put his thermos in his lunch pail. Someone had placed a large stew bone next to the sandwich he insisted be made with Wonder Bread. Truly bewildered, he picked it up and the men burst out in another wave of laughter. Her papa watched the men with their mouths open in big round Os. He closed the lid, forced himself up from his haunches, walked away, tossing the bone aside. The foreman stepped out of his trailer to see what the commotion was all about.

"A real company man," a plasterer said, no longer laughing, watching her papa who began work before the others. Not waiting for the cement truck, Papa scooped three shovels full of gravel into a metal trough, scooped three shovels full of sand, one shovel of cement, the powder bellowing like a cloud. He then ran the water hose to the trough, turned it on, took a handful, and splashed it on his neck, his face, to relieve the sting on his skin. He filled the trough with enough water, then turned it off, got a long poled hoe. He began sloshing the thickening grit. He knew it had to be mixed well for the entrance walk of the Security Pacific Bank they were building.

"Who the hell does he think he is?" asked the truck driver.

"His spic," a welder replied, gesturing to the foreman who stood on the trailer steps and exaggeratedly pointed to his watch, signalling the end of break. The plasterers watched the foreman put his arms akimbo in mock impatience.

"His goddamn spic," the bulldozer driver repeated as the foreman approached them angrily when no one moved. "His spic."

~~~~~

María de la Luz knew thirteen was an unlucky number. It was the number of pills prescribed to her mama and it was the number of cigarettes her mama smoked a day. It was the number of mouths which had to be fed, the number of towels calzones shirts shorts blouses that were washed on Thursday, hung out to dry on Friday, ironed on Saturday, worn on Sunday. And it was the number of nights that María didn't sleep because she waited up for her brothers or the children caught colds and ran fevers and coughed and had nightmares.

On the thirteenth week the truant officer came. His appearance edged the neighborhood dogs into junkyard madness, yapping and growling and throwing themselves against the chain-link fences. The officer stumbled his way into a maze of clean laundry hung on slack wire lines, to the dogs he could not see but heard, felt the stabbing eyes of neighbors behind curtains, peeking between the venetian blinds, asking themselves about this gabacho whose shirt buttons strained to dam back a flooding belly. He loosened his red tie, looked behind him suspiciously, knocked again on the screen door, and the young girl with a runny nose hid behind María de la Luz. The officer addressed her as "Mrs.," and asked why her daughter, "one María de la Luz" (he said the name so that it sounded real crooked to the young girl's ears), had been absent thirteen weeks from school.

"My mother isn't feeling good," she told the officer and he wrote something on his clipboard.

He said, "Is this the kinda life you wanna have, huh? Washing clothes, shoveling dog turd, huh?"

María returned the incredulous stare. Didn't he understand what she said? Her mama wasn't feeling good. The young girl wiped her nose with the sleeve of her sweater, heard his throat-clearing "huh"s.

"Wiping the asses of fifteen kids like some old lady in the shoe, huh? Is that what you want, huh?"

"Fuck off," she told the officer (which also sounded crooked to the young girl's ears) and she slammed the door on his "huh"s, edging in another wave of crazy dog frenzy. Later, the young girl heard María go into the only private room in the house. She peeked in to see María with an open book, paper, and pencil, sitting on the seat of the toilet. María saw her. She marked a page with her finger, closed the book.

"Let me be, so's I can figure this out," she told the young girl. María was sure she had locked the door, but knew too the young girl had a knack for doing things like this. Since her sister didn't move, María tried to ignore her, opened the book, began underlining a sentence with her finger.

"Go, goddammit. Get out!"

The young girl went into the kitchen, passed her mama who sat silently at the table, flipping a stack of playing cards in a game of solitaire, cigarette smoke in a corkscrew above her head. The smoke made the young girl sneeze and she went outside and sat on the porch, watched the hanging sheets flap flap senselessly like sails on a shipwreck.

———

It was her papa's words addressing María. The words came into the bedroom in the form of a white moth, wingspan of her hands and landed on the wall, its wings spreading and rising in slow meditation. The young girl watched. She lay between two sisters; one sister threw her arm over her chest, the other a hefty leg, and she felt smothered like a fly caught in a cobweb of limbs.

María drudged through the fragile thin ice of morning, stumbled over beds and blankets, settled her bones on a roll-away cot next to their bed. Her arm fell to the side, limp, like a dead animal. Outside, the lamppost shone a foggy yellow glow. The white moth fluttered to the window and banged itself against the glass endlessly with dull and scratchy thuds.

The young girl had heard the words from the other side of the door. Mama wasn't well enough to spend Christmas with them.

The girl tried to levitate her body to open the window but was firmly vised between her sisters. She whispered María's name, saw the name mist linger in front of her, then slowly evaporate. She began to see small streamers like molten silver, streak gently downward on the window glass. The moth stood silent, its wings rising and spreading, waiting for her.

Icicles fell like Christmas tinsel from the ceiling. No one would believe that the window bled tears. Her sisters slept soundly and every once in a while one of them would grind her teeth or pass gas. But the girl was the daughter of her mother, and she rose to the occasion until her body banged against the glass, felt the chill against her cheek. She strained to break the window, but felt her arm pulled away, felt weak against the gravitational force, filled her lungs to release.

María opened the window to a blast of cold wind. The moth fluttered out. She slammed the window down.

The young girl cried. If only she had the capacity to walk barefoot on broken and jagged words like María, then she wouldn't have to release the words, and she could smash them into a thousand pieces of glass, just like she wanted to smash the window. But María pulled her close to her, sealed her mouth, hushed her for nothing was worth this much unbroken silence.

~~~~~~

One of the trucks sped by loaded with the last of the scaffolds, leaving dust behind, grinding gravel beneath its tires. The welders worked above him, sparks raining to the sides of them in near completion. Her papa looked up at the building while standing on the top step of the foreman's trailer, admired the erect and shiny structure in all its newness, felt a certain pride, then felt ashamed of that pride. He wiped his boots before entering the trailer. It was unusually hot for a spring day. The foreman swung his chair back, and without standing up handed him an envelope, said in a tight stitched sentence over the buzzing of the air conditioner, "I do weekend jobs, nothing big, a little extra cash on the side, maybe you can work for me then."

Her papa nodded, took the unopened envelope and stuffed it in his back pocket. He wondered if he should leave now or hang around until his shift was over, wondered what to do next. He offered his hand to the foreman who shook it firmly.

Outside the sun blazed, making the smoky air stick to his lungs. Spring was here too soon. If he couldn't find work by summer, they would have to move to where the migrant work was guaranteed: tomatoes in Indiana, asparagus in Illinois, strawberries in Michigan. But until then, he would hammer and shovel the cemented walkway near the laundry lines, make room to plant nopal, verdolagas, chayotes. Of course, things would get better. He was a good worker, one of the best, not afraid to use his back. His lemon tree did not yield this year, but the pomegranates cracked with dark red juice. Things would get better.

He lifted his lunchpail, opened it, saw a bag that someone had placed there, another joke. He poured out the contents of the bag, held a handful of jumping beans on his palm, watched the half moon beans itch and shake in the heat of the sun.

He remembered repeating the joke to María about the drunk, asked that she explain it to him. She said that he worked with a bunch of assholes, and he slapped her for saying a bad word, and she pushed him aside to get out of the house, holding her hand to her cheek. The children cried, judged him with accusatory eyes and he began yelling at them, calling them beggars and leeches and told them to hide or he would kill them all and they scattered, the young girl hiding under the bed where he found her hours later, fast asleep.

It made him wonder about his wife who believed demons possessed her, about his sons who stayed out half the night, the children who scattered in fear, and his beautiful daughter María whom he had slapped with all his might, made him wonder if he was the one being possessed by these jokes he did not find funny.

He decided against throwing the beans out, returned the contents to the bag. He walked home to save the bus fare.

By mid afternoon he entered their small walkway, which led to his backyard. He called the children and the neighbor's children over. They rushed and circled around him, craning their necks to see what Papa held in the brown paper sack. He poured the contents on the porch where a strong beam of sun spotlighted the tranquil beans. The children watched, unimpressed by the beans as still as stones. Suddenly, like popcorn bursting, the beans began to twist, then quake, finally jump, and the children laughed in utter astonishment. "Is it magic?" one of the children asked, and the young girl turned to her papa for an answer.

María de la Luz opened the screen door to look down at the heads watching the beans jumping. "How do the beans jump?" another asked María, for Papa never gave answers. Curious, María picked one up and bit it open against her papa's protest. Inside the cracked opening, a small white caterpillar unfolded its larva body.

"Leave it alone," her papa ordered, but María immediately bit open another and another. It seemed unjust to find enjoyment in the entrapment of other living things. The children grimaced, contorted their faces from nausea as they watched María crack the hard beans between her teeth with delicate force.

"They're trapped, don't you see, and wanna get out."

"Leave it alone," Papa said in a voice the children were afraid of.

"They're gonna die." First the children looked at María cracking the beans, then turned to look at Papa whose voice was turning louder. The young girl panicked, put her fingers to her mouth, began biting her nails. As of today, Papa had no job, no wife, now couldn't even win over his children's forgiveness without being accused of something. He raised his hand at her insubordination, but before he could strike her, before the children began their screaming and crying again, she caught his raised hand in mid motion, and it stunned him, this betrayal of her nature. María had managed to let free all but one caterpillar. She grasped her papa's hand, the one with the blue thumbnail, opened it. Her eyes melted with red anger. She pressed the single bean in the palm of his hand, steadied her trembling voice.

"Go ahead," she said, a tear streaming down her cheek, "if it means that much to you."

Go ahead and what? he thought. What was he supposed to do? He had to make of her an example for the rest of the children. If he let the caterpillar go, she would certainly feel she had won, which would be only the beginning of her rebellion. If he killed the caterpillar, let it bang itself inside the brown bean, something else would die as well. He just couldn't figure out what. The children stared at his every move and he stared at the single bean.

The young girl shoved her way closer to her papa. She looked up at María de la Luz, her nose running, looked at her papa, small and twitching and frightened, looked up at the black doorframe where her mama should be standing right now and putting a stop to all of this madness as she had done in the past. Without thinking, the young girl swept the bean from the palm of his hand. For once, everyone's attention shifted to the young girl. She put the bean in her mouth and swallowed it.

～～～

The day her mother returned from the hospital was the day the young girl tasted the sweetest, reddest, juiciest watermelon she had ever had. Her mama looked pale, her cheeks fallen and waxed, her nose red as if she had suffered a cold. She looked nervously about at her brood of children, but smiled just the same. The children, the smaller ones like the young girl, stiffened up, shoulders back, mouths quiet except for a whispering question here or there. For them it was such an unnatural position that even María de la Luz and Papa felt their bones contort. Mama decided it was best that she sleep first, then get up and make some *arroz con pollo*, fresh tortillas. The children clapped and laughed and were relieved for they were tired of María's Hamburger Heaven, Beto even calling it Hamburger Hell. They felt the rigid air ease when Mama left the room, felt the lazy heat make their eyes sleepy.

They had packed the clothes in boxes and piled them up like a pyramid in the walkway, ready to load them up in the borrowed pickup. But that was tomorrow. Today, María plugged in an extension cord and dragged her prized radio outside and tuned it to her favorite oldies station. Papa changed from his salt-and-pepper suit to a paper-thin speckled shirt which he didn't button, and which flapped open from a slight desert Santa Ana breeze. Spreading some newspapers on the porch, he placed the green watermelon, green as the brine of the Belvedere Park lake, on top; and then he plunged the knife in, the watermelon cracking like thunderbolts into two halves, the juice bleeding droplets on the newspaper. He carefully removed the seedless center of the melon and put it on a plate for Mama who always got the heart. After that, Papa sliced and gave, sliced and gave, and the young girl chose to sit next to María, who sat crossed-legged on the little patch of grass, her dress over her knees; her sister, María de la Luz, spat out the seeds, using her ducking brother as a target.

The young girl bit into the red flesh of the watermelon slice, juice dripping from the sides of her mouth, and she wiped her mouth with María's dress, and María scolded her in such a funny way she could do nothing but giggle and giggle the rest of an almost perfect afternoon.

La Promesa

Guy Garcia

Tom Cardona had been in Mexico for exactly forty minutes when the old woman approached his rental car and pressed her face against the window. Flattened by the glass, her cheeks were like weathered mahogany, cracked and pitted by the elements, and framed by a curtain of stringy hair. She opened her mouth to speak, but her voice was drowned out by the roar of a landing jet. Assuming she wanted money, Tom leaned across the seat, rolled down the window and placed a five thousand peso bill in her hand. The claw-like fingers retracted, then returned, groping for the door handle. It took Tom a second to realize that she was trying to get into the car. Panicking, he grabbed her withered paw and pushed it away as his foot hit the gas pedal. The car bolted forward, but when Tom looked in the rearview mirror the toll plaza was empty.

He joined the torrent of traffic and consulted his map, Guanajuato was roughly 200 miles from Mexico City, a trip that he calculated would take at least three to four hours. Even if he started now and skipped lunch, he would be lucky to get there before dark. Which meant there was no way he could avoid spending the night, which meant that his return reservation was useless.

"Terrific," Tom muttered to himself, suddenly annoyed at the traffic, the smog, the absurdly heavy Mexican coins that tugged on his trouser pockets. The whole God-forsaken country. The tangled freeways and flat skyline—so eerily similar yet different from Los Angeles—only heightened his sense of dislocation. He was a stranger in a strange land, except that the natives looked just like him. He felt uneasy in his own skin. This is what he had feared, this was why he had procrastinated for years, telling himself that he couldn't afford the airfare, couldn't spare the time. No one could blame him for putting his job and family first, for taking care of the home front instead of Estella's pointless goose chase.

Two hours out of Mexico City the terrain became Alpine, a vertical landscape of sheer gigantic peaks and evergreen pines. Sunlight blinked through the treetops, casting helioscopic patterns on the rock cliffs. Eventually the mountains gave way to rolling hills and the road opened up, giving Tom a view of the broad sloping valley that led to the flatlands around Queretaro. Off to the west he could see a thunderhead moving swiftly across the plain, a dark funnel of rain dragging behind it like a widow's veil. A stubble of young corn grew over freshly-tilled fields and if it weren't for the pitiful shacks lining the road Tom could have been back in the Golden State.

He missed it already. His wife and kids and friends were all back there, waiting for him while he wandered unmarked roads in a foreign country in a rented car. And all for what? The futility of it had struck him from the moment his grandmother had pulled the box of pictures down from the closet and showed him the faded photograph of a light-skinned Mexican girl with wide oval eyes and arching eyebrows. "That was my nanny, Blanca Morrell, who raised me when I was a little girl. We told each other everything, even the deepest secrets."

Estella had paused, searching Tom's face for a reaction, but he only shrugged, trying to stifle his impatience. He was just home from college and anxious to unpack and call his girlfriend.

"That's great, grandma. But I've really got to go."

But Estella had held him there, clasping his hands in her own. "I told her that no matter what happened I would never forget her," she said, her voice thick with emotion. "But for years my letters have been returned unopened. I will not rest in peace until I know what has happened. I would go myself, but I'm too old. You are young and strong. You can go to Mexico and make sure she doesn't need anything. Not now; don't worry. Later. I'll give you the money. There's no hurry. Promise me, mi'jito. Promise you'll put your grandmother's soul to rest."

It came up a few more times in the ensuing years, always when Tom and Estella were alone, always with the same conclusion. By the time Tom was married and his visits to Estella's house limited to holidays and funerals, her references to Blanca became less frequent. And after the birth of his first child, to his great relief, she had dropped the subject altogether.

The day Estella died—they found her in her garden, her arms spread as if in mid-flight to heaven—he had assumed the whole matter was moot. There was no one left to care, least of all himself, who regarded the fate of his grandmother's nanny about as relevant as the courting habits of the Aztecs. After all, he was an American, the son of an American, born and raised in the elevated suburb of Fullerton Hills. His house had a swimming pool and two cars in the garage—three if you counted the tri-wheel off-roader he'd bought for laughs the summer before. He listened to classic rock and roll, cheered for the Lakers and had voted Republican in the last two elections. He'd gone to night school for his engineering degree and had worked hard to become regional sales manager for the world's largest tire manufacturer. You wouldn't see him with his hand out for welfare. He cringed whenever a robbery suspect on the local news was identified as a "Hispanic male."

It was just that he considered his ethnic origins a footnote, a given part of the social equation. As a second-generation Chicano he had moved from point A to point B, just as his children would go on to point C. And on and on until it didn't matter where you came from or who your grandparents were. That was progress, the American way. Point A, the past, the world of Estella's youth, was dead and buried under the parched hills of central Mexico, deep in the silver-plated heart of the country. Or so he had thought. Then the lawyer called about the money and Estella's posthumous request.

His grandmother's instructions were unsentimental and succinct: "I hereby leave $30,000 to my grandson, Tomas Cardona, on the condition that he travel to my birthplace of Guanajuato, Mexico, and ascertain the fate of my childhood nanny, Blanca Morrell."

Tom told himself that he wasn't doing it for the money, that he was doing it for Estella. But who was he trying to kid? Thirty grand was thirty grand. Within minutes he was resigned to the journey, mentally booking a plane, packing light. He had to hand it to the old girl. Unable to persuade him while she was alive, Estella, in death, had finally bent him to her will.

Making good time, he pulled abreast of a young Mexican family in a silver Mercedes sedan. A little girl, her neatly-braided hair gathered in ribbons, waved to him from the side window as he passed. Tom waved back. It was hard for him to believe that the girl and the wizened crone at the toll booth were from the same century, let alone the same country. The thought of rich Mexicans stirred something in him, a twinge of pride that said brown-skinned people could drive German cars. Tom mentally applauded. *Drive fast, don't look back.*

The sun was slouching over the horizon when Tom reached the turn-off to Guanajuato. The land had become hilly again and he traveled past small towns perched on steep inclines, their stucco church belltowers anointed by the day's dying rays. The road dipped into a narrow canyon bounded by oak and flowering cactus and the car was soon shuddering over the cobblestone streets in the center of town. Even in the murky twilight Tom could tell that Guanajuato was an unusually beautiful city. It was just as Estella had described it: ornate colonial buildings painted in orange and lime pastels, narrow, winding streets and tree-lined plazas with gurgling fountains. And there, off to the right, was the famous Alho'ndiga de Granaditas, the grain warehouse where the Spaniards made their last stand during the War of Independence.

Tom followed Estella's written directions, driving back to the main square and into the descending ramp that became Calle Miguel Hidalgo. He had read about Guanajuato's mummy museum and underground streets, but was still amazed to find himself driving through a subterranean causeway, its jagged rock walls illuminated by an occasional lightbulb. The road snaked under the city, twisting and looping like a giant's entrails. Then the mouth of the tunnel suddenly yawned and Tom was back on the surface. He followed the street into a well-to-do neighborhood of proud mansions and serene villas draped with clusters of bloody bougainvilla. He found the house, a faded pink manor decorated with stone statues and urns, on a quiet avenue that limned a placid lake. The lights inside were on, and through the slightly parted curtains Tom spied the seated profile of a young woman, her hands fluttering like doves as she spoke to an invisible listener.

Tom lifted the heavy brass knocker and dropped it against the door. A resounding thud echoed through the house and a few seconds later he heard the scrape of a chair being pushed back on the wooden floor. Footsteps approached and the door swung open. The girl was in her early twenties, her hair and clothes fashionably up to date.

"May I help you, please?" she asked in Spanish.

"*Hablas Ingles?*"

"Yes. Can I help you?"

"I hope so," he said. "My name is Tom Cardona. I'm here because my grandmother used to live in this house. Her name was Estella Cardona, and I'm trying to find out what happened to her nanny."

The girl let out a high giggle of disbelief.

"Are you serious?" she inquired in English.

"Yes, I am. I know it sounds crazy, but it was my grandmother's last wish. She died two weeks ago. I flew here today from Los Angeles."

The girl opened the door a notch wider.

"I'm not from around here either," she confessed. "I'm studying at the University. But Mrs. Velasquez—she's the lady who lives here— might know something. The house has been in her family for ages. Please, come in."

She ushered him into the paneled foyer and asked him to wait. He could smell the inviting aromas of dinner, and Tom's stomach noisily reminded him that he hadn't eaten since breakfast.

The mansion, which he guessed was at least two hundred years old, had not aged gracefully. There were watermarks on the plaster ceiling and the floorboards creaked from a million human footsteps. But the furniture had been freshly dusted and the cut-crystal chandelier sparkled. A servant slipped into one of the rooms carrying a silver coffee service. The place reeked of old money—the miserly, slightly tarnished lucre of wealth no longer interested in appearances or the effort required to keep them up.

Tom could hear the girl speaking to someone in the dining room. When she returned she was smiling. "You should feel lucky," she said as she escorted him in. "Mrs. Velasquez doesn't usually receive visitors without an appointment. But when I told her you were visiting from America, she agreed to make an exception."

Mrs. Velasquez was a paraplegic woman of some 65 years, with long braided hair and an imperious manner. A pair of half-moon reading glasses dangled from a silver chain around her fleshy neck. The girl introduced him and Mrs. Velasquez nodded impatiently.

"I think I can assume that you've already met Celia," she said in slightly nasal English. "She comes twice a week to read to me and keep me company in my old age."

"You are not old, Señora," Celia protested.

"Oh, hush, you young thing. What do you know about age? Your life is still ahead of you. The world is your oyster, and I am just a shriveled up old clam."

Her tirade over, Mrs. Velasquez turned her attention back to her guest. "Mr. Cardona," she said pleasantly, "would you like some coffee?"

"*Muchas gracias.*"

"*Hablas Español?*"

"Only a little."

"*Qué lástima.* It's a pity when we lose the tongue of our ancestors."

A servant appeared with a cup and saucer. The service was of delicate china decorated with a coat of arms that Tom assumed was the family crest.

"Are you by any chance familiar with the name Morrell?"

Mrs. Velasquez regarded him over the top of her glasses.

"My dear, the Morrell family built this house. My father bought it from them in the 1940s, long before you were even born. Sugar?"

"Are you sure?" Tom said.

Ms. Velasquez made a sour face. "Of course, I'm sure. I may be a crippled old woman but I'm not senile yet."

Tom groped for the words. "I'm sorry... It's just that... You see I'm here at my grandmother's request. Her name was Estella Cardona and her nanny was named Blanca Morrell."

Mrs. Velasquez's face became a mask of scorn.

"I don't know what you think you're doing young, man, but your joke is not the least bit amusing."

"So you knew Blanca Morrell?"

Mrs. Velasquez rattled her cup in her saucer and leaned forward. "I didn't have to meet her to know that she was a disgrace to her family. They tried to save her by sending her to live in the United States but she had to come back and humiliate her relatives. It's because of her that the Morrells sold this house and left, so maybe I should be grateful."

The cup suspended in Tom's hand became impossibly light, as if it would float away if he didn't hold on tight.

"Do you know where the Morrells went after they left Guanajuato?"

Mrs. Velasquez placed her hand on her sequined breast.

"My dear boy," she intoned. "I had expected you to tell *me*. If they had any sense at all, they went back to France. That's where I would have gone." Her voice acquired the tinny echo of a vintage gramaphone. "They say that the French are cold, but I disagree. I'd take Paris any day over Rome, or even my beloved Madrid. How I miss the charms of the Champs Elysées, the Louvre, the Eiffel Tower. Ah, now there is a city made for summer dreams." Her gaze focused again. "I must say that I fail to understand why on earth anyone would want to know anything about Blanca Morrell."

"It's just that I'd assumed she'd be poor."

"Ha!" Mrs. Velasquez grimaced through layers of rouge and lip-stick. "She was a rich woman with common characteristics."

"What do you mean?"

"She lived a whore's life and died a whore's death before she reached thirty."

Tom leaned back in his chair.

"But it doesn't make any sense."

"What sense can there be in self-destruction, the final sin of a damned spirit?"

"She committed suicide?"

"Yes." Mrs. Velasquez reached for her cup with a trembling hand.

"Can you tell me how?"

She shuddered, as if shaking off a bad memory. "I'm sorry, I can't help you. I'm too old to consort with the devil's darlings. If you are smart, you'll go back to America, Señor. Those who wake the dead pay the demon's due. Goodnight!"

Before Tom could respond, she closed her eyes and started to moan. "Celia!" she called. "I'm getting another attack!"

Mrs. Velasquez's hands were still over her face as Celia wheeled her through the door and disappeared down the receding hall of mirrors.

~~~~~~

Tom was famished. Even his disturbing audience with Mrs. Velasquez had failed to blunt his appetite. He retraced his path into the center of town and checked into a small hotel on the edge of the central square. The evening was cool, but not unpleasantly so, and the sidewalks were alive with children's voices and lovers strolling hand in hand down the bustling avenues. Tom took a lungful of the fragrant mountain air, so unlike the smog that smothered Mexico City, and felt the muscles in his neck unwind. A person could live well here, a long and happy life, unless something intervened and cut it short. Something that caused old women to cover their eyes and grow faint.

Determined to get himself a proper dinner, he followed the aroma of grilled meat and cilantro to a crowded café decorated with pottery and Indian blankets. Taking a seat near the kitchen, he ordered enchiladas suizas and pork carnitas and two Dos Equis to wash it all down. The food was rich and intoxicating—nothing like the fast-food burritos he was accustomed to—with a pleasant chile afterburn that left his whole mouth tingling. His hunger finally sated, the implications of what he had just been told began to sink in. According to Mrs. Velasquez, his grandmother's nanny was a rich woman, a suicide, and a whore. Impossible. But why would the old woman lie?

Tom paid the check and ventured out into the square. Most of the restaurants and stores had closed, but the bars were still full and he could hear the distant strain of mariachi music coming from a saloon at the end of the block. Unaccountably, he had a momentary sensation that he'd been here before. When Tom was a baby, his parents had traveled with him in Mexico, but that was such a long time ago. Had they come to Guanajuato? He couldn't possibly remember. And yet . . . .

He was about to turn back toward the garage when he noticed a storefront with the lights still burning. A sign over the door identified it as a venue for the construction and sale of funeral caskets. Succumbing to curiosity, Tom approached the threshold and poked his head inside.

"Come in, come in," urged a mellifluous voice. "Don't be timid. Take a look around. If you don't see your size we can have one custom-made to fit your dimensions."

Tom did as the voice asked. The room was long and narrow and filled from floor to ceiling with rows of polished coffins. There were ornate coffins with gleaming lacquer patinas and brass handles, simple coffins made of unfinished pine, coffins in basic black and others in powder blue, purple and cream. There were long skinny coffins, extra-wide coffins and coffins that looked small enough to bury a doll.

An overstuffed man in an overstuffed chair beckoned from the end of the room. He had jovial eyes and a wide, licentious mouth. His body was series of convex forms culminating in a spherical belly that tortured the buttons of his starched guayabera. When he spoke his ample stomach jiggled in agreement. His plump fingers held a similarly-shaped cigar.

The fat man smiled and shifted his bulk in the chair. "It's obvious you are not from Guanajuato. Texas?"

"California," Tom said.

"Ah, California," the fat man pronounced the word like something delicious. "The Golden Gate. Hollywood. Mickey Mouse. *El ratón Miguelito*, we call him. I lived in Texas for a while, many years ago. But it is not the same, I think."

"No. It's not the same."

"You are too young to be shopping for yourself. A relative perhaps? I have many customers there. Shipping is no problem. If you do not see what you like, I can build it for you. Very fine workmanship. You cannot find quality like this in the U.S.A., not even for double the price."

The man fat pointed to a casket with an open lid. "Take a look," he urged. "We use only the best woods, the finest silks, the most luxurious quilting. All the stitching is done by hand."

"It's very nice," Tom said.

Having made his pitch, the fat man settled back in his chair, struck a match, and started to relight his cigar stub. "So, if it is not Molina's quality coffins that bring you to Guanajuato, then what does? You have come to see the mummies, perhaps? They are hideous but very interesting—

preserved by the special minerals in the soil. I can arrange for a personal tour if you wish."

Tom shook his head. "I'm looking for somebody, a person who was born here."

Molina nodded through a cloud of blue smoke.

"Then you've come to the right place, my friend. I know everyone in Guanajuato—alive or dead."

"I'm glad to hear that, because this person is deceased. At least, I think so."

Molina exuded empathy.

"Do you have a name?"

"Yes, her name is . . ."

"No," Molina interrupted, "I mean your name."

"Tom Cardona."

"Tom. Like the actor Tom Cruise?"

"Yeah, like Tom Cruise."

Molina's belly jiggled with amusement. "I know a Cardona family— a very respectable family—that lives near the University. Professor Cardona was buried in one of my coffins. It was silver, with brass handles and a dark blue lining. . . ."

"The person I'm looking for had the surname Morrell. She was my grandmother's nanny. I think she was known as La Blanca."

Molina's belly inflated. "Ah, naturally. *La Blanca.*"

"So you knew her?"

"Everybody knows La Blanca."

"What do you mean?"

"Please," Molina waved Tom to a chair. "Sit down. Would you like some tea? A cigar perhaps?"

"No thanks."

Molina produced a fresh Havana, snipped off the tip, and torched it with a Bic lighter, sending smoke rings floating toward the ceiling. As he inhaled, his throat made the raspy whistle of air being forced through a narrow aperture.

"Everyone knows the legend of La Blanca. A Mexican ghost story. They say it's true." Molina hunched his bulky shoulders. "After all, the

Morrell family certainly existed and the house still stands out by La Olla, the pot—that's what we call the municipal reservoir."

"Out by the Velasquez place."

Molina's mouth stretched into a leer.

"You know Doña Sara?"

"We've met."

"There are stories about her, too," he said with a wink. "But that is not what you came to hear."

"No."

Molina sucked on his cigar.

"According to the story," he began, "Blanca was the only daughter of Alain Morrell, a retired French soldier who owned several bakeries, and Rosa Vega, a Creole girl whose parents owned a silver mine north of town. Blanca was vivacious, reckless and blessed with almost unbearable beauty. She was the flower whose perfume made the bees dizzy. The suitors came and went. Blanca would meet them, let them do their best to woo her, then reject them. She broke many hearts and made enemies that would one day contribute to her ruination.

"In any case, news of this unapproachable beauty spread through the mountains and reached the ears of Eugenio Sanchez, the dashing heir of a wealthy cattle family from San Miguel de Allende. Eugenio's father, Don Arturo, had served as ambassador to France and the family traced its lineage to the Bourbon court of Spain. The Morrells were prominent, but the Sanchez clan was both rich and aristocratic. For Blanca's parents, it was an ideal match. With her looks and his money, the offspring of their union would be like royalty. An introduction was arranged, and Eugenio was instantly smitten. An expert horseman, he invited her to go riding with him and they were seen galloping together on the vast lands of the Sanchez estate. Two months later, Eugenio asked Blanca's father for her hand in marriage. Blanca's father accepted, and the town braced itself for the wedding of the century.

"The ceremony was to take place at the Cathedral with the Bishop presiding, the reception in the lobby of the grand Teatro Juárez. The guest list numbered more than one thousand, including many of Mexico's most distinguished families. To feed the hordes, Don Morrell had ordered five

hundred chickens, fifty sides of beef and twenty barrels of beer, not counting brandy and champagne. An orchestra of thirty-six mariachis from
Guadalajara had been hired to entertain, along with an assortment of
dancers, mimes and strolling magicians. The wedding cake alone weighed
twenty kilos, and Blanca's dress, a rippling river of white brocade, lace
and silk, was on its way by steamship from one of the most exclusive
salons of Paris.

"In the final weeks before the wedding, Blanca stopped going to
the Sanchez hacienda and locked herself in her rooms, refusing to come
out. For three whole days a terrible sobbing shook the house. Finally,
when her parents threatened to break the door down, she emerged and
told them that she could not marry Eugenio because she loved someone
else. 'If you force me to go through with it,' she told them, 'I'll kill myself.
I would rather be dead than married to that man.'

"Two weeks before Eugenio and Blanca were due to march to the
altar, the wedding was called off. The fiasco cost the Morrells hundreds
of thousands of pesos and brought great shame to the family. Don Morrell became a laughingstock and his business suffered. Partly as an act of
retribution and partly to shield her from the outpouring of scorn, Blanca
was sent with her nanny to live in America. It is said that she had a child
out of wedlock. A pocho bastard. A few months later, the Morrells liqui-
dated their holdings, sold the house and left Guanajuato forever."

"The nanny," Tom interrupted, "Do you remember her name?"

Molina's brow furrowed in concentration. "I believe it was Estella,"
he said.

The slurred Spanish of two passing drunks intruded through the
open door.

"Is something the matter?" Molina asked.

"No. I was just wondering, would you happen to remember the
nanny's surname?"

Molina's brow creased in concentration.

Tom said, "Could it have been Cardona?"

Molina's head bobbed in confirmation.

"Yes, I believe that's it! What a strange coincidence! Are you sure
you're alright, my friend?"

"I'm fine. Please go on."

"Perhaps it is the altitude."

"Yes, the altitude. Tell me the rest of the story."

"Well, several months passed. Then the most extraordinary thing happened. At first, no one could believe it was her, that she had the audacity to come back to the scene of her dishonor. It was like seeing a ghost. Not only that, but she had taken a cheap room at the edge of town, not far from where we sit, a blue house with two balconies on Calle Ramona. It was unheard of for a lady of her breeding to be living alone in such a place. As you might imagine, the gossips were in paradise. Some said that she had gone nuts and had been sent away to the United States to be put in an asylum, from which she had escaped. Others held that she had murdered her nanny and child. The more pious observers contended that the gringos had made her into a prostitute and that she had returned to ply her wares. In any case, polite society treated her like a leper, which seemed to suit Blanca just fine. The truth is, with her emerald eyes and long brown hair, she never looked more beautiful.

"Soon afterward Blanca was spotted riding with a handsome dark man. The following Sunday the couple was seen again, this time drifting in a rowboat on La Olla. Spies soon identified the man as Juan Fuerza, a mestizo laborer who worked in the silver mines. Then someone remembered that Fuerza's previous job was as a stable boy at the Sanchez hacienda. Yes, he had worked there when Blanca used to go riding and even served as her guide on more than one occasion. Well, you didn't have to be a genius to figure out that Fuerza was the mystery love who had foiled Blanca's marriage to Eugenio Sanchez. Had Blanca and Fuerza tasted forbidden fruit in the trees of the Sanchez property, as some claimed? Or had they merely planted the seeds of a romance that would blossom much later. Who can say? Blanca took the answer to her grave. What is certain is that within a few weeks of Blanca's return, the outcast couple was living together in sin at the flat on Calle Ramona."

Molina paused and used a match to revive his cigar.

"Are you sure you are enjoying this story, señor? Would you like a glass of water?"

"Thank you, no. Please go on."

"Anyway, as you might have guessed, we are near the end. As soon as Eugenio Sanchez learned the identity of Blanca's new lover, he began to plot his revenge. Fuerza was a soulful boy with a firm jaw, straight black hair and eyes like coal. His body was lean and hard from working in the mines all day, but he also had an artistic temperament and liked to play his guitar and sing romantic ballads. On Saturday nights he would leave Blanca's house and join his friends for a song and a drink at the bar right here on the corner, which at the time was called El Espejo Oscuro. It was a warm, moonless night, and when Fuerza left the bar with two buddies he was in high spirits. At the intersection, Fuerza bade his friends goodnight and started alone down the sidestreet, the one over there with the light, on his way home to Blanca's house. The neighbors could hear him singing, as young drunks, and even old drunks, will do. Then the singing turned to shouts of terror. A band of assassins had been waiting for Fuerza, and when he turned the corner they attacked him with their machetes. It was over in a minute. Blanca ran out of her house and found her lover's butchered body in the street, his blood draining into the gutter.

"It was at that point, I believe, that she did actually go insane. When Blanca saw that Fuerza was dead, she let out a horrible scream, a guttural wail that gathered force until every dog in town was barking and people were quaking in their beds. Mad with grief, Blanca went to the police station, but the police had been bribed by the Sanchez family and they told her to go home and forget about it. There would be no protest, no outcry, no official investigation of any kind. It was as if the killing had never happened, and who could prove otherwise? The body, or what was left of it, was disposed of in secret, probably at the bottom of a mine. Even Fuerza's birth certificate vanished."

"What about Blanca?"

"A terrible end for such a beautiful girl," Molina lamented. "My father, who was a boy at the time, never stopped having nightmares about it. All through the night, Blanca walked through the town like a zombie, her hands and dress soaked with Fuerza's blood, screaming for a doctor, for the police, for anyone who would help her. But people only locked their doors and drew their curtains. By now she had become an almost supernatural figure. To touch her would be to touch the devil, to look into her eyes would be to glimpse into a living hell. It is not an opportunity that the God-fearing strive for, I assure you. In any case, she wandered through the city for hours, scaring the daylights out of people as she pounded on their doors and beseeched them to let her in, like a succubus, then moving on to the next street, the next house. She came at last to her childhood home, which was now owned by the Velasquez family. Doña Sara, who had hated Blanca ever since she stole Eugenio Sanchez away from her, opened one of the windows on the second floor and threw cold water on her, causing Fuerza's blood to stain the cement in front of their door. The next morning, they found Blanca's body floating in La Olla. The authorities reported it as an open and shut case of accidental drowning. For months, no one would go boating there, and for a time people tried to avoid drinking water, fearing that Blanca's deranged spirit would somehow enter their body. There were those who also believed that the blood on the Velasquez steps was a curse of some sort."

"A curse?"

"Well, my professional efforts notwithstanding, we Mexicans are not very good at burying our dead. They live with us, behind doors, under creaking beds, in the cobwebs that cling to the walls, watching, judging. . . . Ah, but of course you don't believe me. It is fashionable in this day of computers and moon landings to pretend that what I just told you is merely a myth, that none of it ever happened. And, who knows, maybe it never did. But this much is certain: the stain on the Velasquez steps is still there, and parents still invoke the ghost of La Blanca to keep their children from playing near La Olla at night."

"Where was she buried?"

Molina seemed annoyed by the question. "In the municipal cemetery," he said. "No one claimed the body and she was interred in a pine box that my grandfather donated. There is no marker on her grave. There is nothing to see. Trust me, going there would be a waste of time."

~~~~~~

The municipal cemetery was on the outskirts of town, at the end of a dusty road that coiled up into a dry gully. Several of the tombs were built above ground in the shape of small buildings with tiny windows and doors. Others were marked with a simple wooden or iron crucifix. All the graves, from the richest to the poorest, were adorned with bouquets of plastic flowers—yellow, blue, red and pink. Wildflowers had grown up around the ersatz blooms so that the two appeared to be growing from the same roots. In the hammering sunlight the colors were almost unbearably bright, and they stabbed at Tom's eyes as he wandered through the rows of strangely festive graves, his ears ringing with the drone of flying insects. Most of the plots were unidentified and Tom quickly realized that he would never find what he was looking for without some help. A few yards away a shirtless young man was raking dead leaves and rocks into a neat pile. Tom approached him and smiled.

"*Buenos días.*"

"*Buenos días,*" the man uttered without looking up. Tom strained his memory for the Spanish word for grave.

"*Por favor, dónde está la tumba de la Señora Blanca Morrell?*"

"*El entierro?*"

"*Sí,*" Tom said, "*el entierro de Blanca Morrell.*"

The man looked at Tom as if he were mad. "*Aquí no está,*" he said. Then the man put down his rake and fled.

"What did you ask him?" The question was posed by an elderly bearded man in a plain black suit. His starched collar was tattered but clean and he held a bunch of fresh carnations in his hands.

"I asked him to show me the grave of Blanca Morrell."

"Oh my," the man remarked. "No wonder he ran away. The Indians are very superstitious, especially when strangers ask to see the graves of ghosts."

"She's not a ghost," Tom replied acidly. "She was a woman who lived here and died here and was buried somewhere in this cemetery."

"Yes, I've heard that story too. It could very well be true. But I've been coming here every Sunday to leave flowers for my wife, and I've never seen a tombstone for Blanca Morrell."

"I don't think there ever was a marker."

"So the family never claimed the body?"

"I don't think so."

"When did she die?"

"I'm not sure. A long time ago."

The man removed his hat and wiped the sweat from his brow. "You know, it's just possible . . ." The man left the sentence unfinished.

"What's possible?"

"Well, you've heard about the museum of the mummies, haven't you?"

"It was mentioned in my guidebook," Tom replied. "Something about bodies that were preserved by the minerals in the soil."

"That's what I'm saying. You see, the city's policy has always been that unclaimed bodies would be buried for five years. After that, if the family failed to claim them, they could be exhumed and cremated. But some of the bodies never decomposed. They are on display in the museum. I'll tell you, it's really something to see."

The midday sun pressed down with a vengeance, sapping the blood from Tom's arms and legs. "You're telling me that my grandmother's body might be on display as a tourist attraction?"

The man blanched. "Your grandmother? Good God. Forgive me, I had no idea."

"Neither did I."

It took him a few minutes to muster the courage, but once he decided to go, it wasn't hard to find. Halfway back into town a small sign announced *Momias* with a hand-painted arrow pointing to the right. Tom had to back up to make the hair-pin turn, then he was climbing a one-lane road carved into the side of a hill. As he neared the entrance, a gaggle of children ran alongside the car shouting, *"Las momias! Las momias!"* the museum was situated in a dirt plaza ringed by souvenir shops selling mummy T-shirts and plastic goblins. As Tom climbed out of the car, another gang of youngsters surrounded him. *"Momias de dulce,"* they yelled, hawking ghoulish candy skeletons mounted on a stick and packaged in clear plastic wrappers that looked like body bags. Tom waved the children away and tipped the parking lot guard to watch the car.

After standing in line to pay for his admission ticket for the English tour, Tom was ushered into a windowless waiting room with about thirty other visitors. An American boy wearing a Yankees baseball cap asked his mother if there was really a restaurant where you could look at the mummies while you ate. "I hope not," his mother said with revulsion. Tom wasn't feeling so well himself. His head throbbed and the huevos rancheros he'd had for breakfast were churning in his gut, undigested. He told himself it was the stuffy room or nerves or the altitude— anything but the real reason. The night before, he had hardly slept. He had driven back to the hotel in a daze, refusing to believe that his father was the bastard offspring of La Blanca Morrell, the raving witch of Guanajuato. On the road, he'd narrowly missed hitting a goat. It sprang into the headlights out of nowhere, its eyes lit with panic.

A stern-looking woman entered the waiting room and introduced herself as their guide. She addressed the group in Spanish first, then English, both spoken with supercilious precision. "For some reason," she explained, "perhaps because of the high mineral content of the soil or the dryness of the air, the bodies left in the crypt of the Pantheon, or municipal cemetery, did not decompose. Instead, they mummified."

"Excellent," the boy with the cap exclaimed.

"Until recently, any corpses that remained unclaimed in the municipal cemetery were taken to an underground crypt, where they became preserved in a most unusual state. The museum exhibit includes nearly one hundred bodies, some of which date back to the turn of the century. No flash is allowed. Now please stay together and follow me."

Tom followed last, lingering at the edge of the group.

The museum seemed to be made up of a series of interconnecting rooms, each one of which contained a dozen or so cadavers displayed in glass cases. Tom steeled himself and crossed the threshold into the first chamber. Most of the corpses were naked, their withered and dusty private parts plainly visible. Others sported the moth-eaten remains of their burial suits and dresses. One woman still had her stockings on, her emaciated legs disappearing into a pair of once-fashionable boots. Only a thin sheet of glass separated Tom from the countenance of death. The eyeless sockets stared into space, the lipless mouths yawned open. The poor lighting and horizontal arrangement of the display cases only added to Tom's claustrophobia.

The group seemed to be moving in slow motion. As he waited for the crowd to file through the narrow doorway, a young woman asked him to take a picture of her and a friend in front of one of the bodies. The pair mugged as if the carcass were some sort of decomposing celebrity. Tom clicked the shutter and felt another wave of nausea.

As the tour group meandered through the adjoining chambers, Tom tried to imagine what Blanca might look like after time and death had sucked the sweetness from her features. Could she be that one over there with the sunken cheekbones and startled expression, as if mortality had come as an unpleasant surprise? Or maybe that one in the corner, with the faded ribbon still knotted to the wiry strands bristling from her cranium? It was hopeless. Blanca could never be any of the ghastly fossils around him; she had gone to a place where no one could see her.

The guide beckoned the group into the next room. "This is a particularly interesting mummy," she noted, "for as you can see she was buried alive. By mistake, of course."

There were gasps from the group and Tom felt something nudging toward his esophagus.

"We believe that the woman probably suffered a stroke or heart attack and went into a coma," the guide explained in a slightly jaded monotone. "She was mistaken for dead and buried. But, of course, she was still alive. If you look closely at the hands you can see that the nails were damaged when she tried to scratch open the lid."

Tom felt his blood congeal. The curdled face, its black lizard lips stretched into a silent scream, was the very same that had pressed against his car window at the airport parking lot. The beseeching black sockets, more accusing than eyes, bore into him, drew him closer. Her expression tore at his intestines, gnawed at his bones, until something lurched in Tom's belly.

Across the room, the guide was eyeing him suspiciously.

"*Por favor, señor.* Please don't touch the glass."

"Where is the exit?" Tom gasped.

"We are almost to the end of the tour, sir. If you could just wait one moment."

Instead of answering, he pushed his way through the crowd and staggered out the exit into the garden, where he doubled over and heaved his breakfast into a bed of blooming marigolds. His vomit was volcanic, an eruption of rich food and denial that had taken decades to reach the surface. Blinded by the Aztec sun, Tom bowed like a believer as the violent spasms emptied him, cleansing him of pride and worldly pretense. He gagged and heaved until there was nothing left, nothing but an aching void and the fragrant embrace of the sweet, forgiving earth.

The Baseball Glove

Víctor Martínez

One summer my brother Bernardo, or Nardo, as we used to call him, flipped through more jobs than a thumb through a deck of cards. He was a busboy, a dishwasher, then a parking attendant, and, finally, a patty-turner for some guy who never seemed to be in his hamburger stand more than ten minutes at a time (my mom believed he sold marijuana, or did some other illegal shamelessness). Nardo lost the first job for not showing up regular enough, the next for showing up too regular (the boss hated his guts). The last job lost him when the owner of the stand packed up unexpectedly and left for Canada with a whole month of his wages.

The job he misses most, though, was when he worked as a busboy for the Bonneville Lakes Golf and Catering Service. He says it was the only time he ever got to touch elbows with the rich people. The parties they catered served free daiquiris, hard drinks, and iced beer (really iced, in big barrels choking with ice). In some, like the one he got fired from, they passed out tickets for juicy prizes like motorcycles, TV sets, stereos, and snow skis. This particular party featured a six-piece band that once opened for Jimmy Durante and a great, huge dance floor so the "old fogies" (as my brother called them) could get drunk and make fools out of themselves. The way he tells it, you would think he did that man a favor working for him.

It turns out he and a guy named Randy took off their busboy jackets and began daring each other to get a ticket and ask a girl to dance. Hell, Nardo said, the guy bet he wouldn't, and he bet he would, and after a two-dollar pledge Nardo steered for the ticket lady.

"I could've hashed it around a bit you know, Manny," he told me. "I could've double- and triple-dared the guy a couple of times over, then come up with a good excuse. But that ain't my style." Instead he tapped the guy's fingers real smooth and walked up to the ticket lady. She looked out from behind the large butcher paper-covered table at the blotches of pasta sauce on his black uniform pants and white shirt—which were supposed to look clean along with the catering service's light orange busboy jacket, but didn't—and said, "Ah, what the hell," and tore him a tag.

Then, before the little voice nagging inside him could talk some sense, he asked the nearest girl for a dance. She was close to his age and had about a million freckles and enough wire in her mouth to run a toy train over. They stumbled around the dance floor until the band mercifully grinded to a stop. She looked down at his arm kind of shy-like, and said, "You dance real nice."

Now my brother had what you'd call a sixth sense. *"Es muy vivo,"* as my grandmother used to say about kids born that way, and with Nardo it was pretty much a scary truth, because he could duck trouble better than a boxer could duck a right cross. He made hairline escapes from belt-whippings and scoldings, just by not being around when punishment came through the door. So I believed him when he said something ticklish crawled over his shoulder when he looked across the dance floor, and in front of the bandleader who was about to read an announcement over the mike, he saw his boss, Mr. Baxter—and boy, was he steamed!

Mr. Baxter owned the catering service, and sometimes, my brother said, the way he'd yell at the busboys, it was like he owned them too. Mr. Baxter didn't say anything, just pointed to the door, then at Nardo, and wrote a big, imaginary **X** across Nardo's chest. Just like that, he was fired.

"Don't you ever get braces, Manny," my brother said, as if that were the lesson he learned.

At first he refused to go to the fields (although my mother insisted that my father was insisting), not because of pride, although he would have used that excuse at the beginning if he could have gotten away with it, but because like anyone else, he didn't like sweating over clods of dirt under an 105-degree sun.

That summer was a scorcher, maybe the worst in all the years our family lived in that desert, which our town would've been if the irrigation water pumped in from the Sierras was turned off. I could tell how searing it was by the dragged-out way my mom's roses looked every morning after I watered them. The water didn't seem to catch hold, and the roses only sighed a moment before the sun sucked up even that little breather, leaving the stems to sliver, curl up, and turn ashen.

Everyone else in my family worked, and it was hard to remain inconspicuous when my sister Magda always returned home from the laundry slumped over from feeding bedsheets all day into a monster steam press. I hustled fruit with my Uncle Louie, who owned a '58 Ford pickup. Together we sold melons, apples, peaches, oranges, whatever was in season, from door to door. But Uncle Louie hurt his leg tripping over some tree roots in our front yard, and it was all swollen blue and tender at the ankle. For a while, he couldn't walk at all except to hobble on one leg to the fridge or lean over to change channels on our black-and-white. He didn't go to the doctor because he figured nothing was broke, so why pay good money to some old fart just to write something on a piece of paper.

Anyway, the only one not working was my brother Nardo. But after a while, no one really expected anything from him. The truth of the matter was that he was just plain lazy. Whether one tried threats, scoldings, or even shaming (which my mom tried almost every other day), nothing worked. We all gave it a shot, but none more than my dad. He'd yell and stomp around a little space of anger that he'd cut out in our living room, declaring to the walls what a good-for-nothing son he had. He'd even dare Nardo, sometimes, to at least be a man and get up off his ass and go join the Army.

My dad's English wasn't so good. Some words he just couldn't say right. Instead of saying "watch," he would say "wash," and for "stupid," he would slip in a bit of Spanish, "estupid." But when he said "ass," or "ounce," stretching the S with a long, lingering slowness, there was pure acid in his teeth.

"If only Bernardo had jus' whuan ounss, whuan ounss . . . ," my dad would say, making the tiniest measure between his thumb and forefinger, but using a voice the size of our entire block.

After a while everybody gave up on poor Nardo. It was too bad, really, especially for my dad, who truly believed that with enough yelling and jumbling of the veins around his neck he could correct the error that was his son. When he finally woke up to the fact that it wasn't ever going to happen, his heart crumbled into bitter, disappointed pieces. From then on my dad acted like Nardo was just empty space.

Nardo, for his part, stayed home lifting weights, doing push-ups and sit-ups, and tenderly nursing any piddling little pimple worth a few hours of panic. He was a nut for health and fanatical about his handsome looks. He must've combed his hair at least a hundred times a day in the mirror.

I wasn't like Nardo at all, and my dad reminded me of it every time my brother's name boiled up from his lip. I suppose fourteen years of not knowing what, besides work, was expected from a Mexican, was enough to convince me that I wouldn't pass from this earth without putting in a lot of days. I was of my Uncle Louie's line of useful blood. All his life, no matter what the job, my uncle worked like a man trying to fill all his tomorrows with a full day's work. He didn't like sitting on the couch, didn't like TV one bit, never laughed at Skelton or got sentimental over Andy of Mayberry—mostly because he didn't understand them very well. The first chance my uncle got, he started fumbling about the house fixing sockets and floor trim, painting lower shelves and screwing legs back onto tables and chairs. He was a genius with clay tiles, and during that time he and my dad laid down the kitchen floor, which is still there to this day.

But with my Uncle Louie crippled, I was empty as a Coke bottle. I needed money for school clothes and paper supplies. I also wanted a baseball glove so bad a sweet hurt bloomed inside a hollow place in my stomach every time I thought about it. Baseball had a grip on my fantasies and wouldn't let go. There was an outfielder's mitt in the window of Duran's Department Store that kept me dreaming downright dangerous, diving Willie Mays catches. I decided to stir up Nardo to see if we couldn't go pick some chili peppers.

"You can buy some weights," I said a bit too enthusiastically, making him suspicious right off the bat.

He looked up at me from the middle of a push-up.

"You think I'm lazy, huh?"

"No," I lied.

"Yeah, you do. You think I'm lazy," he said, breathing tight as he pushed.

"I said no!"

"Yeah, you do!" He forced air out of his lungs, then got up misera-bly and wiped his hands. "But that's awright, college boy, if you think I'm lazy. Everybody else does."

He started picking at a sliver in his palm.

"I'm not really lazy, you know. I've been working."

He began biting for the sliver now, moving his elbow up and down like a wing, trying to get a better tooth on it.

"If you want me to go with you, I'll go, if that's what you want. But I'm telling you right now, if it gets hot, I'm quitting."

With that miracle we woke up the next morning, borrowed my uncle's primered pickup (which Nardo knew how to drive despite the tricky gearshift), and got some cans from our dad, who was pretty cheery over me getting Nardo out of hibernation. He practically put a birthday ribbon on the large brimmed hats from Mexico he gave us to protect us from the sun.

When we arrived at the chili field, the wind through the window of the pickup was burning warm on our shirtsleeves. Already the sky was beginning to hollow out, the clouds rushing toward the rim of the horizon like even they knew the sun would soon be the center of a boil-ing pot.

The foreman, wearing a pale yellow shirt with a black leather vest and cowboy boots curling back almost to his ankles, refused at first to hire us, saying I was too young, that it was too late (most fieldworkers got up while it was still dark), and besides, all the rows had been taken hours ago. On top of that we looked too much like kids strolling out for a picnic. He laughed at the huge lunch bag bulging under Nardo's arm.

Although he could fake disappointment better than anybody I knew, deep down I figured Nardo wanted to give picking chilies a try. But a good excuse was a good excuse, and any excuse was better than quitting, so Nardo didn't hesitate and hurriedly threw his can in the back of the pickup. He made a flourish to open the door, and seeing him so spunky and bouncing, I couldn't help but think it nothing less than pure torture when the foreman said that fortunately for us, there was a scrawny row no one wanted next to the road.

The foreman must have thought it an enormous joke giving us that row because he chuckled and called us over with a sneaky offer of his arm, as if to share a secret.

"*Vamos muchachos, aquí hay un surco muy bueno que pueden piscar,*" he said gesturing down at some limp branches.

The row had a coat of white pesticide dust and exhaust fumes so thick I knew our hands would get stained right away. The leaves were sparse and shriveled, dying for oxygen. Even the plants slanted from the road as though trying to hustle away from the passing traffic of people and trucks.

My brother shrugged. His luck gone, there was not much else to do. The foreman hung around a while to make sure we knew which peppers to pick and which to leave, not that it mattered in that row.

We had been picking for about an hour when the sun began scalding the backs of our hands, leaving a pocket of heat like a small animal crawling around between our shirts and skin. My fingers began to stiffen; it seemed forever before I reached the center of my can. Nardo, on the other hand, topped his can before I did, patted the chilies down, and lifted it over his shoulder, setting his rock of an arm solid against his cheek.

"I'm gonna get my money and buy me a soda," he said, and strode off over the rows toward the weighing area, carefully swishing his legs through the plants. I limped behind him straining with my half-filled can of lungless chili peppers.

The weighing area wasn't anything special, just a tripod with a scale hook hanging from the center. People brought their cans and sagging burlap sacks and formed a line. After the scale pointer flipped and settled, heaving with the sack's weight, the sacks were unsewn and the peppers were dumped onto a table bed where slits between the slat-boards let the mixed-in dirt and leaves sift through. There was a line of older women and young girls, some with handkerchiefs masking their faces, standing along the sides cleaning and kneading the chilies through the chute at the end. When a sack was stuffed, one of the foremen unhooked it from the nails and sewed up the opening. Then he stacked it on a pile near a waiting truck, whose driver lay asleep in the cab with his boots sticking out the window, blurring in the waves of heat.

Standing near the table bed was sheer hell. Dried leaves and the angry scent of freshly broken chili peppers made my eyes flare and my nose dribble a mustache across my lip. No matter how hard I tried to keep my breath calm, I kept coughing and choking as if someone had stuffed a crushed ball of sandpaper down my throat. I wondered how the women were able to stand it, even with the handkerchiefs.

The only good thing about the weighing area, really, was that they paid a minute after they announced your load. This lured families and workers from Mexico needing quick cash for rent payments or emergency food, and people like me who had baseball mitts to buy. It also brought business to a burrito truck behind the scales owned by the labor contractor. It sold everything from tacos, chili beans, and egg burritos, to snow cones and ice cream bars. The prices, though, made my brother complain loud: "You know how much I paid for this!" he exclaimed, when out of earshot of the foreman. "Eighty-five cents! Eighty-five cents for a damn soda! And it's one of those cheap jobs to top it off, no fizzle or nothing."

We picked steadily on, but by noon both Nardo and I were burnt out and a good sprint away from the nearest picker. Farther up, under where the clouds were like water boiling on the horizon, there was a staggered string of men working two rows apiece.

"They're wetbacks," my brother said as explanation. "They pick like their goddamned lives depended on it."

I looked over at the Mexican working the four rows next to ours and nodded agreement. The man used two cans, trading handfuls from one to the other. He went up two rows, then down two others, greeting us occasionally on his return with a smile and a shy wave. To save time, he placed sacks every twenty feet or so, and every half hour he'd pour a loaded can into the closest one. Behind him, three sacks already lay fat and tightly sewn. We eyed him, fascinated by his quickness.

"Maybe that's what we should do," I suggested.

Nardo shook his head. "Are you crazy?" he asked with conviction. "It'll take us the whole damn day just to fill one lousy sack."

He was right. We weren't really a threat to pass anyone. We stopped too much, my brother to eye the girls heading for the weigher, and I to watch the man and compare hands. His were wings in a blur of wonder, mine were stirring a pot of warm honey. He kept me mesmerized the whole morning with the way the nerves around his arm twitched as he shifted from plant to plant, his knees out like a triangle, tilting first one way, then another. He was a whirlwind gathering up cans and empty burlap sacks. He could've been a terrific shortstop, I thought, as I marveled at him, almost forgetting my own tiredness, noticing that he never seemed to tire, never seemed to rise much above the plant but hid inside the quivering leaves until with one flickering toss, a rain of peppers would shower the air and drop into his can. I was eyeing him when my brother tapped me on the shoulder.

"Look what's coming," he said, pointing his chin at a van creeping up the road. Cars had been insulting us with dust and fumes all morning, so when I saw how carefully the van approached, like a dog sneaking up on a bush, I knew something was wrong.

The van was green, a dim, starved-for-light green, like the leaves on our row. It had no markings. Its windows were open, and the man behind the wheel had his head out searching for something in the rows.

Suddenly people began to stand up, licking the air and stretching like they were peering over a wall. There was fast talking in Spanish and frenzied commotion as fifty or so people all at once jumped up and started running. They didn't even bother going through the furrows in scissor steps like Nardo had done, but ran in waves, trampling over the plants and tipping over cans. Those who were the last to react brought up the rear. They steadied their hats with one hand while their quickly snapped up coats thrashed in the other.

I still didn't know what was happening. My first impulse was to run, but then I saw three more vans and a large labor bus pop out of a narrow road in the cornfield bordering ours, and I knew that the Immigration had come for the people.

No one had seen the other vans position themselves at points along the cornfield. The people just ran wildly in panic toward them as if their first instinct was to hide inside the stalks. The quicker ones got caught almost at once, their paths cut off by officers holding out their arms. They surrendered without a word. The slower ones veered off into the open spaces of the cordon and dove into the corn. Most were caught in the first sweep, except for the ones who ducked under the arms of the officers and made it down the road. But they, too, were quickly run down by another van and escorted inside.

The few who managed to hide inside the cornfield seemed to have gotten away, and we all cheered and waved our arms as if our side had won. Some of us jeered at the officers, my brother Nardo the loudest. Everyone quieted down, though, when some of the officers formed a line along the field and disappeared into the stalks. A while later, they came out yanking on the shirt collars of those we thought had gotten away. Everybody sighed and said nothing.

The foreman who had given us the scraggly row and who was also the contractor rushed over to see what was going on. He took off in a huff saying "son-ova-beeches" and worse. I thought he was going to cuss those immigration guys off, but instead he stood by, meekly watching the officers corral the people before loading them into the vans. I tried to find the Mexican on the row next to ours, but I couldn't see him. I hoped he had gotten away.

The officer who looked like he was in charge approached the foreman and said something we could not make out, but it sounded like a scolding. Then the foreman came back and knelt down by the water tank.

"Damn son-ova-beeches," he said again, taking off his hat and raising dust as he slapped it against his pants leg. He poured himself some water and glared over at the immigration officers as they packed the people in and roared off in a growing cloud of dust. A crowd of us stood around covering our eyes, but none of us bothered to go back to work.

When the air cleared, a man appeared at the spot where the vans had assembled. He was an older man with a white stubble beard and a long, slightly darker mustache. He tottered back, nursing his right knee. At first I thought maybe he had gotten away, but then someone recognized him and laughed derisively.

"Hey, Joe, you're not a wetback. You're a *bracero*."

Joe came slowly over and took off his hat and covered his stomach as if he'd been caught naked. He shrugged an apology and said he couldn't help it, when everyone else began to run he got so scared and excited that he ran too. He looked down at his legs as if they had betrayed him. He said the Immigration let him go as soon as they saw he had too much meat on his bones to be a wetback. Everyone laughed. Then a family, whose befuddled uncle he was, came over and led him away. My brother and I laughed too, but for some reason I thought he was the best man in the whole field.

Of the twenty or so people left, everyone claimed they encouraged the Mexicans not to run. They said Immigration usually doesn't go inside the fields to check for green cards unless they have a good reason. If you acted like a citizen, sometimes you could fool them. None of those ungratefuls took them at their word, though, and for that they had only themselves to blame.

One of the listeners, a tall pimple-faced guy with blotched cheeks and the skin of a fig, only paler, shouted out, "*Pinches gavachos* don't give a damn about harassing us. *Gavachos* do what they want."

He walked away, not even waiting for a response or picking up any cans or equipment. Everybody watched as he slammed the door of his rusty Buick and drove away.

"I guess he came alone," Bernardo said musingly, then more alert, "We can pick any row we want, now." With the back of his wrist, he rubbed his eyes, even though the dust had died down.

"That guy's crazy. Those people don't live here, anyway," said a fat, moist-face guy with tight, bunched-in cheeks and pants that settled unevenly around his waist. When he walked, one of his legs looked shorter than the other. He went over to one of the rows a Mexican had been picking and lifted up a pair of old shoes. The soles were heavy with mud and the leather scarred and furrowed like the faces of old men who've worked in the fields all their lives. He held them at the tips of his fingers and away from his precious nose. The man who wore them probably took them off in the heat to stick his toes into the moist, irrigated soil. A chorus of laughter went up when the guy held them high, then fell when he dropped them back to earth. He rummaged some more down the row until he found a sack three-quarters filled with chili peppers.

"Hey, I'm gonna keep these," he declared and dug his hands into the sack.

When everyone saw this they all began to clamor around for the other abandoned sacks. They claimed their right by how close their rows had been to the Mexicans beside them. The sacks belonging to the man working on the rows next to ours were lying, already sewn, on their sides. Nardo walked over and placed his hand on the first one. Two other guys came over and began to argue about whom the others belonged to, but my brother was stronger, and after some half-serious pushing and shoving they walked away grumbling.

"Look, Manny," he said excitedly, spearing up his shirtsleeves. He lifted one sack by its ears and pounded it on the ground, packing the chilies down its belly.

"We got more here than it takes us two days to pick," he said. "Hey, you can even buy your baseball mitt."

I looked down at the sacks, then far out in the distance at the little clouds of dust still rising and disappearing where the vans had been pulling away. I wondered how long I would have had to work to fill those sacks, and my weariness stretched as wide as the horizon. I thought of the baseball glove, all clean and stiff and smelling of leather, and of myself in the cool green lawn of center field, like on the Bonneville Lakes golf course Nardo always talked about. I imagined I was already on the baseball team at school, and people were looking at me. Not these people picking chilies or those sent away in the vans, but people I had yet to know, looking at me as I stood mightily in center field.

The Flat of the Land

Diana García

From the roof of her house, Amparo gauged the tilt of the old water tower with the name "Pixley" faintly outlined on the side. It was hard to say how long the tower would still be visible: another week or two, depending on the mud's flow. Not that a missing tower would make any difference in a place where the only off-ramp was at least five miles west and the combination store and restaurant with its dusty lunch counter was on the abandoned side of old Highway 99. Maybe the girl with the blonde hair and freckles who worked at the store or the girl's mother or grandmother would notice when Amparo stopped coming in for an occasional skinny hamburger and greasy fries.

The first time the mud caught Amparo's attention, it looked like a harmless bubble in the ground. It was an April morning, and she'd been hanging the wash out to dry on the clothesline behind her house. She had scarcely paid attention when the mud burped at her, distracted at the time by the breeze whipping the clothes on the line and thinking that the shadowy clouds overhead might contain some rain.

That had been almost six months ago. Amparo turned and studied the flat expanse to the east and the Sequoia foothills in the distance. At the point where the mud had first appeared, the bubble had grown to the size of a pond. Here the land sank into itself and followed the outline of some long-ago river, a few scattered cottonwoods the only clues to its crumbled banks. From this source, the mud had developed an easterly flow that skirted the stand of cottonwoods. Amparo wondered why the mud had left the trees untouched.

On the land next to hers, bulldozers had carved foundations for a style of house popular forty years earlier. From her roof, the excavations looked like archaeological digs. By the time Amparo moved here, no one was left who could tell her why the development had been abandoned. All that remained of the original site was the water tower and the water main to her house. The only other trace of water was the mud; how else would the mud keep rising and spreading the way it did?

When the dimple of mud turned into a smile and then a six-inch wide crevice that threatened to swallow her clothesline, Amparo began to sense a possible threat to her hideaway. Up until now, she had kept her brothers and parents at bay by giving them a Fresno post office box address. She visited them as often as twice a month so that they wouldn't press her for more information about where or how she was living. They seemed satisfied knowing she was living alone and that her disability income was more than adequate for all her needs. She never talked about her son or her former husband, so they assumed she had laid those memories to rest. That damn mud, though, might spoil everything. At first she talked to it.

"What do you think you're doing? You have no business out here in this weather. The sun will bake you before the summer is over and then you'll have done all this work for nothing." When the sun didn't bake the oozing crack to a dry, light finish, she started asking, "Why don't you go downhill?"—indicating a direction opposite her house—"It's much easier than going uphill." The crack widened, its banks thickening and hardening, creating an impenetrable barrier within a few days' exposure to the sun.

Amparo trained herself not to think about the spreading mud. She listened to the Mexican stations on the radio. At night, she'd lie in bed and pretend the coyotes were talking to her instead of to the foothills and the jack rabbits. She'd answer, "Yes, manzanita does make the best cover," and, "No, the easiest way to get yourself killed is to expose yourself." She rarely turned the lights on after dark, afraid someone might see the glow and learn she had discovered the house.

The house was no secret, really. A developer had built the two-story structure as a marketing device and then abandoned it as too expensive: adobe walls like those of a Pueblo ruin and energy supplied by an underground cable and a solar-powered generator. At one time, someone else must have lived here. Perhaps it had been a retired construction worker, some laborer or cement finisher destined to end his days sweeping dust from the compacted dirt floors and enjoying the cool feel of the dark tan walls, secure in the knowledge that no one would look for him here—no former wives or children with grandchildren to bother him.

Now it was Amparo's house. She washed her clothes in a wringer-washer like the one her mother had taught her to use when she was a little girl, like the one she had used when her son was born, the one in which she had washed his diapers. She admired, as if they were someone else's, the bookshelves carved into the sixteen-inch-thick walls of the living room and bedroom. When she felt the need for exercise, she'd run up and down the steps to the second floor loft and master bedroom, chanting "upstairs and downstairs and in my lady's chamber." And, of course, there was the six-inch plumbing throughout, wide enough to handle anything, even a pot of scorched beans.

Not that she ate much these days. She still enjoyed her plain Cream of Wheat for breakfast every morning—her *atole*, she called it. For lunch and light snacks she had learned to eat seasonally, buying all her produce at the roadside stands along old Highway 99. There were almonds and raisins year-round; strawberries, peaches, tomatoes, and peppers during the summer. By early May she was tired of apples and oranges but with June came early corn and sometimes a melon or two. Dinner was always corn tortillas, beans, and rice. She made a pot of beans and another of rice every Sunday. Sometimes she'd toss some bits of chicken or beef along with a handful of garbanzos, some chopped onion, and cilantro into the steaming rice. Her biggest craving was grease; once or twice a month she'd drive to Pixley for a hamburger and fries at the store's lunch counter.

The day the mud licked the left front tire of her old white Studebaker Lark station wagon, Amparo drove to the store for a "grease bomb"—that's what she called the hamburgers. It was the first official day of summer. By then, the mud-filled crevice was about twenty yards long, six inches wide, and about a foot-and-a-half deep. That day at the lunch counter she'd asked the young girl's mother, "Did they used to have a mud bath around here that you know of?"

"What do you mean, mud bath?" the woman had answered, poking a few loose strands of dark brown hair underneath one of the pink foam rollers on her head. At least the rollers worked better than the torn hair net the woman usually wore. "You mean the hot springs?"

Amparo checked her fries for stray hairs before she dipped them in ketchup. She knew about the dots on the map called Fountain Springs, California Hot Springs, and Miracle Springs. No water at any of them. "No, not water. Mud. Did they ever have mud baths over by the old water tower?" Amparo asked, trying not to sound too curious.

"No, no mud. This is a desert." The woman had a droning voice, like an old record player at slow speed. "The only water for mud would have to come from the creeks. We haven't had enough water for the creeks to run in almost ten years."

The woman's mother had interrupted, "The last time I saw the Chocolate River—that's the old riverbed over by your house—was when I was still a girl at home. That was about seventy years ago when the flash flood tore out the old road right after the war." Almost as an afterthought the old woman had added, "You know, a long time ago, when my grandmother's grandmother came here from Illinois, it was all tule marshland like Three Rivers."

That was when Amparo began parking her Studebaker on the side of the house away from the cottonwoods.

After the mud ate the clothesline and then the smallest manzanita bush, the one farthest from the house, Amparo consoled herself with the thought that at least the muddy flow didn't interfere with her sewer line. By the Fourth of July, when the crevice reached a foot wide and the dried banks on each side made a slick sidewalk cooler than the surrounding earth, she had made some allowances for its existence. That night, she lit sparklers in the starlight. She jumped and danced from bank to bank, playing a cheery game, a combination of hopscotch and jump rope, remembering incantatory lyrics from first grade.

> Mother, Mother, I am sick.
> Call the doctor, quick, quick, quick.
> In comes the doctor, in comes the nurse,
> In comes the lady with the alligator purse.
> Out goes the doctor, out goes the nurse,
> Out goes the lady with the alligator purse.

In the morning, the crevice was fifty yards long—Amparo estimated this from the thirty-foot foundations on each side of her lot—and anywhere from three to four feet deep, depending on where she pushed an old mop handle into the ground. Much more than four feet deep and Amparo wouldn't have anything long enough to measure the depth. As it was, when she pushed the mop handle into the section closest to the biggest manzanita bush, her fingers could touch the slowly rising mud.

It was such fine, clean mud—no worms or sharp rocks. "How would you like some roses, an old grandiflora, a wine- or cinnamon-scented bush? Would you like that? I could plant a row on each side of the front yard, use some of your mud for fertilizer. I bet you'd make good fertilizer?" This last a question. It was hard to say what the mud wanted.

On July 15, her forty-fifth birthday, Amparo washed her bathtub and sprayed it with rosewater. When the sun was at its highest, she started dragging buckets of warm mud to the tub, climbing the stairs to the master bathroom, careful not to slosh too much onto the floor. Not that it mattered. Once the mud set, it was hard to tell where the original dirt floor ended and the new layer of mud began.

Amparo patted the mud to remove any air pockets, then took off all her clothes. She combed her long, still mostly black hair until it sparked with static electricity. Carefully she packed mud into her hair, arranged the entire mass into a turban on top of her head. Then she delicately dipped her right toes into the mud. Thick, lukewarm liquid squeezed between her toes. She lowered herself into the tub and let the mud ooze above her knees, her crotch, her belly button. Eyes closed, she finally sank to her chest and leaned her head against the back of the tub.

She thrilled to the sensation, like that of someone holding her without making contact. It was as if she had lost half her body weight. She felt an unnatural buoyancy, an inability to touch the very bottom of the tub. With smooth, even strokes, she massaged a thick layer of mud on her face and behind her ears.

She felt her skin tighten as the mud dried. When the mud grew cooler than her body, she pulled the plug and watched the mud make its way down the drain in small gulps. Then she padded downstairs, mud dribbling in small clumps wherever she stepped too hard.

Amparo sat outside in the late afternoon sun, her legs stretched in front of her, the heat baking her body mask to a glossy finish. She studied the effect in the hand mirror. As long as she kept her body perfectly still, she looked like an ancient statue. All the wrinkles were gone, the deep lines around her eyes and forehead, the cellulite. And her back pain was gone.

Amparo stretched from her waist to touch her toes. Where the mud started to crack, she carefully peeled it away, conscious of the adhesive-like grip that caused her skin to redden wherever there was too much hair. Her skin had the firm smoothness of a ripened peach fresh from the tree. The pores on her nose had disappeared and her hair shone in the sunlight. She remembered how Sammy, her ex-husband, used to tell her that the first time he spotted her running her old black German shepherd in the park, the sun made her black-brown hair look like a comet. "How perfectly you've caught me," she told the mud, its slick surface stamped with the lines of her body. That night she fed the mud her leftover beans and rice.

In early August she spotted a possible hairline crack just to the right of the main crevice. She brushed the line with a manzanita branch and it seemed to go away. It was hard to say. By late August, when the hairline crack had lengthened to form a thin leg to a V, she was sure. This leg was aimed at the opposite corner of her house, and like the first leg, it pointed in the same direction. "Ahh, you want the foothills," she whispered.

At first, the mud's flow was indiscernible unless she sat for several minutes, her eyes focused on a mark she'd scratch into the still-damp sides of the widening cracks. Another trick she used to measure the mud's movement was to make little paper boats from old Christmas wrapping paper and watch them gently float and bob on the barely moving surface. By early October the mud flow was obvious—a steady movement east despite the three-year drought.

When she first found the house three years ago, its biggest attraction had been the roof, the easy access along the molded staircase that climbed in profile up the east wall of her second-floor bedroom to the roof escape. Amparo had always thought she would like to live in a house with a hidden staircase to some underground study; now she knew that her real dream had always been of such a skylight escape. She enjoyed climbing the stairs in the morning, sliding the double-construction sky-lights open. She'd clamber over the lip of the stairs and eat her *atole* on the roof, watching the day take hold. It was as if the house had been designed just for her.

Now she made the roof her lookout post; the mud would need guid-ance. "Foothills to the east, say 15 miles, straight flat land, hardly any sage," she announced her first day on the job. She listened to the mud's distinctive sound. She could hear it humming and swallowing, no longer baffled by its inability to lay claim to the house. There were no windows or doors on the east side of the first floor of the house. The mud waited at the weep holes and joints, sensitive to the loosening of a corner as the house gave ground.

The coyotes' yips and cries grew more distinct. She counted how long it took their echoes to reach her, much as she would count the space between a thunderclap and a lightning flash. When they lurked too long she belittled them, smirking at their mangy coats, "Try a little mud in your fur. You'll kill a few fleas that way, I assure you," and "I once had a jacket with a red fox fur." She relented when they turned tail and skulked away. The next night she left a pile of freshly grilled chicken breasts sea-soned with rosemary.

On the day of the harvest moon, Amparo drove to the Fruit Patch produce stand and bought the last of the zucchini, now over a foot long and four inches in diameter. She chose a pumpkin the size of her head, as well as a garland of dried red New Mexico chili pods and a selection of Indian corn tied with twine.

At sunset, Amparo climbed to the roof and arranged the offerings on favorite plates. She poured a mixture of *atole* topped with raisins and walnuts in a mixing bowl. When the moon was full overhead, she placed the plates and bowl in a star-shaped pattern, one for her head, the others for her hands and feet. Then she lay on the roof enjoying the cool breeze overhead.

To the mud she tossed an inconsequential aside. "Isn't it nice not to have to worry about cleaning and cooking and washing and worrying about someone all the time?" When the mud withdrew like a sulky child and refused to respond to her chatter, she confessed, "Yes, I give you credit for going uphill away from the riverbed. I never would have thought of that."

To the house she offered soothing counsel. "We'll ride it out together, the two of us. You'll see. I'll take good care of you." The mud hiccupped and poured a thick sheen over the lot. Amparo imagined how the land might have looked as an inland sea. "Just think of all that water." She felt the house shiver.

In Amparo's dreams that night, a stand of cottonwoods turned into a grove of ancient trees. Where a clothesline once twirled like a giant umbrella, clumps of tule rushes danced in the surge of a waxing moon. In the distance, the flat roof of a house bobbed above the flat of the land that stretched toward the foothills.

And as she slept, the mud came close and caressed the base of the house. It told of the excitement of heat lightning cast on the horizon on summer evenings; of the tenderness of misty sighs heaved from a roiled earth on snow-swept mornings; of a world best viewed from a height of 1500 feet.

In turn, the house recounted the thrill of water tumbling over a bed of smooth-ground gravel; of air so cold in autumn that spawning salmon gasped when they broke the surface.

House and mud lingered over shared secrets, reveling in this moment of discovery. The house openly admired the reflection of stars on the moist surface of the mud. In turn, the mud thrilled to the crusted surface of the house, each trowel-stroke another mystery to be explored.

In the predawn hours, Amparo awoke to the lurch of the house lifting and settling on a wide river of mud. House and mud paused as she clambered to the roof. They allowed her time to adjust her stance to the house's uncommon roll, then the house made a slow 180-degree turn from the old highway to the foothills.

Like a swimmer learning a new stroke, the house muscled through the mud, at first tentatively, then with increased fluidity. Loose pieces of masonry scattered as the house and mud picked up speed. The mud wash kicked up nearly one story high, flattening sage and manzanita.

"We're coming, we're coming, it won't be long before we're there," Amparo shouted to the hills. To the sun she complained, "We need some light over here. How do you expect us to see where we're going if you wait until six o'clock to get up?" To the house and mud she instructed, "Faster, go faster, we're almost there! Don't worry about me." As they drew closer, a cleft in the foothills parted, and house, mud, woman squeezed through in an eruption of closely contained forms, aiming for the tree-laced meadow above.

Through the temporary opening could be seen air so clear the sky looked like cut crystal, a passage so smooth that a traveler could press one hand against each side and never feel the moment of contact.

Glossary

~~~~~~

The following is a list of Spanish words and phrases and their English translations, arranged by story and by order of appearance. Parentheses indicate literal definitions rather than translations.

In the stories, words in Spanish may or may not be italicized, depending upon the style of each author.

Introduction

movimiento movement

vato loco crazy dude

campesino farmworker

Pocho (a child of Mexican parents, born in the United States)

No Se Lo Tragó la Tierra
He Didn't Just Vanish
(literally, The Earth Didn't Swallow Him Up)

Sí se puede. It *can* be done.

One Holy Night

panadería bakery

dar a luz have a baby

sinvergüenza hussy

demonio devil

Alegre Merry, Blithe

The Pan Birote

Pan Birote Bread Roll

mamás moms

El Güero y El Prieto
(nicknames for a light-skinned and a dark-skinned child, respectively)

en bola in a herd

nalga(s) behinds (buttocks)

espantos ghosts

No dejan ni alistarse! En lugar de dar gracias a Diós están peleando en día de misa? Ya verán!
You don't even let me get ready! Instead of giving thanks to God you go and fight on a Sunday? Just you wait!

paciencia patience

como el demonio like the devil

pan para los pobres bread for the poor

alacranes scorpions

víboras snakes

los niños the kids

como si no tuvieran ojos
as if they were blind
(literally, as if they had no eyes)

Ay, Diós mio, ayúdame!
Oh, God help me!

y iban a hacer malas caras
and they'd turn their noses up

que coman caca let them eat shit

se iban a morir de calor
they'd die in that heat

172

La Mala The Mean One

Cállense! Hush!

calzones panties

el día de pan para los pobres
the day to give bread to the poor

gorda fat lady

la gente people

libros de misa missals

chillando screaming

Los dos gallitos, un güero y un prieto,
pero los dos de sangre de jalapeño
The two cocky boys, one light and one
dark, but both with jalapeño blood

Ya venían mugrosos.
They were already dirty.

remolinos gusts

Anden cabrones! No les pagues atención!
Go on, you brats! Just ignore them!

Déjalos cabrones. Stop it, you brats.

Ya que lo manaciaron todo, que se
lo coman! Now that they've put their
paws all over it, let them have it!

Porque así son los hombres.
That's the way men are.

Pues, ya ves, así es el mundo.
Well, you see, that's life.

No quiero. I don't want it.

Cómetelo tú, mi'jita.
You eat it, honey.
(literally, my daughter)

Ya, no necesito más.
There, that's all I need.

los dos jalapeños the two jalapeños

Somewhere Outside Duc Pho

vieja old lady

chorros torrents

ese buddy, pal

pendejos assholes

Pobre Poor

The Closet

Tía Aunt

Mira Look

Pa' más canas.
Like I need more gray hair.

pero ya sabes estas muchachas
but you know how these girls are

mire las florecitas
look at the tiny flowers

Que match, ni match.
Forget about matching.

las muchachas de tu Tía Mage
your Aunt Mage's girls

Cómo estás, Rufina?
Hace tanto tiempo . . .
How are you, Rufina?
It's been a long time . . .

vecinas neighbors

comadre (name by which the mother
and godmother of a child call one
another; by extension, a female friend)

Qué lástima How sad

curandera healer

Doña (title of respect given
to a mature woman; equivalent of
former English use of "Lady")

Mi Minga (nickname for Dominga)

Esta no sabe nada. Nunca aprendió,
nomás pa' mitotear y componerse
la cara. She doesn't know anything.
She never learned anything but to
gossip and paint her face.

varsoviana (a folkdance originally
from Poland, similar to the mazurka)

Don, Doña, Mano, Mana
(*Don* and *Doña* are titles of respect for
mature men and women, respectively.
Mano and *Mana* are slang for "brother"
and "sister.")

Tú sabes, vivían en Cheyenne
You remember, they used to live
in Cheyenne

Hermana de la Josephina, tu vecina?
Your neighbor Josephina's sister?

cómo se llama? what's his name?

Su vida fue muy triste, muy pesada.
Siempre la tenían sembrando, escardando.
Her life was very sad, very hard.
They always made her plant and weed.

Carajas Rascals

té de oshá Oshá tea (medicinal brew)

me mandó mamá mom told me

Pero But

Sí, pero esa uñas largas comes to see
him con interés.... Ramona ya
tiene los ojos rotos de tanto llorar.
Yeah, but that greedy woman comes to
see him out of selfishness.... Ramona's
eyes are ruined from so much crying.

Se murió. He died.

Quién? Who?

Pues, era el mero de Washingtón.
El Presidente. The bigshot from
Washington. The President.

Que jardín tan lindo.
Such a pretty garden.

Y que me muero y no me muero y
allí estoy. So there I am, dying
but not dying.

Y esa ventanita?
What's that little window?

piojos lice

lombriz worm

almorranas piles (hemorrhoids)

pecoso mocoso snotty freckle-face

chingado fucked-up

Pa' tu cuartito.
For your little room.

Enero

Enero January

la doctora doctor

Via Crucis (Way of the Cross, the
route taken by Jesus to His crucifixion
on Mt. Calvary; a simulation of the
pilgrimage procession performed as
a church devotion)

cocido meat and vegetable stew

el lavadero laundry room

calzones underwear

zapetas diapers

cosecha harvest

sopa soup

café coffee

gerente manager

novios boyfriends, suitors

en el otro lado
on the other side, across the border

Americanas American women

la hija del patrón the boss's daughter

el norte the North
(i.e., the United States)

lonchera lunchbox

Aquí todo es diferente
It's all different here

servilletas napkins

petaquilla trunk

No es ... It's not ...

la Iglesia the Church

muy ranchero too vulgar

el vicio alcoholism
(literally, the vice)

mole (sauce made with chile,
sesame, and other spices)

capirotada bread pudding with
raisins and almonds

Qué tanto miras en las nubes?
What are you looking at in
those clouds?

Nada. Sólo me gusta ver para afuera.
Nothing. I just like to look out.

Hija mía My dear daughter

Smeltertown

carne asada barbecue

Ni modo Too bad

Chula Beauty

mi'jita sweetie (literally, my daughter)

tierra-café earthy-coffee color

guayabera (loose-fitting dress shirt of light fabric, worn untucked)

te sales! you're too much! (literally, go away!)

mi'jito dear (literally, my son)

Bueno Well

La Abuela Grandmother

Ay qué Américo Oh go on, Américo

la perla de los mares pearl of the sea

Borinquen querido beloved Borinquen (alludes to a well-known song about Borinquen, a major port town in eastern Puerto Rico)

Buenas tardes Good afternoon

gallo rooster

jíbaro peasant, poor farmer

javalina female boar

Ay señora Oh my

deschavetado lunatic

arroyos creeks

chongo chignon, bun

barrio neighborhood

Summer League

cacahuates peanuts

Hollywood!

burros donkeys, asses

saguaros (tall desert cacti)

piscadores pickers, harvesters

mijo son

Easy Time

huevos balls

La Loca Santa

La Loca Santa The Mad Saint

Ave María purísimas Holy Mother of God

velorio wake

comadres (name by which mother and godmother call one another)

compadres (name by which parents and godparents of a child call each other)

padre priest

idioma language

Hombre necio, pendejo! Stupid bastard!

O si no, qué, hija? Or if not, what, daughter?

gabacha white girl

El Milagro The Miracle

susto fits

pelos hair

maracas rattles (testicles)

nuevo mexicanos new Mexicans

curandera healer

novia girlfriend

acequia irrigation ditch

vieja old girl

La Gritona The Screamer

carne adobada marinated beef

Dios mio My God

mi'jita honey (literally, my daughter)

The Jumping Bean

arroz con pollo (traditional Mexican dish of chicken and rice, with tomatoes, onions, and spices)

La Promesa

La Promesa The Promise

mi'jito my son

Hablas Ingles?
Do you speak English?

Muchas gracias. Thanks very much.

Qué lástima. What a shame.

El raton Miguelito Mickey Mouse

La Blanca (a name that carries
the suggestion of "The Fair One"
or "The White Lady.")

La Olla The Pot

El Espejo Oscuro The Dark Mirror

Buenos días Good morning

**Por favor, dónde está la tumba de
la Señora Blanca Morrell?**
Excuse me, where is the tomb of
Blanca Morrell?

El entierro? The grave?

Aqui no está. It's not here.

(las) momias de dulce
candy mummies

The Baseball Glove

Es muy vivo He's very sharp

**Vamos muchachos, aquí hay un
surco muy bueno que pueden piscar.**
Come on over, boys, here's a really
good row for you to pick.

bracero day-laborer

pinches gavachos damn white guys

The Flat of the Land

atole (traditional Mexican drink
made from cooked corn that has been
milled, strained, and boiled)

Contributors

Daniel Cano returned from Vietnam in 1967, where he served in the 101st Airborne Division. After completing studies at the University of Granada, Spain, and California State University, Dominguez Hills, he held several administrative positions. He now teaches English at Santa Monica College. His first novel is *Pepe Ríos*.

Ana Castillo was born in Chicago in 1953 and earned her Ph.D. degree from the University of Bremen, Germany. Her many prose and poetry collections include *My Father Was a Toltec*, *Women Are Not Roses*, *The Mixquiahuala Letters*, *Sapogonia*, *Massacre of the Dreamers*, and *So Far from God*.

Sandra Cisneros was born in Chicago in 1954 and raised there. She is the author of three books: *My Wicked Wicked Ways*, *The House on Mango Street*, and *Woman Hollering Creek and Other Stories*.

Edna Escamill, born in 1941 in Calexico, was raised in both Tucson and Baja, California. She is the author of the novel *Daughter of the Mountain*.

Carlos Flores was born in 1944 in El Paso, Texas. He received his M.A. degree from the University of Texas at El Paso and currently teaches at Laredo Junior College.

Diana García was born in 1950 and raised in Merced, California. A graduate of San Diego State University, she in now a bilingual legal consultant in San Diego and a part-time English instructor.

Guy Garcia was born and raised in East Los Angeles, and attended the University of California, Berkeley and Columbia University. He is the author of *Skin Deep* and *Obsidian Sky*, as well as numerous short stories and articles.

Dagoberto Gilb was born in 1950 in Los Angeles, where he was raised. He now divides his time between Texas and California. A journeyman union carpenter, he is the author of the collection *Winners on the Pass Line*.

Jack López was born in Lynwood, California, in 1950. A graduate of the writing program at the University of California, Irvine, he teaches at California State University Northridge.

Víctor Martínez was born in 1954 and raised in Fresno, California. He is a graduate of California State University, Fresno, and is the author of the poetry collection *Caring for a House*. He presently lives in San Francisco.

Rosalie Otero was born in Taos, New Mexico, and raised there. She received her Ph.D degree from the University of New Mexico, where she now works.

Mary Helen Ponce was born in Pacoima, California. The author of *Taking Control* and *The Wedding*, she earned her Ph.D. degree at the University of New Mexico.

Alberto Alvaro Ríos was born in 1952 in Arizona, where he still lives. A graduate of the University of Arizona, he is the author of the short story collection *The Iguana Killer* and several poetry collections, most recently *Teodoro Luna's Two Kisses*.

Danny Romero was born and raised in Watts, California. He graduated from the University of California, Berkeley.

Gary Soto, born in 1952 in Fresno, California, is the author of thirteen books, the earliest, *The Elements of San Joaquín*, and the latest *Local News*. He teaches occasionally at the University of California, Berkeley.

Helena María Viramontes was born in East Los Angeles in 1954. She was educated at a now-defunct Catholic college. She is the author of *The Moths and Other Stories* and the work-in-progress *Paris Rats in E.L.A.*

Acknowledgments

wwwwwwwwwwwwwwwwwwwwwwwwwwwwwwwwwwwwwwwwwwwwwwwwwwwwwwwwwwwwwwwwwwwww

"The Waltz of the Fat Man" copyright 1991 by Alberto Alvaro Ríos. The story first appeared in *The Kenyon Review* and is used by permission of the author.

"One Holy Night" is from *Woman Hollering Creek and Other Stories* (Random House, Inc., 1991, and simultaneously published in Canada by Random House of Canada Limited). Story first published in *The Village Voice Literary Supplement*, 1988. Copyright 1991 by Sandra Cisneros. Used by permission of the author and Susan Bergholz Literary Services, New York.

"The Pan Birote" copyright 1992 by Edna Escamill. Used by permission of the author.

"Somewhere Outside Duc Pho" copyright 1992 by Daniel Cano. Used by permission of the author.

"The Closet" copyright 1989 by Rosalie Otero. Used by permission of the author.

"Enero" first appeared in *Stories from the American Mosaic* (Graywolf Press, 1990). Copyright 1990 by Mary Helen Ponce. Used by permission of the author.

A version of "Smeltertown" first appeared in the *Rio Grande Review*. Copyright 1990 by Carlos Flores. Used by permission of the author.

"Summer League" copyright 1992 by Danny Romero. Used by permission of the author.

"Hollywood!" first appeared in *Fiction Network*. Copyright 1987 by Dagoberto Gilb. Used by permission of the author.

"Easy Time" copyright 1992 by Jack López. Used by permission of the author.

"La Loca Santa" copyright 1991 by Ana Castillo and is taken from the novel *So Far from God* (W. W. Norton & Company, 1993). Used by permission of the author and Susan Bergholz Literary Services, New York.

"The Jumping Bean" copyright 1992 by H. M. Viramontes. Used by permission of the author.

"La Promesa" copyright 1992 by Guy Garcia. Used by permission of the author.

"The Baseball Glove" copyright 1992 by Víctor Martínez. From the work-in-progress *Parrot in the Oven*. Used by permission of the author.

"The Flat of the Land" copyright 1992 by Diana García. Used by permission of the author.